SO-ARP-628

THE BOY

THE MASTODONS: BOOK I

THE BOY

JAMES STRAUSS

FIVE STAR
A part of Gale, Cengage Learning

GALE
CENGAGE Learning

Detroit •   ie • London

GALE
CENGAGE Learning™

Set in 11 pt. Plantin.
Printed on permanent paper.

LIBRARY OF CONGRESS CATALOGING-IN-PUBLICATION DATA

Strauss, James.
    The boy / by James Strauss. — 1st ed.
       p. cm. — (The Mastodons ; bk. 1)
      ISBN-13: 978-1-59414-813-2 (hardcover : alk. paper)
      ISBN-10: 1-59414-813-9 (hardcover : alk. paper)
      1. Boys—Fiction. 2. Children, Prehistoric—Fiction. 3. Prehistoric
peoples—Fiction. I. Title.
    PS3619.T7433B69 2009
    813'.6—dc22   2008053579

First Edition. First Printing: April 2009.
Published in 2009 in conjunction with Tekno Books and Ed Gorman.

ACKNOWLEDGMENTS

Frank Samuelson and Suzanne Lamon, world-class artists of the Northwest, who helped me visualize the incredible world of prehistory revealed in this novel.

Prince Mongosuthu Buthelezi, of Kwa-Zulu Natal in South Africa, for letting me walk the canyons and lands of his people, and supporting this effort.

Bradley C. Hodge, for his lifetime friendship and grand sense of honor and integrity, which you see mirrored in this novel.

Jeremy Rosetta, better known as Raincloud, is a Santa Domingo Indian and silversmith of high regard, and the friend who sat with me day by day as I wrote the first draft.

David Milch, producer of *Deadwood* and *John From Cincinnati*, for introducing and training me in the art of screenwriting.

David Shore, producer of the television drama *House*, for his examples of vision and imagination necessary to conceptualize the story set forth in this novel.

Barry Machado, PhD, and his wife Anise—Dr. Machado, professor emeritus of Washington and Lee University, is a noted historian who has helped me cage together enough rational historical thought to make this novel relevant.

John Helfers, my editor and friend, who made so many corrections and added so many valid changes that his name might just as well be with mine on the cover.

Harvey, my cat, who added all those typos, which John Helfers had to work so hard to remove.

Acknowledgments

Hanley Kanar, Executive Director of the Love Is Murder writer's convention, for introducing me to the right people and befriending me to herself and other notable literary personalities.

Dr. John Bair, psychologist of the North Chicago Veterans Center, who provided an invaluable psychological profile of the protagonist.

Jody Mikkelson, editor and friend, who helped me make it all have cohesive meaning and direction.

DEDICATION

This book is dedicated to my wife, Mary, without whom I would never have pursued the actual writing nor had the belief in myself to continue writing. Also, to my children, Michael and Julie, who both heard the earlier versions of these stories every night as children, and made me continue to make up and tell more. Finally, to my parents, Bill and Irene, who made me what I am and continue with their solid support of my efforts.

PROLOGUE

He ran as he had never run before, his full attention devoted to the rounded rocks that lay strewn unevenly about the confines of the old river bed. Where the stones did not protrude, there were pockets in the suppurating mud around them, and the only possible way to move as fast as he could was to run across the rocks' dry, curved surfaces. Not even the most fleeting thought of injury from such reckless abandon entered his mind, already closed by fear. The sound behind him, deep and unending, pushed him forward, his slim, upper body extended at almost a bent forty-five-degree angle to the muddy ground, and his wildly beating feet padding rapidly from rock to rock, their bare soles transmitting no feeling up through his paralyzed nerve fibers. Panic drove him with a singular purpose. *Escape.* The conscious thought of what he might be fleeing from never made any attempt to materialize within his energized mind. The process of thought did not occur until he was given a choice, and then his body halted as if on its own, and he listened.

A new sound, ever growing in strength, had entered his awareness. The boy looked back for the first time, but saw nothing to explain his panic.

The great cliff rose to the left, as he looked down the almost dry streambed. It had always been there and nothing appeared changed. But a faint sound from ahead drew his head back around. Wind had joined the rushing, rising whisper. It was somehow a normal sound, even though he had never heard anything like it before, and his decision was made. The deep gong behind him, coming from within the earth itself, was not to be faced, no matter what lay ahead. He plunged forward, into what appeared to be a heavy rain, until his single moment of rational thought fled completely.

When his senses returned, he knew that although his arms and legs were moving, he was no longer running. He was cold, but he could see nothing. He could not remember being struck, but he knew that his worn, cast-off skins were gone. And he fell and fell, endlessly, into a cold blackness, the pain all over his body growing dimmer and dimmer as the coldness replaced it.

His eyes opened and full consciousness came instantly, along with pain in his right elbow, left hip, and ankle. The boy stared up into blue sky, unable to remember what it was like before everything had changed. Had it been blue? A low squeal came out of his mouth with an outflow of breath, yet he seemed removed from the sound, as if someone else had made it. He looked down at the offending elbow and marveled at the slimness of the Y-shaped branches entrapping it. Slowly, grimacing, he pulled back until his joint slipped through the tight wedge of the small, bent branches.

The thought of "tree" did not cross his mind until he was falling. End over end he catapulted down, not understanding even the reason for his rotation. His hip and leg had come loose at last. He got out one long groan before he struck the ground, and blackness took him once more.

CHAPTER I

The sound had begun as a long series of hollow echoes, and the boy awakened to it now, his eyes snapping wide open, his ears alert to the noise nearby. He remembered that sound and shivered. Pain radiated from his back, elbow, and leg, bringing his mind to full consciousness. He tried to rise, but only managed to squirm within the soft, barely yielding substance that encased him. He pushed his good arm up and out, while at the same time staring up into the bare branches of a huge tree looming over him. He finally recognized the substance all around him. It was mud. Above, a brown haze had replaced the blue sky of prior memory. The deep sound continued. It was the burble of water rushing in the distance, but in a volume he could not quite comprehend. Ever since he could remember, the tribe had always been short of water, and had always waited impatiently for the inconsistent, sparse rains.

The boy ceased his struggles with the wet, sucking mud, and laid back. Most of his head was uncovered. He rested and thought fleetingly that he might be dying. His eyes squinted with the effort of trying to remember what had happened. He had been lying on the uneven floor of the cave where he lived when a surge of sound had come radiating from deep within the dark environs below, and with it had come the penetrating cold. It gripped him, and shook him, but he was used to the uncontrollable shaking of his limbs, that came with the nights. Ten summers had passed in his life, with adulthood still far in front of him, and the warrior's role he could only dream of. His status as a child in the tribe did not merit even the slightest skin covering for protection, only the frayed leather of a child's knee-length garment.

He had awakened to the feel of the sound throbbing through his body, and an instinctive fear had filled him. The cold seemed to withdraw and his muscles had ceased shaking. Aware now, he was determined to find the source. His short stature was a significant advantage within the dark cave complex. He could move anywhere fully upright without striking his head. It was one of the most frequent sources of pain among the fully-grown males.

Without a sound, he had easily moved among the humps of robed backs seemingly strewn haphazardly about the cave. His ability to move at night was almost that of a nocturnal animal, quiet and sure, and he had awakened not one sleeping figure during his passage to the nearest cave entrance.

The pre-sunrise light of dawn had greeted him while his head cocked this way and that to determine the source of the sound. He had looked at his feet, realizing he had felt the sounds better than he had heard them. They suddenly stopped, and the wind gusted in. His nostrils had flared as he sampled the unlikely, clear wind. Wind was common with the setting sun but not with the rising. His long, brown hair had lifted with the breeze, but the sound's drumming and wind's rising at the same instant had caused the small hairs on the back of his neck to rise. He had stepped out of the cave to look up and down the escarpment. The three cave openings, one after the other, had revealed nothing. He had stared up the many, many man-heights of the steep cliff face in both directions, and then across the valley to the cliff on the opposite side, a full day's journey away, and that for a seasoned warrior.

The streambed lay below, quiet and dry. Only occasionally

had the rains filled the deep bed with wonderful, babbling water. Green plants grew on either side of the moist banks, taking their life-giving liquid from the water almost always hidden deep below.

The boy's eyes had shifted upstream in time to catch a bright blue flash of light, more powerful than even a close lightning strike. He had been stunned. There had been no clap of following thunder and not a single cloud could be seen in the sky. Fear had choked him.

And then the ground had moved. And then, just briefly again. It had left him swaying in shock and terror. Ground did not move. It had never moved.

Automatically his arms had risen up to the level of his small shoulders for balance, but he had not been aware of this at the time. And then had come the impossible wave. His eyes had been focused downstream when it had appeared. He had played in the infrequent ponds of the running stream with the other children enough to recognize a wave. But this had not been a wave of water. It was a something else moving up the valley, a wave of ground. That had brought forth his only remembered scream, and then his terror-ridden flight. He had run from the wave, but had not gotten far. It had caught him in the streambed and thrown him into the air. Rocks, plants, and debris had been thrown up with him. Then it had passed. He had landed still running, staggering blindly through a dense cloud of dust and dirt.

Lying on his side, embedded in the mud, he remember nothing more except for the pain and cold from whatever he had run into. With his free hand he removed chunks of dried mud from his chest, then his waist and thighs. The mud was actually crusted and almost dry near the surface. He crunched some of it between his fingers as he came to a sitting position. It was not the sandy material he remembered from the streambed, but more solid and clay-like. He stared around, the wet clay still turning slowly between his fingers. The old streambed was gone, as if it had never existed. In its place was a surface of almost smooth clay, interspersed with laid-over branches and piles of green, pounded brush. Except for the huge tree.

Above him it towered into the air, blocking most of the brown sky. Only then did it occur to the boy that his last, strange feeling had come from falling. Quickly he worked his way out, twisting and popping great chunks of crusted mud all about him. He knew he was bruised, but feeling all about his body revealed no great cuts or breaks. Tired, he sank to his knees, noticing his nakedness for the first time. Not only his worn old ribboned skins, but even his breechcloth had been stripped away. He had only a brown glaze of mud to cover him, although he was no longer cold.

The feel and sound of the rush of water dominated his senses. It was almost overwhelming in its intensity, demanding immediate attention. He forced himself back to a standing position. Everything hurt, but his elbow hurt most of all. He cradled it with his good arm but not before pushing back his mud-encrusted hair. With his back to the tree, he looked first to the left and then to the right. The escarpment was plainly visible above the mounds of green brush debris to his right. It was the same, yet somehow different than he remembered it. To his left lay only piled, broken saplings and more heaps of brush. He limped toward them. Slowly he worked through the dying plant matter until coming to a flat of green reeds. Somehow they had survived the deluge, like the great tree. Shifting his gaze, his eyes met a sight that confirmed his hearing, but left his mind in utter disarray.

The boy stared at a rushing body of water that extended from the end of the reed flats well into the visible distance, which seemed to rise up in its passing. A boom sounded, and then another distant one followed. For an instant the boy thought it was more of the unearthly sounds that had frightened him so badly before. Then came another, and he understood. The water was filled with debris of all manner and size. Even large trees hurtled by with a speed that he couldn't have matched with his best run. The great booms were rocks from the old streambed, now underwater. He felt rather than heard it just as one boulder the size of his father's head was thrust up out of the water, and then swept around the edge of the reeds by the force of the surge. It was a mesmerizing scene, which he almost could not tear his eyes away from. But the other sound of water . . . with just the beginning of comprehension, he retraced his steps back past the tree, breaking into a gentle lope as he worked around the jagged stumps beyond it, until he came once again to rushing water. It was almost the same as the other side, except that the far shore seemed tantalizingly close. It only took another short time to cover the remaining directions. He was on an island, which measured no more than a hundred man-lengths wide and was in the middle of a huge, raging river.

He looked up at the tree branches high above. There had been so many huge trees along the length of the old streambed. As a child, he had never once strayed far enough from the caves to climb any but the closest. He thought for the first time of the family. Had they or any members of the tribe survived? He looked up again. If he could climb high enough, he might be able to see the base of the cliff.

The brush all around the base of the gnarled, old trunk was thick, having been thrown up by rushing water. While he worked his way up, the boy realized for the first time that he owed his life to somehow ending up in the tree's highest branches. Nothing could have survived the crush of the water and debris he had watched churn by, much less the higher and faster waters.

The bark was hard even against his calloused and muddy fingers, but the runnels between their twisting rows gave him purchase. Inserting the toes of his good foot, he reached up to begin the climb. All of his muscles froze, and he pressed himself into the broad surface of the tree trunk. The boy carefully and slowly turned his head until his right ear was pressed into the bark, and his left outward, to catch the smallest sound. A low animal croak repeated itself. The volume and depth of the sound sent renewed shivers up and down the boy's body. The sound was nearby, and from the depth of its timber, the animal had to be very large.

The boy was not alone on the island.

CHAPTER II

He turned his head until the tip of his nose touched the wood. No other part of his body had moved. The sound came from the other side of the tree where the packed brush rose much higher than he could see. The sound came again. It was a deep snuffle that trailed off into a watery blubber. He felt the low timber of it reverberate through his gripping hands. Fear built up until he almost could not bear it. He breathed in deeply, and then held the air for a moment before letting it out. His father had trained him in that single warrior tactic. When he expelled the air it came out with a soft, whispered "father" through his lips.

The boy concentrated energy to his hands and then down to his splayed, gripping feet. His body sank to the hardening mud at the base of the collected bracken. Hunched down, he took inventory. He had nothing, not even a breechcloth. Certainly nothing close to a flint chopper or point. The sound came again with unceasing regularity, and another surge of apprehension rolled over the boy's body. But as he waited, terrified, it suddenly ceased. He simply sat and listened, his skinny, ten-summer limbs clutched about himself in hiding.

Why? He wondered. *Why has it stopped?* His father had said that the deep breathing allowed the mind to think right through fear, and never had he been more afraid in his life. He breathed again and tried to think. His mind's conclusion came with a shock and did nothing to diminish the terror. The wild animal on the other side of the tree had sensed him and had stopped making noise because it too knew that it was not alone on the island. The boy knew that he had been quiet to the extreme, which meant that the animal must have the acute hearing of a hunter. A predator. And there was only one prey trapped with it on the small piece of land.

Big animals ate small animals. With few exceptions, it was a rule of life. Even armed warriors seldom returned to the tribe with killed prey larger than they themselves. Around the cave fires, the quietly spoken reason for this was the difficulties of attempting to haul large carcasses long distances. Thoughts flitted through his mind, even the pleasing idea of some giant monster plastered against the other side of the tree trunk in fear of the slight sounds the boy had made. That brought a silent snort and a quick smile to his lips, which were as fleeting as his imagined picture of the beast.

He waited one hundred breaths, and then another hundred, but there was no sound except that of the rushing water with its occasional, bell-like underwater rock vibrations. He could run or fight. As small and barren as this island was, there was no place to run or hide. He could not remain crouched down behind the tree; hoping that the thing never came after him, never got hungry, that it was not bigger than he. He might swim, but just the thought of the raging water's brown jumbled mass made him shiver convulsively. There was no choice.

He had to fight. The decision made, he turned and pressed his back against the heavy bark. He dug into the nearby mud, searching for a proper throwing rock. The fingers of his right hand closed over a wedge-shaped object, a little bigger than his palm. He picked the object up and hurriedly scraped the mud off. It was a piece of natural, white limestone with broken edges as sharp as those laboriously chipped by the tribe's weapon maker. It was an uncommon find. He whispered his second word since awakening on the island.

"Omen . . ." came forth low and quiet, spoken into the surrounding brush. He had listened to the warriors sing praises of such singular and fortuitous events. Omens only happened to the greatest of warriors in times of their greatest dangers. It defined them.

Fear subsided from the boy's shoulders as he gripped the weapon tightly, its long, sharp edge forming a near straight line along the bottom of his clutched hand. A warm feeling spread from inside the depth of his empty belly. Although he was certain to die in moments, he had been given the great honor of an omen. He would die a warrior, not some thin, cast-about boy.

With a death grip on his new weapon, the boy lowered himself into the mud of the bracken pile surrounding the tree, its brittle surface giving way as he wallowed down into the wet sludge beneath. Ever so slowly, deep breath by deep breath, he worked his way between the branches and leaves toward the still, silent beast on the other side of the tree. Little light penetrated the interlaced brush above him as he slithered, trying to keep his injured elbow from further harm, pausing only to listen after moving each full body-length.

What he knew to be a short journey seemed to take forever. Part way through his next move, he was confronted with a great wall that blocked his path and seemed to push the crushed mass of branches back toward him. The light was so poor that he had almost blundered right into it with his forehead.

The wall moved. His eyes a hand's breadth above the mud and not even that far from the wall, he observed the strange effect. It moved slowly toward him, and then away. Just the slightest rise and fall, but it was moving, he noted. Bile rose into his throat the instant the boy recognized that he was staring at the side of a living thing.

Without conscious thought, the boy's body began to work backward, away from close contact with the living monster. Very briefly, he considered attacking the unprotected side of the beast with his new weapon, but immediately concluded the futility of such an effort. Even if the beast remained still, it would take too long to do more than wear away at the hide of such a creature. And he instinctively knew that it would not remain motionless.

He maneuvered backward until he was fully clear of the bracken. The beast was no more than three body-lengths from the base of the tree. And its hide was covered in brown fur. That thought, and the fact that he might have encountered the largest bear ever known to exist, caused him to lie there and consider his situation while he fought to control his rapid breathing and equally rapid heart. The tribe used bear hides as coverings against the cold nights, and the greatest warriors wore its hide as clothing. But the boy had never before seen a live bear much less one that was probably larger than one of the three great cave openings.

Once again, he concluded that he had no alternative options. The bear would hunger. There was no other game on the island that the boy had seen or heard. He had to attack the beast and quickly find some soft, vulnerable point for his sharp blade-like flint knife. The attack must be overwhelming in its intensity and ferocity. The warriors bragged of such intensity. Many times their prey simply stood in terror, paralyzed under such an attack and thereby proved very easy to slay. Or so the stories went when retold around the fires after the hunt . . .

The boy closed his eyes and gripped his weapon, trying to imagine such an attack, but could not conjure up the image. He just could not do it. His eyes snapped open, as the beast once again made its fearful sound. It had somehow sensed him in spite of his stealth and care.

CHAPTER III

Casting all thought from his mind, the naked, mud-covered boy pushed himself quickly to his feet, the small flint blade gripped tightly in his weakened right hand. He plunged forward and then around the edge of the brush pile surrounding the base of the great tree into the very shadow cast by the bulk of the brown monster.

The great warrior shriek he had intended came out as a broken croak, the unintended screams issued during his hysterical flight up the streambed having worn his vocal cords raw. The ferocious attack unraveled rapidly from that point onward. The boy broke free of the cloying vines protruding from the very edge of the bracken. Slipping as he rounded the brush, off balance from encountering the vines, and with the diminishing croak coming from his open mouth, he plummeted forward and fell. Still attempting to recover, the boy shot his feet forward and extended both of his small arms out to the sides, but to no avail. He collapsed into a sitting heap before the great, brown-coated beast, the senseless croaking that only caused more pain in his throat dying away.

Miserably, his shoulders slumped in defeat and his knife-wielding hand resting slack by his side, he stared up at his doom. It was the stuff of his most terrible tribal nightmares. Standing a full two man-heights tall and nearly as wide, its dark skin was covered with a deep brown and densely smooth coat, even thicker than that of a bear in summer. A short, broad trunk

21

hung between two short stubs of pure, white ivory. The eyes seemed to stare out to the sides, but the boy knew that the creature's full concentration was on him. He sat no more than five feet from the pink end of the trunk and felt as if he could reach up and touch it. But he could not move. He was paralyzed with fright.

It was a Mur. Only in awed whispers did even the bravest of the warriors ever even speak of the Mur. There existed two great, lumbering creatures, the boy knew. The Doth were giants, taller than wide, with stringy hair all over their grayish-black hides. Great ears waved and flapped as they swung their weary, ponderous heads. With huge trunks they swept entire thickets clear of bushes and small trees. The warriors of his tribe sought them for prey, but were rarely successful.

But the Mur were a different matter entirely. They would eat tender brush, that much was known, but what was also known was that they ate smaller animals, including warriors. They were much faster than a man, could hear for unbelievably long distances with their large, funnel-shaped ears, and their acute sense of smell allowed them to track the spore of prey long after the animal had passed by. The boy children of the tribe were threatened with being staked out for the horrid monster should they fail in their duties or disobey any elder. The one good thing was that no tribal member, other than far-roving warriors, had ever even seen a Mur. They were unknown in the valley of the caves.

The boy tried to breathe deep, as his father had taught, but he could not.

His breath came in short, shallow gasps as he waited to die. He was unable to take his eyes from the beast, but could not move even when its snout dipped forward and down, the pink end exposing two holes that seemed to sniff back and forth as the trunk swung before his face.

Nothing more happened for many moments except once more the snout of the thing returned to its place back between the two small ivory knobs. The boy did not know what to do. But he understood what a hunter or warrior was supposed to do.

He would not wait passively for his fate. He would meet it as the omen seemed to direct, as a warrior.

"Well?" he said aloud, gaining confidence slowly from simply hearing his own voice . . . alive. "You have my smell. You heard my cry. What now?" he asked, wanting to laugh at the ridiculousness of the question. He got to his knees by first leaning forward and getting onto all fours. Then he brought his torso up so that his head was at the same level as the creature's eyes. The Mur didn't move, but simply continued regarding him without making a sound.

"You're not as big as I thought," he said, his thoughts turning more analytical as he began to examine the beast.

The sense of great mass was due mostly to its girth, he realized, and how solidly it was built. Whatever its size and strength, it did not seem predatory . . . or even threatening. It was no better a hunter or warrior than the boy.

"You're a baby monster," he breathed out, the conclusion coming more as a surprise than of deliberate realization. As if in answer, the beast let out another cry. This time the sound did not terrify the boy. Being so close and no longer threatened, the boy gauged the cry to be more sad than frightful.

"Yes," he mused, "You're a baby Mur all right. How did you ever come to be here?" He waved his newfound flint in the air as he talked, but no longer was even aware that he still held it or that his elbow hurt so badly. The boy walked before the Mur in semi-circle, back and forth, occasionally stopping to peer at some other aspect of the animal. His fear gone, he concentrated on attempting to understand the mystery of the animal's presence and the coincidence of his own.

"What's wrong with you?" he voiced to himself. The Mur regarded him steadily with one large, round eye. The top lid was framed by long, black eyelashes and the area around the eye's pupil was brown with small, black flecks. It did not blink as the great head turned slowly to follow the boy's movement. He noted how the front legs were planted deep into the mud, set straight down like great pillars, while its rear legs were slightly bent, as if ready to catapult the body forward.

The boy dropped to one knee and peered at the front left leg of the beast.

"You're hurt." A tear in the animal's fur ran from just below its shoulder down almost all the way to its foot, planted deep in the mud. The boy was surprised that he had not noticed the wound immediately, as it oozed red and clear fluid to such an extent that no dirt could be seen within. The Mur let out one of his strangled bellows that ended in wet flutter. The boy took the utterance to be either agreement or a complaint about his being too close, so he rose and stepped back a pace.

"Here," he said formally, "here is my weapon," and he tossed the small flint knife into the mud at the base of the Mur's injured leg. It made no move in response to the gesture, only the turned head with one unblinking eye continued staring at him.

"Okay," the boy said hesitantly, waiting another short time before advancing a couple of steps.

The Mur's head moved and the swinging trunk caught the boy solidly on his right shoulder, almost knocking him from his feet. The pain shot straight up from his damaged elbow, causing lights to explode behind his eyes.

"Hey," he yelled, clutching the arm, but then had to duck as the trunk came back across for another attempt at knocking him aside. Once again the baleful single eye regarded the boy, but there were no more swings of the heavy trunk.

"Okay. I understand," the boy intoned gently, extending his hands forward slowly with palms upturned. There was no reaction from the Mur.

"I don't see anyone else here trying to help you," he finally stated, turning and looking in all directions. There was no movement except one small flick of the beast's trunk and a very quiet grunt.

The boy knew from his father and listening to the warriors that very few animals could be taught words of the tribal language, and wild animals of any sort were not among them. But he also felt something from the Mur. That somehow, they were communicating, even if it was not possible to understand how.

As he watched, the Mur finally blinked.

"Why am I bothering?" the boy said quickly, and then waited, his hands still outspread before him, as if expecting some definitive answer. The Mur only blinked again, which made the boy smile.

"I guess I'm still alive," he whispered as he gently eased forward to inspect the damaged leg more closely. The Mur merely canted its head over further to the left and continued to regard him with its great right eye.

"Hmmmm," was all that came out of him as he explored around the injury. He saw right away that it was a deep crack in the skin and tissue. The blood coming out was sparse and leaking from the bottom of the fissure. He touched the fur, and when the Mur did not react to this intrusion, he worked his good left hand through the surface hair and onto the skin.

"Wood. You feel as hard as wood," he marveled. Deep down in the wound he spotted a long sliver of white. The boy felt sick to his stomach but did not turn aside.

"Bone. I can see the bone," he reported to the Mur, looking up into its staring eye. He knew it could not possibly understand, but then the animal blinked again. The boy stared. It seemed like for all the world that a tear had formed in the great eye. He had always meant to ask his mother if animals cried, but had never gotten around to it.

The brief thought of his mother caused the boy to back away from the Mur and reflect anxiously. His mother was the tribe's healer, although their Shaman in truth believed she was his servant and he the real healer. He looked wistfully in the general direction he knew the caves to have been.

He thought of his people. His family. "Mother?" he spoke softly, not wanting to break down but coming very close. He looked back at the Mur. There was nothing to be done for his family unless he could get off the island and get back, and that could not be done until the water went down—if it did.

The boy straightened his shoulders and peered back at the animal's wound. Once more he stepped to the shoulder area and dropped to one knee.

"How did we get in this mess? Your left leg is hurt and my right arm." He thought for a moment about the possibility of that being a second omen, but then discarded the idea. He looked into the Mur's eye and spoke directly. "I'm not going to hurt you." He bent forward as he said it, cleaning the mud from his hands on the fronds of a nearby bush. His mother said that mud was bad for wounds, except certain muds that were actually good for them. Gripping the edges of the wound by grasping great handfuls of the thick fur, he tried to pull the crack shut, but only partially succeeded. The Mur let out a loud snuffle, but did not pull back or try to assault him once more with its trunk. He tried again, straining with the effort, but his right arm simply could not put forth any strength . . . any more than it would have allowed him to climb high enough into the tree's lower branches to allow him to attempt to see around the island, he realized ruefully. He let the edges of the wound open again and felt the Mur shiver with pain. It almost seemed to travel in a small wave through the beast's rich fur. Once again, the boy was reminded of the catastrophic event that placed them so unbelievably on the island.

"Sorry," he said gently, then patted the Mur reassuringly on its exposed right cheek just below its tear-filled eye. He stepped back from the animal to think.

CHAPTER IV

The boy's eyes caught the edge of the speeding water out beyond the reed bed when he absently looked up. The sound of the rushing water from both sides was still nearly overwhelming in its intensity.

"That's it," he exclaimed to the Mur, and it snuffled right back at him, but he paid it no mind as he once again began his pacing.

"You were caught up in it too, weren't you? You must have come down in that, somehow," and he pointed out toward the swirling water. He was pleased to see the Mur attempt to look in the direction he had waved, even though the brush and the tree blocked any possible view of the island. But the boy was more pleased by the conclusion he had come to than from the response he had gotten to his question. "No wonder you're hurt," he said, "I can't believe anything living could have survived what you must have gone through." He pictured the great body roiling and twisting, caught in the raging river's terrible grip. When he had felt the animal's skin, it had been almost as tough as a warm surface of flint, but it could not be much of a match for what lay in those rushing waters.

"Still," he continued, "if you could survive it once, then maybe there is hope of our getting off this island before we starve." Then he realized what he had said. "Well, before I starve anyway."

He walked back to the Mur and retrieved his flint, cleaning

the chunks of dried mud that had adhered to it as it lay. "I think I can help fix that wound," he said, pointing at the animal's damaged leg, "but I can't do it unless you stay still. I need some things first, but I don't need you following me around." The last had sounded good, and he smiled to himself as he set off toward what had to be the rock tip of the island. He smiled. It was not as if the Mur had moved one step since he had heard its presence on the island, but it made the boy think that he was in control of something. It was a good feeling and there was a spring to his step that had not been there since before the catastrophe had occurred.

He made his way back to the open mud area near where he had first fallen from the tree. The day was bright and warm and the mud was now hard enough on the surface to walk on without sinking. The imprint of his body lay nearby, looking almost like a burial pit, he thought gloomily. With his back to the tree, he looked up at the central rise above the piles of bracken. He climbed as best he could with the weakened elbow and with his hip still hurting. The collected debris was filled with disguised pitfalls among the split and broken tree trunks that made up its foundations. Finally, he reached an area above the plant matter, and he knew at once that he was at the same level the water had reached earlier that morning. He looked back in awe. Although the water had risen to only half the trees' great height, it was still astounding to gaze out and realize just how much must have flowed through the valley.

"Impossible," was all he could say. The wind blew directly into his face as he completed the climb. As he had suspected, the rise was a singular rock outcrop with its forward edge splitting the great river into two diverging currents. He leaned carefully forward, his muddy stomach pressed into the rough surface, and stared down to the water below. The edge of the rock was like a great flint knife, he realized, literally cutting the water in two. He noted the split of water was uneven; the part that broke to his left and flowed past the reed bed was the greater of the two, almost twice as broad as the narrower band that split to his right.

He watched a giant tree flow directly toward him, its trunk only partially above the brown swirling surface, and its root system towering halfway as high as the rock itself. It was hypnotic, and he could not take his eyes off of the speeding mass until it struck the rock's edge.

It was not cleaved in half, as he had expected, although he felt rather than heard the impact. Instead, it was pushed immediately under the surface, with even the root system disappearing completely, but only for an eyewink of time. Then the entire tree seemed to spring upward as it reared half its full length up and then past the side of the rock surface. With a roar, it crashed back into the rushing water and was immediately swept aside and down the right portion of the island.

The boy let out his held breath. He had reared back physically and tensed himself for a blow, even though the huge object had never been close to his lofty position. The depth and the power of the river had been demonstrated once again, and he knew that there would be no crossing it unless it subsided. The sounds of the low, bell-like boulders, crashing unseen into other rocks under the seething rapids below, sealed his conclusion. He slumped in disappointment.

Peering back, he saw the brown flat back of the infant Mur protruding up above the pressed brush surrounding the tree. Its great furred head turned to permit the left eye to observe him, unblinking again, above. He instinctively waved and began the descent, his original intent on climbing the rock again at the forefront of his mind.

The great rock had always been beside the streambed, its location of particular importance as one side had always been covered with a thin surface growth of plant material that the boy's mother used in her healing poultices. He crawled to the edge again and peered down. Halfway down the face. he saw the familiar yellow-brown lichen. It was too far down to retrieve any from above, but the special plant wrapped just a bit back from where the water had worn it away below.

The boy's eyes flicked over toward the near shore and were instantly drawn to a thin column of smoke. The gray-black tendril rose in almost a direct line from the great rock to where the caves had been located. He thought of his family. Someone from the tribe had survived to stoke the cooking fires or to move one or more out from the escarpment. His heart soared. The pain of even thinking about what might have happened to all he had known was great enough to cause tears to well up in his eyes.

"No," he whispered, wiping one eye with the mudstained back of his good hand. "I can't cross the water. Not yet. I'll help the Mur," and with that thought he was already moving back down the rough surface of the rock.

Near the bottom, he placed his stronger right leg onto one of the broken chunks of wood that had been swept against the base by the torrent of water, then brought the remainder of his weight down and plunged through several layers of the collected debris.

He came to rest in what seemed like a darkened pocket within the maze of branches, leaves, and drying mud. He eased into a scrunched, sitting position, proud that he had not screamed as he had plunged into the pile. His left side lay against the rock surface, so he pushed against the pile with his right and pulled himself upright. The fingers of his left hand grasped a rounded handhold on the rock surface. The boy stopped in mid-climb and settled back. A perfect, round semi-circle lay under the fingers of his left hand.

Quickly he cleared away the collected leaves and dirt that stuck to that section of the rock. He pushed his back into the pile and pressured backward to give the muted light enough room to illuminate what he had uncovered.

For a moment he did not understand what he was staring at. Then it came to him. It was an artificial carving of some sort, made deeply and smoothly into the surface of the flint-hard rock. He had been holding his breath in while staring, he realized, and upon realization let it slowly out.

"That's not possible," he said as the air left his lungs. He was certain that in all the years he had been with the tribe, no one had ever even attempted such a feat. It was rumored among the children that the warriors made drawings on the back walls of the caves, but only using the ends of burned sticks. Tentatively he traced the entire design of the carving, wondering what could possibly have been hard enough to cut into solid rock. Some rocks cut into other softer rocks, but the great cliff face was not soft rock. The boy had watched the old flint maker work the pieces of special rock found in parts of the streambed. Even they had to be heated under the cooking fires for long periods before being rapidly cooled in water. Only then could the blanks that would become spear points and knives be chipped into the required shapes. The process was closer to Shaman work than warrior work he knew.

The boy angled his head to better understand what he was looking at, but it seemed to make no difference. A perfectly round circle, deeply indented, with what looked like exactly straight deep lines raying down from it. At the bottom, almost three hands down, were horizontal lines that were closed at each end like the haft of the warrior's knives. He would try to remember the exact shape for his mother. She was always interested in new things that nobody else bothered to understand or try to explain.

He clambered out of the bracken, adding substantially to his collection of small cuts, abrasions, and scratches. The broken ends of the smaller branches were sharp and yet impossible to work through without some contact. Once free, he rubbed the worst of his injuries, and then moved toward the water on the tribal side of the rock. As he got closer to where it rushed past the side of the island, the noise increased to the point where nothing else could have been heard except maybe the deep, resounding beat of the underwater boulders. The current leaped up in its mad rush past, after being cleaved by the sharp prow of the solid rock face. He stared at the seemingly solid wall of water racing by at the height of his head. It quickly dropped as it passed, disappearing into the rough collection of great rocks and broken trees lining both sides of the island.

Where it broke or was cut by the rock prow, a wedge-shaped area was left between the side of the rock face and the moving water. Wet mud lined the bottom of the pie and it was near the top of that mud that the boy saw what he was looking for. The plant that grew on only one side of the rock held healing power only where it was in contact with water.

"Well, there is certainly enough of that," he said as he moved into the thick mud. His eyes only momentarily left the wall of speeding water. He felt if he reached out to touch it, he would instantly be swept to a painful death.

He crouched, his feet sunk near to his knees in the sucking mud of the wedge-shaped area. Hugging the rock, he reached down with his right hand and detached a great chunk of the thick wet moss, ignoring the twinge of pain in his elbow. The water splashed higher, closing the gap, causing him to flinch as it surged and retreated, but it never did. Then, just as he had the heavy piece firmly gripped in his hand, the mud under that foot gave way and he plunged face first onto the very point of the wedge. The water grabbed his hair and pulled, but the boy

33

retreated in panic. With both hands wrapped around the precious chunk of healing growth he lunged backward away from the terrible deluge.

It took many breaths, just sitting in the drier mud, before he could retreat further. Slowly and ponderously, he slung the great wad of moss over his good left shoulder. It clung to his back like the thick fur of the Mur.

It seemed to take forever to make his way back to the clearing before the tree. The Mur's head protruded just over the top of the debris pile, its gaze still attentive.

He approached the beast and slung his load down near its injured leg. The thick trunk of the Mur swung down and lightly tapped him on the head, then continued wandering through the air. The boy grunted, staring into the animal's eye.

"You don't look very smart, you know," he said and waited, but the Mur did nothing different. "I think you are, though. I think you know I am trying to help, but I guess we'll see." He turned and examined the rest of the clearing closely until his eyes were drawn to its edge back the way he'd come in hauling the moss from the rock. He walked over and began sinking his fingers into the drying mud, first in one place and then another.

"Come on. I know you're here." He searched until his fingers closed on the object he was looking for. Out of the mud he pulled a length of thin vine, its ends both disappearing in opposite directions.

"Got you," the boy exclaimed happily. The vine was one of the essentials of tribal life. Its fibers held skins together, and even tied spear points to shafts. He pulled handfuls of the thin, tough material from the mud until he had collected a small pile. With his newly acquired flint knife, he sat and slowly abraded the ends of the vine until he had one long, continuous section free.

"It cuts with a flint, but you can't break it almost any other way," he said, smiling at the Mur and holding up one end. He realized then that he had completely lost his fear of the animal, in fact, he could not even think of it as a monster anymore. Gathering the vine into a long coil, the boy moved back to where he had left the moss, thinking the whole way. Maybe it was the catastrophe, he thought, or the deep fear regarding the survival of his family that he could not allow to surface. Maybe it was just that the Mur was cute in its own way. He looked up into the animal's unblinking eye.

"Maybe it's just because I'm not alone," he said, and took it for a sign when the Mur blinked.

The boy sat at the base of the animal's wounded leg and began to work. The vine ran a perfect single arm length before it angled slightly and a tuft grew forth from the point of that junction. He pulled tuft after tuft from the strong plant until he had one single, long length. Normally, the tufts sat on the surface of almost any exposed area the plant grew on, while the connecting vine ran under the surface, connecting them all like a giant puzzle. The children of the tribe often played a game to see if they could tell just what tuft was connected to another specific tuft, as they were not always connected to the closest.

"Now for the tough part," he said, looking up at the Mur's swinging trunk. He rose and stepped forward to the side of the giant baby's great head, patting the skin just under the large eye, wondering what the animal thought of him, or if it thought at all.

"I'll do the best I can," he mumbled, not knowing what else to say. Leaning over the moss, he divided it up into three long, narrow slices with the edge of his right hand. The bottom of the plant that hugged the wall was pure white and ran from the thick, green mass of surface material. It was laced with roots almost too thin to see, and that was the portion, the boy knew, where the healing strength was contained.

"Hope you don't mind this too much," he said, up toward the carefully watching eye. Then he leaned down and began to pack the moss into the wound near the creature's foot. When he had the entire first length bulging out from the crack, he tied the vine, using the only knot he had learned, around the very base. Breathing hard, his right hand and left hip hurting again, he worked the vine around and around the thick, furry leg. He pulled it as tightly as possible for him on each circle until that part of the wound was completely covered in the thin wrapping.

As he worked, the boy marveled at the incredible animal. Even though it was much younger than he himself, he could not make his hands meet on the other side of the leg. It was that big and it would grow to be so huge that he could not imagine it, the boy knew.

CHAPTER V

The entire job took so long that when he was finished, the boy saw the shadow of the great tree above him had become much longer. He had crammed the entire mass of healing moss into the wound and used his single knot over and over again to secure the tightly wound vine to the leg. He had stopped looking up at the Mur's eye because he could not take seeing the liquid collected there. The low, whimpering sounds the animal made while he had worked were bad enough.

"There," he said, stepping back to admire his handiwork. "It might heal," he went on, darting in to move a loose end. "Well," he considered, his weak arm still cradled with his left, "it heals for us, anyway." What would work a Mur was beyond even thinking about, and he knew it. How the animal even lived was beyond him. With its wood-hard skin, strange, soft fur, and then a big trunk getting in the way of everything, he could not even guess how it had come to be in the world.

"But I have to call you something," he mused. He paced back and forth before the animal, its head turning slowly to follow his progress. The eye had dried up and it had stopped making noises, which he took it to be a good sign. He thought deeply.

"We," he began tentatively, "are human beings." He patted himself loudly on the chest with his clenched left fist. "We are the people . . ." and his voice trailed off, ". . . well, the people that are." He expelled his breath and dropped his fist, realizing that he had no idea what he was talking about.

"We are the people and that is our tribe." He raised his right arm and pointed back toward the tendril of smoke he had seen from the great rock. The Mur's only reaction was to tilt its head slightly in the direction he was pointing. His arm came down. There was nothing to be seen from their level except broken trees and piles of heaped-up branches, leaves, and debris of all kinds. The boy felt ridiculous.

"You are a Mur," he tried again, tapping the animal on the center of its trunk. The Mur tapped him right back on the forehead with its soft pink trunk-tip.

"Alright," the boy said, stepping back and pushing the trunk aside. It was the strangest feeling in his life to be touched so willingly and so benignly by such a huge wild beast, even if it was a baby beast.

"Let's see," he said to himself, thinking. "Yes . . . you came by the water." The boy wrestled with his language to get the meaning right. Among all the members of the tribe names held special meanings and were only assigned after considerable thought and analysis. He would not be named until he entered training for warriorhood.

"Murgatroyd," he said, then pulled it apart sound by sound.

"Mur, of course, and then 'ga' is 'comes from,' and 'troyd' means water." He turned up his hands toward Murgatroyd's attentive eye, revealing the good sense of such a name. The animal blinked and the boy patted him once more under the eye and endured another glancing blow from the pink trunk-tip.

"Okay, it's Mur of the water then, and you can call me . . ." and the boy stopped. He had no name. Until he reached adulthood in two more summers he could not hope to have anything resembling a name. That was the stuff of warriors, and, as with the omen, was something that could only be confirmed by the warrior council and the fates. He thought wistfully of the warrior training ahead and how he could not bear to spend two entire summer periods playing with the other children.

"Boy." The name popped out of its own accord. "You can call me boy, I guess." Even the use of that single word to describe him was a transgression, but he shrugged the thought aside.

"Murs can't talk," he said, accepting a swat from the trunk and a singular blink as assent. Feeling free to say whatever he wanted all of a sudden, he leapt back and pranced before the Mur in a deadly predator's crouch.

"I am Wolfkiller," he growled with his face scrunched up and his hands stretched before him as talons. He did not really know what a wolf was, as the warriors only spoke of the groups of padded and silent animals that stole their prey if they were not careful. The tribe's children were properly afraid of the wolf packs, as it was one of the assorted animals that they were threatened with being fed to if they didn't behave.

The boy looked at the Mur for his reaction but the beast did not move or stir.

"Not Wolfkiller, huh?" he said and dropped back to his normal standing position. "Bear Tooth?" tried tentatively, but still the Mur did not react. The game he played in front of the animal made the boy think of the tribe and what had been all his life. He stopped his cavorting and turned to face the direction where he had seen the smoke. His body moved almost of its own accord toward the backside of the island where he could view the far shore unobstructed.

Carefully, he worked through the piles of debris, climbing where he could not readily step and then threading his way around the twisted, smaller saplings with their sharp, broken edges. His already scratched and skinned body was sensitive to even the slightest touch. Only one cut had been added to his collection, and that from a broken sapling where the crook of broken-off branches resembled nothing more than a bird claw.

Finally, he stood on a bare area of rock where the water

rushed by, not a man-length from his feet. The speed of its passage still drew his eyes hypnotically downward, until he forced himself to look into the distance.

The smoke tendril was still there, although the far shore blocked all view of the rising area that ran between what had been the old streambed and the cave entrances. Behind him was the now familiar snuffle of the Mur, but he could not tear his eyes away from a continuous search up and down the shore for any sign of movement or life.

Murgatroyd snuffled more loudly than he had, which caught the boy's attention first. Then he heard the sounds of wood breaking and heavy objects moving. What turned his head finally was not the sounds, but the feeling. He felt the Mur's steps. Slow, deep plunges through the muck until the great beast struck rock or hard clay. Nothing else on the island could have overpowered the sound of the rushing water, he knew. A momentary shiver of fear went through him. No matter how docile the Mur had been, it was now many, many man-weights of moving, wild animal.

The boy thought of retreat, but one quick look around was all he needed to abandon the idea. There was really no place to hide or escape to, as the great animal proved by lurching right through a head-high pile of debris that he had laboriously climbed. The boy retreated to the water's very edge as branches flew in both directions and Murgatroyd towered before him. The Mur raised its trunk and blew a hissing, low roar that raised the small hairs on the back of the boy's neck. He'd even left the flint knife back where he'd treated the Mur's leg.

The trunk of the animal swung down and once again the delicate pink nostrils lightly touched his forehead. Instinctively he batted it away, as before, relief flooding over him as he relaxed his tensed shoulders.

"Hello Murgatroyd," he said, looking the Mur in the same

eye. "What do you want?" He said the last absently to himself, however, and at the same time he bent on one knee for a close examination of his handiwork.

"Not bad." He smiled when he said it. His mother would have been proud. The binding had seemed to even tighten a little with the Mur's movement. The animal held the injured limb straight instead of with the slight bend of its right leg he'd noted before. He straightened and turned back to the shore once more.

"You know we're trapped here," he said as he gazed across the water, but really talking to the Mur behind him. Glancing down at his feet, he found that the water had somehow made its way across the flat stone, and was only a hand's breadth from his left foot. He had not considered the water rising again.

"Let's go back to the tree," he said, turning to face the animal. "At least I can climb that if the water keeps rising." The walk back was much easier as the Mur had cleared and flattened a path right through the worst of the debris field. He felt more than heard the animal take up right behind him. He looked back once, but only to see how the animal was handling the bandaged leg. It dragged just a bit and the Mur held it stiff, but other than that the vine and moss seemed to impede it not at all.

Once at the tree the Mur took up its old position, backed in next to the trunk and now facing outward toward the clearing. Much of the brush that the boy had worked so hard to quietly penetrate had been trampled into a mat not much thicker than prairie grass. Using some of the extra pieces of sturdy, thin vine and some of the crushed leaf debris, the boy fashioned a rough garment at least sufficient to cover his nakedness.

"It's not much," the boy said as he modeled the uncomfortable breechcloth before the Mur. No amount of pulling, pushing, or adjusting would make it completely acceptable, so he gave up. At least it was not likely that he would have to endure the ridicule of the other tribe children—if he got back to them. "It will have to do," he said, standing with his hands on hips.

At least the vine belt gave him a place to carry his flint knife, and he carefully placed the sharp blade between several of the windings just in front of his right hip.

The Mur seemed to agree with most of what the boy did, complimenting his movements and work with frequent snuffles and pointed directing of its agile trunk.

The boy looked up at the setting sun and realized for the first time that he had not been truly paying attention to the totality of his situation. It was already late in the afternoon and the sun was descending below the great rock. The fine dust that had settled out of the air and clouds now dotted the sky. Life appeared normal, at least when he looked up. But the water gave no indication of subsiding anytime soon, and the thought of its recent small rise moved the boy to action.

Feeling almost like normal again, he explored the rest of the island by moving to the far side and checking out the flat, solid-rock area where the reeds had somehow survived. The Mur followed close at his heels, its trunk-tip sweeping to touch the boy occasionally on the back of his head or shoulder, almost as if it had to make sure he was still there.

He looked back to see how the Mur's leg was holding up and was pleased. The miraculous healing power of the moss was his mother's single greatest contribution to the tribe. It not only healed open wounds but it also dramatically decreased pain, allowing greater movement. Without the ability to move under their own power, most of the males injured during the frequent hunts did not survive to return to the tribe. The moss also helped keep the Shaman in his place, the boy knew. They frequently argued, although the boy only heard of the conflict by listening to his parents talk. The current tribal Chief often sided with the Shaman, especially if his mother recommended any kind of immobilization or gentle form of treatment for the warriors. The Shaman was openly outspoken in his belief that the Earth needed warriors returned to it in order to allow more to be trained and confirmed.

The boy's mother had once intimated that the Shaman himself was the one that needed to be returned to the Earth. Her presence at tribal councils had been forbidden following that incident.

The boy smiled as he looked out over the racing waters beyond the reed bed. His father had taken the side of the Shaman and their part of the cave had been the scene of a quiet, hissing argument. His father had insisted that his mother was opposing the will of the Chief by refusing to curtail her feelings and opinion about the Shaman to all that would listen. She was threatening the very existence of the tribe by attacking the authority of the Chief.

A cold, uncommon silence had lain over the area until the night preparations for dinner. When serving from the heavy stone soup bowl, his mother had dropped it on his father's foot, causing him to howl and leap about the cave on his one good leg, holding his damaged limb in both hands. The long laughter into the night and the retelling and reenactment of the event had ended the argument, but the boy knew the issue had only gone underground.

His thoughts returned to the island as his eyes caught the angle of the waning sun, and more importantly, how he was going to escape it and rejoin his people.

CHAPTER VI

He looked back, past the following Mur, to the clearing set between the rock face and the great tree. The piles of brush beyond gave away the limits imposed by the small size of the island. With the Mur close behind, he made his way to the edge of the rushing rapids, the water strangely still appearing to be higher than the solid ground they stood upon.

"It must be due to the water's speed," he mused to Murgatroyd, but the Mastodon maintained its usual silence, not even a snuffle or trunk tap to indicate its agreement. Together they made their way around the only unexplored edge of the small piece of land.

After encountering the difficulty of the brush piles again, he allowed the Mur to lead. The large animal simply butted the higher piles aside and then trampled what was left into the semblance of a rough path. It took no time at all to circle the tree, pass through the clearing, and then once more stand upon the flat, hard rock surface before the reed bed.

An early evening wind had picked up and the only clean part of his body, his long hair, cleansed by its near fatal entry into the passing river, blew back from his face. It was a wind from over the top of the escarpment and he was used to the nightly summer event, the familiar breeze now giving him some comfort.

The tendril of smoke reclaimed his attention once more, as it was now identifiable without climbing anything. The wind blew the gray wisp out and across the river below them. A surge of emotion swelled up in his thin, muddy chest. There was so much to tell his family and the tribe. The omen, all about the Mur, and possibly of even greater importance, the strange, unforgettable mystery symbol carved in rock.

The Mur snuffled and brought the boy back to reality.

"Where did you come from?" he suddenly asked the animal. "Why are you here? How big is your mother?" He shot the questions out as fast as he could think of them, and then stopped, staring back into the left eye he was accustomed to communicating with. "I guess what is really bothering me is why are we here together?" He shook his head and then the Mur did the same. Until now, nothing out of the ordinary had happened during all the boy's days. He looked up and around.

"And then this?" He waved his hand at the island at large, the wonder of the past day's events causing his mind to blank with the shock and enormity of it.

After a moment, he dropped his arm and looked at the slate-flat bed of rock. Here and there were round river rocks polished to near spherical perfection by the action of the water. They ranged in size from ones as large as his head to those as small as his closed fist. He bent down and selected one of the fist-sized stones. Without preamble or comment, he reared back with his right arm and flung it out over the water. His throw had been good and the rock landed with a distant, visible splash almost a third of the way across. Nothing could be heard over the rushing hiss and boom of the quickly passing water. The Mur looked out to where the impact had occurred, and then looked down at the boy once again.

"This, my mother says," the boy stated, instructively, leaning down to find another of the small specimens, "is what makes us different." He held the rock up to Murgatroyd's attentive eye as he spoke. Extending his left hand, he flexed his fingers back and forth, first making a fist and then spreading them out.

"This hand allows me to grasp things and throw them. It is what makes me special." With that, he heaved the stone as far as he could throw and then stood to watch its flight. It impacted this time almost halfway across the wide river. Then he turned with raised chin and met the Mur's unblinking stare, about to add something, but he stopped before he even began. The Mur snuffled and searched around the surface of the rock table for something.

The trunk came back up, holding a rock almost the size of the boy's head and large enough to cause him to step back a pace. The delicate trunk end had the stone firmly grasped with its two soft pincher type ends and then half-circled by the trunk.

"What . . ." was all that the boy got out before the Mur reared its great head halfway around and snapped its trunk out toward the water.

They stood in silence as the stone disappeared, swiftly becoming a small black dot in the air up above the river. It traveled so far that the boy could not quite make out where it impacted on the ground, well past the edge of the water. Finally, he looked at his own right hand, flexed it briefly, and commented, "All right. So a big, long nose can do some things . . ." he did not know what else to say. "Long . . ." he said to himself, again flexing the hand, then bringing his eyes up to the Mur's gently waving trunk. He suddenly remembered the particularly strange piece of sapling that had cut him earlier.

"C'mon," he said to the Mur, and ran back along the path to the far side of the island. He arrived only moments later, the great animal thumping its pillar-like legs and feet so solidly behind him that he turned in fear of being overrun. But the Mur stopped just as abruptly, gathering leaf piles with its trunk as if it had only rushed to that very spot to enjoy a snack.

"You're eating!" the boy exclaimed, while the Mur ignored him as it stuffed leaves and branches into its mouth. "That's a good sign," he went on, and then focused his concentration on trying to recall exactly where he had been when he had seen the curious-looking tree part. It took considerably more of what light was left in the day than he had hoped to find the piece. Murgatroyd slowly moved about, turning the area into a green, padded clearing.

"Got it," the boy exclaimed, holding up the tattered mass. Clutching the slender body of the sapling, he quickly stripped the small branches and leaves away. The broken ends near its top were what had so painfully caught his attention. Five separate shoots that not only branched out from one point, but also curved back together, forming a kind of natural wooden pocket. While he worked the wood with his flint knife, he walked slowly back toward the clearing in front of the tree. Peeling the green bark was easy but using the knife to carefully trim the smaller branches so that the "claw" nature of the pocket was not damaged was more difficult.

Finally, he finished, and then flourished the instrument in the air in front of the Mur. "Ha, now you're not the only one with a long nose." He ran back toward the slate-flat rock they had stood on earlier, the nonsense of his statement lost on the following Mur.

Arriving at the stone area, he hunkered down and began searching. Stone after stone failed to pass his inspection, and each was quickly cast aside. Finally, he found one. He had been matching each stone with the general size of the cup at the end of his severed and trimmed wooden shaft, which now measured just over once again his own arm length.

He slipped the stone into the cup, turned his back to the water, and lightly swung the wood over his shoulder and out. The rock traveled ten body-lengths before plopping through the crusted surface of the muddy clearing.

"It works," he breathed, looking at the Mur for some sort of endorsement or confirmation, but the animal only stared back at him. The boy ran to retrieve the stone and then repeated the exercise again and again, each time throwing the round stone farther and farther across the clearing. Out of breath, he ran back from getting the missile, which had nearly made it to the far side of the island.

"Now for the test," he said grandly, smiling at the silent Mur. Facing the river again, he loaded the five-fingered pocket, leaned backward as far as he could, and swung the cup up and over his head. The rock sped into a great arc across the water, while he stood clutching his elbow. Although he had not had to bend his wounded arm at the joint in heaving the stone, pain radiated from the stress he had placed on the entire limb. But he whooped anyway, and then danced around the rock surface in a tight circle.

"It worked. It worked," he kept repeating. The missile had landed on the far side of the river, not having traveled as far as the Mur's, but clearing the water.

"Wait until I show my father this," he went on, working the shaft a bit with his flint. His enthusiasm was only slightly curbed by the knowledge that the warriors of the tribe did not necessarily take to new ideas unless they were put forward by the Shaman or the Chief. Even his father's senior warrior position did not allow him to suggest much in the way of change.

He worked the point of the flint into the end of the wooden shaft. The full-strength throw had almost cost him the stick itself, which he had just been able to hang onto. A strap of vine was the answer, and it took just a short time to fashion it. There was no way to carry the object in his state, so he also tied a piece of the vine that ran all the way from its pocket to the end of the shaft.

"The rocks . . ." he said aloud, the weakness of his new idea becoming immediately apparent. It needed specially shaped and sized rocks to work at all. The little wooden pocket would be useless with stones either too large or too small, and even rough stones probably would not fly true. It took more time to search the flat surface around the stone for more of the little, black spheres. He found six before giving up and retreating back to the base of the tree, hugging the stones to his chest as he went.

The Mur joined him under the branches' wide expanse. Suddenly an additional stone plopped onto the boy's small pile. The Mur had made his contribution, and the boy was once again stunned. The stone was just exactly the right shape and size.

"You are either very intelligent or very dumb," he said up to Murgatroyd's gazing eye. The boy shook his head. Nothing in his life had prepared him for the Mur or almost any of what had transpired in his day on the island. No experience, not any conversation with his family, or among the tribe's children. He felt tired down to his very bones. The light was swiftly disappearing as he worked the last sections of vine into a basket pouch for the stones. Tying the pouch to his left outer hip and loading the seven rocks made him feel heavy. He had come upon the island naked, but now he felt almost too heavy to move comfortably about. But he would not part with any of his new things. He was excited and fatigued all at the same time, and still deeply worried about his family and the tribe.

He stood and looked about him. Soon it would be dark. He had been taught since birth that a human being never slept in the open if he had a choice. Predators hunted in the night, and a sleeping human would be instant prey. Even though the island had been explored to his satisfaction, and he was sure there wasn't anything on it that could hurt him, he wouldn't have slept on the ground.

And then there was the water, he realized. If it rose again, which it had seemed to have stopped doing, then he would be defenseless. It made him shiver to think of being caught in the pull of the river's plunge past the island.

"It has to be the tree," he said, looking up.

With most of the brush trampled by the Mur it was much easier to examine the thick, ropy bark of the great tree trunk. No matter how the boy approached it, he could not get enough purchase with even his bare feet to overcome the weakness in his right elbow. And the experiments with the throwing stick had not helped at all, he realized. He backed off and examined the problem from a few body-lengths' distance. Then he looked at Murgatroyd facing him from only half a body's distance from the bark.

The lowest reachable limbs of the great tree sprouted out a full three body-lengths above him. The Mur stood two or even maybe a bit more.

"That's it. I'll climb you," he said, immediately stepping into the breach between the tree and the tough, furry side of the Mur. Murgatroyd turned his head to follow him but did not move. The boy grunted with the effort of pushing his feet into the bark and slowly working his back up the side of the Mur. With one last great heave he slid up onto the flat back of the great beast. Afraid the Mur would move away, he then leapt up to grasp one of the great radiating branches. He was up and over the limb just as the Mur moved out from under him.

He laid stretched out with his belly over the thick limb and his arms dangling. He fought to pry his throwing stick loose from under his hip and crotch. The flint knife dug into his side and he had almost fallen because of the weight of the stones on his hip. He was too tired to move once he got all the objects into some kind of less painful position.

In the near dark, he finally worked up the energy to climb to the easier middle branches of the tree. By the time he found a natural crook of three branches sprouting out together, he could no longer see down through the leaves and darkness. He heard the snuffle of the Mur below, adjusted his battered body as best he could in the pocket, then fell into an immediate and deep sleep.

CHAPTER VII

He awoke with first dawn. Sleep left him reluctantly, as he slowly moved the different parts of his aching body. The solid wood was hard beneath his back and thighs as he rolled carefully, making sure to keep his torso close to the main trunk of the tree. A fall from this height would be fatal.

The view below was magnificent as he surveyed almost the entire island. The boy was fully awake before two facts fought for his immediate attention: the island was slightly larger than he first thought, and the Mur was gone. The water sounds were also different. He watched the moving water closely as it heaped up to make its strange way past the escarpment side of the huge rock. It was quieter, slower, and there were no sounds of great boulders moving within it. There even appeared to be little in the way of floating debris compared to the day before.

The light was gathering enough for the boy to look straight down and make out the deep tracks of the Mur, but there were so many from their traversing back and forth that he could not make out any particular direction it might have gone. His heart skipped a beat and he sat back. Until that moment, he had not realized just how much the young Mastodon meant to him. He had sensed its complete acceptance of him and a bond he could not explain.

Making sure his new equipment was secure, the boy climbed higher into the canopy of the tree. Near the top, several small limbs clustered together, allowing him to brace his lower body and push his shoulders clear of the leaves. Only after arriving did he think to consider that he would have had an easier climb if he had left everything at the base of the tree.

The early morning sun illuminated the vast escarpment with a muted, yellow light. As he had suspected, the great cliff had been changed by the rushing torrent of water. It was now cracked in many places, and he saw huge chunks had broken off and plummeted to the floor far below, leaving debris spaced unevenly up and down the course of the river.

But smoke still poured from the cooking fires above the caves. He could not see the area of the entrances or the slow rise of ground before them. Momentarily he panicked, then realized that the sun was not high enough in the sky. The base of the escarpment and the rise that led up to it was still cloaked in a band of darkness.

Something had been nagging at the back of his mind, and he turned around on the branch to survey as much as he could. Then it came to him. The water had receded considerably and both shores were visibly closer to the island. With slower water, a lower level, and seemingly little debris in the river, he might be able to cross. Taking one last long look at the smoke wafting slowly up the cliff face, he started descending the tree.

His new equipment hampered him considerably less on the climb down than it had on the way up. He thought of the Mur and how different his life would be without the great beast in it. They had only spent a single day together, but somehow he felt a bond with the beast that he had felt for no human, other than maybe his mother.

Hanging by both arms from the lowest branch, the boy let go and fell straight down to land in a heap in the thick pulp made earlier by Murgatroyd. The bag of stones had turned in midair to land under his bottom and he rolled onto his belly holding the injured area with both hands.

"Where is a Mur when you need him?" he asked into the muddy leaves. He had to do a better job of remembering that he was carrying some hard, knobby equipment now. He got up, holding his throbbing right buttock. The balance of the earlier injuries in his elbow and hip made him sway strangely from side to side as he walked toward the water. Only after thought did he reflect on the simple fact that he would not have had the equipment problems if he had left everything at the base of the tree before his climb.

The water had dropped at least a full man-height. The only sound of its passing could be heard coming from the prow of the great rock that split the river into two channels, but it had been reduced to just a quiet, swishing noise now.

He tried to gauge the depth by walking into the river, but only went a few feet before he realized that he was being foolish. He had already made the decision to attempt the crossing, so it did not matter how deep the water was at all. Backing out, the boy searched the shore.

It took only moments for him to find a thick, broken section of water-worn tree. The ends had already been rounded by the pounding journey down through the maelstrom of the river's recent wild flood. The large piece floated high in the water when he wrestled it from the shore, and he tested it further by pushing it into deeper water. Judging the bare trunk sufficient, he guided it back to the mud bank and then sat on it to prepare for the crossing. Hunger tore at his belly, and he realized he had not eaten since the day before last. Fear and pain had affected his normal longings. He needed sustenance to make the journey across the river. He pushed himself up and searched for small vines to fashion a net. He hurriedly wove a small piece of net and attached it to a branch that he could use to sweep out into the current. The fish catcher was ragged and weak, but only had to work one time.

Back at the edge of the river, he waded out knee deep into

the softly flowing current and after only four attempts had a nice, medium-sized fish in his net. He quickly trimmed it with his flint knife, very pleased with himself, and thought about building a small fire but he had none of the special red rocks to strike his knife against. He ate the fish raw and started to prepare for his river crossing.

It took only a short time to decide that his new equipment would stay strapped to his body rather than attached to his flotation log. His adventure on the island had changed his life in a way that he could never have imagined, and the resulting tools had quickly become as much a part of him as his hands or feet. They felt right to him, so deep down inside that he could not fully grasp the emotion, but he could still somehow appreciate it. A single last tendril of vine was used to add a cord to his precious flint knife, which he hung around his neck. He was ready.

The boy sat facing the far shore as it stretched from the water's edge to the base of the high cliff face. Most of the area he had roamed his entire life had been along the gentle slope beyond the bracken piled up from the river's tremendous rise. He could only remember, when the streambed still existed, one time that he had ranged as far up as the rock face that now cut the water like a giant dull knife. With the now gentle flow of the water, he calculated his landing site on the far side. He might even be able to go ashore right at the shallow wells located straight down from the cave dwellings.

He looked back at the island that had been a home to him for such a short but momentous time. His heart ached over the loss of the Mur, and the status it would have brought him. Both of his brothers had quickly demonstrated the inherited size that helped make their father the senior warrior of the tribe. The man stood a full head above any other warrior and most of his sons would no doubt follow. Except for one. The boy took after his mother. Dark-haired, blue-eyed, and slight, but willowy and quick. The only thing even close to being big about him was his rather larger than normal forehead.

He rubbed where the Mur had so often brushed his head with the soft tip of its trunk. Absently, he wondered if any other human being in existence had ever been so touched. No, he thought, remembering back to some of the cooking fire stories. The warriors spoke of only sighting one of the beasts far in the distance, mingled with a group of the more pacified plant eaters they so desperately wanted to hunt. They also told tales of an adjoining upstream tribe that claimed to have hunted the dreaded Mur, but even they admitted that they had never killed one. The boy's father thought it was laughable that they bragged of having lost nearly two hands of warriors in the engagement.

His attention swung back around to the far bank, and to the task at hand. He had to find his parents, if they still lived, and his tribe. He looked down at the debris strewn along the shore and began looking for just the right chunk of driftwood. It had to be light and small enough for him to be able to lift it easily but also big enough to let him float with it. Finally, he found the perfect specimen.

Slowly, the boy pushed the log before him. The water's pull felt cool and gentle as he walked until it reached his chest. Then he kicked off and began running underwater, pushing the flats of his feet as much as he could against the water's weak resistance. It was slow work, but not exhausting, even in his condition. The paddling did not irritate his hip or elbow, and even the sting of his different small cuts quickly faded as he got used to the cooling water.

It was easier than he had expected, and he settled into a comfortable rhythm until he saw the snake. He froze in terror when he recognized the sinuous animal gliding toward him. Unable to move his legs, his unnaturally balanced body rotated under the unstable, round wood. He had seen the snake coming from upriver, but it had looked almost exactly like a floating piece of wood with one end thrust out of the water. It came directly at him, and there was nothing he could do except whimper.

Not even the unknown threat of the Mur on the island had filled him with such debilitating fear, and he was defenseless. Clutching the log, his weapons were useless. The serpent's tongue forked out briefly, a bright pink flash, and then its head, nearly half the size of the boy's own, turned slightly away, and the long, thick creature disappeared under the water.

The boy thrashed his feet in terror. There was no need to consider whether the snake was poisonous or not, as by its size alone—at least twice as long as the boy was tall—it could probably handle an adult quite easily. The boy glanced about wildly. It was somewhere underwater, waiting to strike. He kicked out every way he could until his legs were so tired he could barely move them. Finally, he fell still, except for the soft foot paddling that kept him upright. The snake had never resurfaced. He waited and waited, but somehow the animal had passed by underwater and then kept going without being seen.

Or so he hoped. He looked back once over his shoulder to the island, but it was already upriver from his position. The water was moving faster than he thought, and looking at the shore again, he realized he would never make the landing he had been aiming for.

He was well past the halfway point, and the far shore was becoming tantalizingly close when he once again heard the rush of water. At first he thought nothing of it, but then felt what seemed like a deep, continuous tremor in the liquid itself. He stopped paddling and listened. The sound came from no particular direction that he could fix upon. He rested for another moment and then squinted his eyes and peered downriver. Yes, there was something there. He saw a white cloud that rose majestically above the water's surface. It seemed far downriver, and not threatening in any way he could imagine. He went back to his paddling, but his mind sought to retrace the old streambed of his childhood.

The children had never strayed far from the area visible from the entrances to the caves, but on a few occasions they had gone in small parties in the company of a warrior to view the majesty of the escarpment downstream. The boy had made one such sojourn the summer before. He had stood silent, awestruck, as had the other children. The confluence of two cliffs, the smaller dovetailing into the greater and then running out toward the distant plains where the valley expanded and fell into a singular broad horizon. It was overpowering to witness. They had stood just at the juncture, looking out.

A sudden shiver of pure fear surged through his cold body. The snake had scared him near to death, but this was a different sort of fear. The old dry streambed, with its occasional wet patches, had formed a sculpted cup just at the edge of the smaller cliff. Which could only mean one thing . . .

"It's a falls," he almost whimpered, grabbing the log tightly with both hands and starting to kick harder and harder. The vibration in the water and the rushing sound of the falls had changed in the brief time he had spent considering the white, rising cloud. It was now a dull, pounding roar, still muted, but rising steadily, and leaving little doubt as to the enormous power generating it.

He pictured the area he had visited as his legs roiled the water behind him. The impossibly wide and deep river was going to go right over the edge of the cliff. His body would be smashed beyond any hope of recognition if he did not get to shore. The thought of plunging over the abyss spurred on his efforts. His legs were turning thick and numb as logs themselves, but he forced himself to keep moving. Just as the realization that he would not make it hit him, the log hit something so solid that the shock broke his hands free. Somehow, he managed to grab the rounded end of the rough, worn wood and hold on.

It was a boulder, with only a small portion of its rounded surface sticking out of the water. He held on to the log as the pressure of the now faster water pushed him against the great stone. It was a balancing act. If he moved to either side then he would slip by the boulder and continue downriver.

With the last of his energy the boy surged straight up, his upper back and neck arched to follow the curve of the rock. The water's push did the rest and he lay flat, the almost submerged wet surface barely large enough to hold him. The log, with him holding the one end, flowed around to lay bouncing gently in the lee current. He pulled the end up onto the rock and then stood.

The distance to the bank was a good twenty body-lengths, he guessed, and the current was running strong and fast. Unwillingly, he looked downriver. The booming din from the falls predominated everything else over the entire area. The resonating feel and sound seemed to come up out of the water itself, and the rising cloud of mist downriver was cut by a thin, horizontal line. The boy peered at the line until he realized it had to be the exact point at which the water flowed over the cliff. Quickly he looked back and forth between that line and the nearby shore.

"I don't know," he murmured to himself, holding the second knuckle of his right hand up against his lips. He thought he could make it, but he also knew that he was cold and fatigued. His legs had been about to give out when the boulder had intervened. He was momentarily safe, but with the pull of the water and his growing fatigue, there was no hope of staying where he was for very long. Carefully he examined the water downriver again.

"Yes," he whispered with a hopeful half-smile. His hand dropped to his side and he knelt to ensure that the log was not being dislodged from its precarious balance on the edge of the rock.

Downriver at an angle from him and closer to the bank was another almost submerged boulder, the water rippling around it. It was smaller than the one he was on, but it still protruded from the water and it was not moving.

The plan came to him in an instant. Pulling the log from the water, he lifted it until it was over his head. His weak elbow felt the strain as the water-soaked wood rose above and over his left shoulder. He bent his legs deeply, leaned forward toward the bank, and plunged as far out into the water as he could.

It was even colder than he thought, and his first breath rushed out of him. But he kicked hard and strong and surfaced, once again pushing the log forward with his hands. The smaller rock rushed toward him, and he was only able to catch it by letting go of the log completely. Chest flat against the stone and hugging it with both arms, he watched as the life-saving piece of driftwood approached the frightening straight line, then disappeared into the booming sound and mist.

The boy turned his head to look at the tantalizingly close bank.

His heart sank. The river curved in slightly just above where he was.

The water was not just rushing past him now, it was pushing a bit outward toward the center of the river, as well. The cold was sapping away what energy he had left, he knew.

Placing his feet as high up on the boulder as he could, the boy pushed up with his arms and then flung his body out of the water toward the nearby shore. He tried to angle a little upriver, but had no time to look as he broke the surface and the current took him.

He fought with all of his remaining energy, his arms flailing and legs pushing. Choking against liquid inhaled as he spluttered through the current, he almost failed to notice his left hand striking hard bottom. Then his right hand hit. He pulled his legs down and thrust forward. A second effort, and he was standing waist high against the river's heavy pull.

"Oh," was all he could get out, standing with his eyes closed and his cold hands clasped together in front of him. The water pushed him still, bouncing from foot to foot toward the cataract. Reawakened to the great danger, the boy grasped whatever reeds were nearby and finally a leaning tree limb. He pulled himself sideways and onto the hard mud of the bank. There he lay gasping, one cheek pressed into a small tuft of grass.

CHAPTER VIII

For a long time the boy sat by the edge of the water, his arms wrapped around his bare, bent legs, rocking absentmindedly while some warmth returned to his body. Slowly, he uncoiled, and took inventory. Everything he had gathered from the island had survived the tearing action of the heavy current, leaving him mildly surprised. There had been no thought whatever for his equipment during the struggles and since leaping from the larger of the two life-saving stones. If he had thought about it, he would have removed the basket of rocks, at the very least. He smiled at his own stupidity as he inventoried everything secured to his vine belts, and wondered what the Mur would have thought about his actions.

The sun was half to full as he stood and absorbed its warming rays. He rubbed his leg muscles but they only ached all the more. "Thank you," he said softly, and then proceeded to check his entire body. His desperate flight through the river had bathed him for the first time since long before the great earth-shaking catastrophe. He shook his head. As the numbing effect of the cold water wore off, he realized there was not one patch of his entire body that did not have some sort of bruise or cut or scrape. But that barely mattered now, given what he had just survived.

The falls drew him like a strong magnet. He made his way over the stones and scattered piles of debris, similar to what had been on the island. The river veered out and left a full ten body-lengths between its edge and the great escarpment wall. The boy stood and looked out over the rushing water as it cascaded over the sharp edge of the smaller cliff. Near its center, it even seemed to heap up in its haste to find the best place from which to drop.

But the full drama of its passage was all below. Even the boy's cold and discomfort was drowned in the cauldron he witnessed. The white cloud was all spray from the collision of all the mighty river's volume into one roiling and tossing pool. The thunder was overwhelming, and he leaned back physically from the sound, but could not look away. He simply stood there, gazing down, waiting for when the curtain of mist was swept away by a passing breeze.

He had imagined a terrible consequence of the falls, but nothing like what he witnessed. There was no living animal that could survive being swept over it, and once again his thoughts turned to the Mur. How had it managed to leave the island? Had it ventured out into the waters and been swept to its death below? The boy thought about it and then discarded the idea. Murgatroyd had proven to be anything but stupid, and the sheer size and weight of the animal would have allowed it to wade in waters that no other animal could handle; although the brute power of the falls itself would make short work of even a fully grown Mastodon.

The boy sat on a convenient rock near the precipice, his body still drying, and stretched out under the sun. Elation at having survived such a terrible fate seeped into him. Near his right side, a small pool formed by an offshoot of the river attracted his attention. Even following such a lengthy immersion as he had just experienced, he was thirsty and the water in the small bowl of rock appeared clean and clear. He bent to scoop some onto his hair, which was spotted with mud from having lain down after his swim. Tying the wet mass together at the back of his head with a small piece of vine, he then leaned down to drink. The reflection on the surface of the water caused him to draw back and snap his head up.

A large, black bird sat on a rock pedestal overlooking the pond from the far side. But the far side was only an arm's length from where the boy sat. It stared back at him with one eye, then squawked loudly and turned its head to view him with the other eye.

The boy noted the protruding, almost comical, wideness of the bird's yellow-orange beak. It looked like the blackbirds that inhabited many of the nooks and crannies above the caves, but the beak was definitely unusual.

In the past two days, the boy had been closer than he'd ever been before to three animals, although he discounted the snake with a shiver. But, even so, there had been the Mur, and now this bird. He thought deeply about the fact that up until these two, he had not known any animal, except to look at from a great distance. "Omens?" he wondered. Then he leaned forward half-across the pool and peered at the bird with his face no more than three hand-lengths from its bobbing beak. He stared and the bird looked back, frequently moving its head from side to side to change eyes. The boy pulled his head back and shook it.

"Well, you're not an eagle. And you sure aren't even a hawk. No, you're just a big, old, black bird with a funny beak." He waved his hand at the shiny black animal. "Shoo!" he yelled at the same time.

The bird squawked right back at him, its voice considerably louder.

"Great," the boy said to himself, checking his battered face in the mirror made by the still pool surface. "Not even a smart bird." The bird squawked again, making the boy frown, as the sound was loud enough to hurt his ears, even above the nearby thunder of the falls. He examined the creature once more and then noted the head angle: the bird watched him just as Murgatroyd had, with his head turned to the left, the single right eye glaring directly at him.

"Strange," the boy said. "This whole world is strange. What happened to create such change?" then he looked around, until his gaze turned upriver, where the smoke still flowed out over the water. He rose, brushing the excess water off his shoulders and forehead, and began walking toward the caves, then unaccountably turned back to face the pool.

"Good-bye bird," he said and waved. With a great squawk and a dramatic plunge backward, the bird extended its long wings and glided out over the rushing water straight into the white cloud of mist billowing up from the cataract below.

The boy worked his way along what had been the old, smooth path, noting the changes that had happened to it. Where the path had been straight and true, it now ran upriver in gentle curves, and twice he crossed areas where the ground had slumped in to form shallow bowls. What had been a mild, open slope from the edge of the old streambed to the base of the cliff was now dotted with boulders of all sizes and shapes. The cliff was just as high and forbidding as he remembered, but it looked so different with its fissures and cracks, and the pile of rubble now seemed to meld the ground into it, whereas before it had been a sharp division of level ground and steep, solid rock.

He walked on, his feet more tender than usual from being immersed first in mud and then water for so long. One new boulder near the water's edge held a curious, black object on its pointed top. It was another of the birds, and he was so surprised that he walked a short way from the path to get a closer look. The bird squawked, and the boy knew immediately that it was the same bird.

"What kind of bird are you? And why follow me?" the boy

yelled, but it lifted off once more, dived straight down before him and then accelerated back toward the water with rapid, audible beats of its powerful wings. The boy turned up and began the last part of his trip home.

The vista that spread out slowly in the distance before him was anything but what he remembered. The smoke flowed out of a single cave entrance, whereas all of his life it had drifted up in the caves and exited through a vent high on the escarpment above. The two additional entrances he had known since not long after birth were simply not there, including the one he had exited only the morning before. Their former presence was marked only by piles of rock debris. Tribe members moved about the area, hauling things out of the single cave entrance and covering the mounds with sleeping and storage hides. There was even an additional fire outside the single entrance where most of the women and children seemed to be gathered. Then the most discomforting element of the scene struck him. He was walking in plain view, and several members of the tribe had turned to observe him, and then gone back about their business. They had to have recognized him, and he almost cried out in greeting to them, but instead instinctively withheld any communication. Something was even more dreadfully wrong than the aftermath of the catastrophe.

As he approached the fire, all discussion ceased and all turned to look at him. An inexplicable uneasiness grew within him, and he did not smile at their welcome faces. One of his brothers stood next to the single cave opening, but he also said nothing. His expression held no emotion whatsoever. The boy stopped and looked from the women and children back into his brother's eyes, and his stomach churned with the acid of worried apprehension. Finally, he stepped forward to face his brother directly, but was nearly run down by his father's huge body emerging from the entrance.

There was no embrace from the huge warrior; instead, his father's powerful right hand gripped him like a soft claw on the left shoulder. He squeezed gently and spoke.

"Where have you been?" The question came out as an accusation, and the boy had never seen a colder or more distant look in his father's eyes. The man had never been truly warm to him as he had to his two other sons, but the boy had never experienced such a glacial demeanor from him. And he had not seen his mother among the women.

"I was trapped on what is now an island in the middle of the river," he answered in a catching small voice. He pointed back with his right arm but did not turn his head from his father's fierce gaze. "I could not get back until the water level dropped."

The big man's head moved slightly as he stared at the river, but he said nothing.

Suddenly his mother appeared from around behind the boy's father, her left hand gently resting on his left shoulder. She smiled a crooked half-smile, and then gently pried his father's iron grip lose, and embraced him. The boy turned liquid inside and tears welled up in his eyes. They both slipped down to a kneeling position, his head tight on her shoulder. Only at the end of her embrace did his eyes take in what they could see of the cave's interior. The roof was much lower and the back somehow all scrunched in. Even the single entrance was much smaller than it had been, yet he could see nothing in the surrounding rock that would allow for that. Warriors came past them carrying all manner of items usually stored in the cave's vast back chambers. It was apparent, however, that they had to slip tightly between the walls of a small crack to gain entrance.

His mother withdrew from the tight clasp, but remained kneeling before him with her hands remaining on his shoulders.

"I must speak with him," his father said ominously from his side.

The boy felt the man's presence more than saw him out of the corner of one eye. He knew that his father still stared out toward the water, and that whatever he had to say could only be terrible news. He looked around for his other brother, but could not find him without moving from his mother's embrace.

"I know," his mother replied at last, and then stood, her hands falling away to her side. Her expression was so sad that the boy wanted to comfort her, but he sensed that the profound sadness gripping her was about him.

He felt his father's uncharacteristically hard grip on his upper arm once more, and he rose to be led into the cave. Once inside, he absently noted the amount of damage and it was extensive. The caves had always been cold and damp, but they had been neat and clean. Now debris was littered everywhere and there was no evidence that portions of the cave system he knew like the back of his hand had ever existed. Questions that he would have normally asked, "Where would they live? What was going to happen to the tribe? Who had been lost in the catastrophe?" he could not, he dared not ask. He said nothing as his father released him. They stood facing one another in shadow, aside from the front entrance.

"You were seen to run from here the morning last. When the earth moved you awoke and fled our home," his father's deep voice paused with a catch in it before he went on, "and you provided no warning to anyone." The boy stood silent, not blinking at all, trying to take in his father's words.

"Then, when so many were trapped and lost under fallen rocks and dirt," the big man gestured to the solid but cracked walls surrounding them, "you did not return to help," he paused again briefly, "until now."

The boy would remember hearing those words for life, but their cutting nature did not approach the tone of his father's delivery. He literally could not speak into the silence growing between them. He could barely even think.

The words had been spoken as if a final interpretation of the events had already been made; as if a sentence had been pronounced in his absence. Tears rolled down both of his cheeks, but he was too afraid to even attempt to wipe them away. His father's eyes were deep, dark pools and remained focused out toward the entrance and the light. He seemed to wait for something, but the boy could think of nothing at all to say. He wanted to say that he was sorry, but he could not even do that. His vocal cords were paralyzed.

Then his father pronounced his sentence.

"It is the decision of the council of warriors and the approval of the Old Bagestone, our Chief that, because of your young age, you be allowed to remain with the tribe."

The boy was stunned into even deeper shock. Banishment? Banishment had been considered? Only the most heinous crimes were punished by this ultimate penalty, and never once in his ten summers had it occurred in the tribe. Yet it had been considered for him. Stories of old, told around the cooking fire, had discussed the application of the most dreaded sentence. The banished member was physically cast out naked on the plain beyond the old streambed and given one crossing of the sun to disappear. If ever seen by a warrior again anywhere, he was to be slain immediately, and without compunction, his body left for the carrion feeders. The stories only whispered of events from long ago, and the children had secretly not believed them, like the story of miscreant children being fed to the unseen and unknown wolves.

The boy's head bowed under the shame and alienation, but his father was not finished. "You will not enter warrior training and you will never be a warrior of this tribe. When you reach the adult age of fifteen summers you will become an adult, and up to that time you will not be allowed to participate in the work of the tribe unless specifically assigned. You will not speak to tribal members in training nor to any of the warriors that they are to become. You are only allowed the privilege of remaining with the tribe because of your age and my status in the tribe."

The words sank in one by one like hammer strikes upon the base rock of the streambed. He would never be a warrior. He would never hunt with the warriors, tell tales of his kills, or attend the all-night sessions of the tribal council. The boy, upon reaching adulthood, would only be allowed to help the tribe if told to do so and, until that time, he would not even be allowed that. In effect he was banished, but not thrown out of the tribe altogether. Banishment would have been more merciful: just a few days or weeks of hunger and regret, and then the release of death or the forgetfulness of a solitary life. But this status as a slave meant a lifetime of shame and loneliness. And how was he to be named, if he could not really be a warrior or lesser member of the tribe?

He would be the only male of the tribe with such status. There had been such men in the past, but they were either not right in the head, injured, or they were those that yearned only for the work of women while wanting the association of men.

It was too much to take in. The words and their impact bore down on him like weighted stones. He ran toward the raging river, passing a small, crippled child as he went. The boy stared at him with bright flinty eyes as he went by. The boy glanced back at him with a frown, then ran on to the edge of the water. Farther behind he could see his father walking in his path. He had eaten nothing but the fish in days, and his battered body could not take the shock of his humiliation and then the short run. He was not even aware of passing into unconsciousness and falling to the ground.

CHAPTER IX

The first few days of his new near-slave status were among the worst of the boy's life. He had awoken from a full day and night's sleep, and had carefully hidden his throwing stick, special rocks, and the flint knife under one of the riverbank piles. He was surprised to not have everything taken from him and remained unsure if the warriors might not come and take them at a later time. He hid them far enough away from the water, in case it rose again, yet not so far from the caves as to be difficult to get to. The boy glumly knew that his experiences on the island would be kept to himself. In the future, there might come a time to share with his mother, but even that did not appear likely, and he was not certain that he would be allowed to keep anything gained during his stay there once he discussed it.

His social exclusion and isolation would have been far more strictly enforced, except for the monumental need for labor required by the greatest tribal building project in its known history. The decision to build artificial caves, well away from the great escarpment, but not too close to the river, had only been made the night before. The boy knew it was his mother's idea, as he could only now listen when among the family gathering, but the common talk of the village was of the Chief's bold, new project. Only his father's ability to sway the warriors had stood up against the Shaman's plan to reinhabit the cave complex by digging them back out. Even with his senior warrior status his father had not wanted to present the plan, because to oppose the Shaman was uncomfortably dangerous. What kind of danger was never discussed, but somehow his mother had prevailed, and his father had taken the unknown risk.

The boy was the perfect work utensil for the building attempt. Only one tribe who lived far up the old streambed was known to live in artificial caves, and those structures had only been examined in the most cursory fashion. Those structures, made like giant upside-down baskets, from the bent wood of small saplings, would be a far cry from the tribe's attempt.

The stream's overnight growth into the great river had eroded the soil all along the bank. In several places, great, flat beds of cracked slate lay strewn about the sand, layer after layer of almost the same finger-width thickness. It could be pulled up, scored with a flint knife, and then broken with a granite hammer into roughly similar square plates. The beds of black-gray rock reminded the boy of the clear area before the reed bed on the island. He bent under his load as one last piece was placed in the braided willow basket strapped to his back. An exception had been made to his isolated status for the building of slate structure, but only until the structure was complete. After that, occasionally, tribal members could make him do things for them, but that would not occur often.

From the sun's rise over the escarpment to its fall down past the distant cliff across the river, he labored back and forth between the warriors, who scored and broke the slate, then up to the women and warriors-in-training who carefully packed each piece atop an already laid line. His own mother had carefully traced out and then dug shallow trenches for the walls of the great enclosure. Inside the structure she worked at laying out inner room walls, each with its own fire ring and smoke tube.

The only time a smile had crossed the boy's face was when the first trial room had been built, to prove to the Shaman that the plan would work. Before the mud had even dried, the warriors had packed in until the walls had almost collapsed from the outward pressure. The experiment had been a success, with only triple-thick walls being added to the plan.

The boy's task would have been impossible except for the help of the children considered too young to do normal work other than chores. Their contribution, with their small, two- or three-slate-plate basket loads, made up the bulk of the work. The boy never stopped, except to drink from the river and eat near the boulder where he had hidden his few possessions. He simply ran, like the other children, back and forth to help carry the slate for the structure.

The day of the third full moon since the catastrophe passed saw the completion of the strange, flat complex. It looked almost exactly like a beaten root cake his mother baked for breakfast upon occasion. The last days of the slate hauling had been particularly difficult for the boy, as the cold of fall was now intense in the early mornings, and the young children could not be of such great assistance because of it.

Bent under his load, he trudged up the gentle rise, winding around the worn branch debris that had been deposited by the Great Flood, as the tribe had come to describe the rising of the water. The branches had proven to be the most important element of the construction. Interlaced in between the topmost slate plates and then bent over and entwined together they had become the stabilizing element and roof of the many rooms. Mud covered the bent branches and then weed grass was laid atop the mud. The result had surpassed even his mother's predictions.

His time had passed, for the most part, in utter exhausted silence. The crush of the heavy labor and the tribe's rush to complete the structure before the onset of freezing cold and snow had limited what little opportunity he had to communicate. Only a few children, running up and down on the same beaten path, had said anything to him at all. His mother had assured him that all would be well over time, but then concentrated all of her efforts into making sure the project was completed on time. There was no celebration or announcement when the sprawling, roughly round structure was completed. Supplies were simply moved inside as well as skins and other belongings. The process of getting settled into such strange "caves" began and stretched through the late evening. Fires lit in individual rooms provided an eerie glow to the work.

The boy slept uncomfortably just inside the door of his family's designated room, then arose early the following morning. He was satisfied that a sufficient pile of slate stood stacked near the upriver side of the structure, and his responsibilities were done. It was the first day of enforced liberty for him, and he intended to spend it away from the company of all human beings.

He stood just outside the door of their exterior wall room. Most members of the tribe did not have an opening directly out, and deep discussions had occurred at council sessions to determine who would reside where. But then, he reflected, that had been no different when they had all clustered inside the many different parts of the caves. The central places, where all could be observed, were occupied by the leaders. The interior parts of the new structure, opening into the central ceremonial space, would be the same way. The warriors would occupy the areas nearest openings for protection and to keep them near the freedom of the open land just beyond.

A light layer of white covered everything within sight, the river appearing as a wide, steaming, black line down the slope. The first snow, and the boy hesitantly kicked at some with his foot. The heavy labor had not only provided a venting solace to his tortured emotions, it had required that he be provided with foot leathers. The skins were not those of the special, triple-thick bear hide as the warriors had, but then he would not be traveling great distances over rough terrain either. He walked in a small circle, and then smiled to himself. They were perfect, and the first positive thing that had come into his life since his return home.

He looked back through the opening. The room was larger than most, and the clean slate floor near the door glinted with the first rays of the morning sun. With the new dwelling had come new rules that only three moons earlier the boy would have complained piteously about: Remove all foot leathers, no spitting, no rock or food throwing. But he complained no more; he did not even consider the new orders harsh. He took all commands or orders now in obedient silence, even from the other children. His low status was no mystery.

He shrugged his shoulders once in dejection, and then padded out across the fresh, white blanket to retrieve his equipment. The further he traveled from the tribal dwelling, the lighter his step became, until he was trotting. The cold dropped away along with the heavy weight of his emotional burden.

It took only moments to retrieve the flint and stones from his hiding place and reattach them to his waist, while it took a bit longer to refashion the sling for his stick. He realized that if he carried it slung on one shoulder with the "claw" swinging downward he could load the weapon much quicker. It rode best on the side opposite his special stones. He squared himself and faced the river. He had not mentioned any of his new equipment to anyone, much less the experiences he had encountered in his time on the island. Far upriver, the small chunk of land, even with its great tree and rock face, was hard to distinguish from the backdrop of the far shore.

The boy turned downriver, adjusted his various vine attachments and then began his journey.

"My own warrior training begins today," he said to the rushing waters as he moved into a gentle, running lope. His right hand seemed to flow with the movement and swing of the throwing stick, while the woven bag of small rocks bounced comfortingly at his left side. He'd lost his tattered, castaway shirt, but he knew the day would warm rapidly, especially atop the escarpment wall, his intended destination. When he had stood at the edge of the thunderous falls, he had seen a portion of the cliff further downriver that might provide enough hand- and footholds to make it all the way up. The danger of falling to his death did not even occur to him as he ran next to the river. He no longer had anything to lose.

He examined the face of the escarpment as he walked the curves of the path. The wall above the old cave entrances and almost all the way to the great falls was smooth, with only a few cracks. The boulders strewn about from the cliff face all the way to the river seemed to be a result of great sheets of rock peeling from the face and shattering on the earth below.

It took only moments at his ground-eating pace to reach the lip of the cataract. He had only slipped a few times in the smooth-bottomed foot leathers, and each time his willowy balance and forward momentum had saved him from landing on the ground.

The falls thundered deafeningly and part of the boy wanted to cover his ears. But he did not give in to the desire. He watched the river pour over the edge and instead of the awed terror he had previously experienced, he felt elation and joy at the churning destruction. He breathed deep of the swirling mist and felt a personal attachment to the entire, tumultuous scene. It was a shock to him, he realized, that within days of having returned to the tribe, the great, noisy cataract was accepted by all without question. How it had come about or where all the never-ending water came from was simply not discussed by anyone, similar to the silence that followed the passing of any tribal member. They were just gone.

Only the Shaman, Huslinth, had brought up the subject of the catastrophe at council, and that had been regarding the replacement of the new structure so as to avoid future disasters. His argument, that the entire incident was the result of the tribe's failing to sacrifice sufficiently to the powers of the earth, had not met with open derision by the Chief, but it had been quietly discounted.

His mother had discussed the exchange one night over the cooking fire. The Chief had listened to all of the Shaman's reasons and then concluded with some of his usual wisdom: "If nature demands a price for its bounty, then who are we to argue." His mother had laughed at the inability of the Shaman to deal with the statement. Thinking that the Chief was supporting him, he had agreed. But the Old Bagestone had gone on.

"And so, nature has spoken. She has come and taken from the tribe those things that she felt were of value. We could not know what those things would be. Nature is satisfied." The Huslinth had bowed his shoulders in defeat.

Movement caught the boy's eye and he ducked as a black shadow cut the air in front of his face. A great fluttering of wings beat the air into gusts of current as the boy stopped, his shoulders hunched in anticipation of being struck in the head. But nothing touched him.

Instead, a bird fluttered to a landing, sitting on the same pedestal across the small expanse of the clear pool. It let out a squawk just loud enough to be heard over the crashing of the falls.

The boy noted that he had just reached the point near the edge of the cataract where he'd first seen the very same creature. No other bird in his existence had ever had such a strange beak.

"You again," he said with some disdain. "The omen of ill fortune. What do you have in store for me today?"

Suddenly the bird fell more than flew to the ground near his feet, casting a small cloud of powdery snow into the air. Instead of walking on its two orange legs, it flopped onto its back and then bounced around before him, as if trying to dislodge something. The boy peered down bewildered and stared into the creature's shiny right eye, and thought he saw pain and fright.

"What?" he said softly, leaning down. The look was so familiar, yet foreign. He knelt close to the bird and its movements subsided, but it did not shy away. He poked at the bird's complex tail arrangement, seeing movement within. Then he saw the small insects. The bird's feathers were infested with crawling bugs. He recoiled, quickly withdrawing his finger. All members of the tribe had a powerful aversion to vermin of all kinds. The women spent a considerable amount of time at the streambed water pits, scrubbing leathers and skins to rid them of the terrible creatures. The boy's mother had proven to them all, except the Shaman, who took credit for any good news, that drinking only clear, pure water and keeping clean from insects prevented sickness.

He looked the bird in the eye and then gripped its body with one hand and carried the surprisingly heavy weight over to the side of the clear pond. Although the animal pecked him hard on the top of that hand, the blow did not break the skin. With his other hand he scrubbed and picked while the bird struggled and squawked away.

"You are the filthiest creature I have ever seen," the boy grimaced, but continued his odious chore. He noted the bird's thick feathers were only black near the surface, while just beneath was a layer of very fine, white material that resembled fur more than feathers. This was the infested layer. Finally, unable to pick all the small beasts out by hand, he dunked the lower part of its body into the water and scrubbed with both hands.

The water was filled with floating bugs when he was done. As soon as he released his grip, the bird's wings convulsed out and back, splashing the insect-filled water all over the boy's face and chest.

"Ugh!" he yelled, falling backward and brushing madly with both hands to get the terrible things off. The bugs seemed to have died almost instantly upon landing in the water, but the thought of them infesting him as they had the bird drove him into a frenzy of slapping and picking. In a loud flurry of flapping wings, the bird took off, circled the area once and then flared briefly and landed back on the pedestal where he had stood when they first encountered one another. It set immediately to adjusting its misaligned body feathers with its thick, wide beak, stopping occasionally to observe the boy sitting on the other side of the bug-filled pool.

"Won't be drinking out of that for awhile," the boy mused after finishing his own cleaning. He sat and stared at the strange animal.

"So maybe you're not a bad omen," he concluded, speaking to the bird as if it understood his every word. "How does it feel to be just a lowly bird, one without bugs, that is," and then he added, smiling, "and one with a fat beak." The bird squawked once, seemingly protesting the last comment, but then went back to its grooming.

The boy stood up and completed rubbing down his own body.

"It's too cold to stay here with you," he said, grimacing from the chill of the fall's mist that had drifted over not only to block the sun, but to release a fine cloud of water all about the area. As he had noted from a distance, the boy watched the mist gather into drops on the outer surface of the bird's feathers and then just roll off. Birds were waterproof, although no tribal member, not even his mother, had ever been able to tell exactly why.

For some reason he felt it necessary to let the bird know what he was doing. The old path had always ended right at the juncture where the smaller cliff ran into the escarpment wall. The boy had noted on his previous visit to the falls that what had once been an abrupt drop was now a steep but negotiable decline of fallen rock and debris. Only the edge and beyond, beginning where the water flowed over, was sharp and flatly defined. It was that observation, and the cracks and depressions further downriver, that had buried the thought deep in his mind that scaling the vast wall might be possible.

"I'm going to climb that, the great escarpment that has never been climbed before," and he pointed almost straight up toward the very top of the escarpment, but the bird only gave the direction a brief glance before going back to grooming itself.

"Humph," the boy said to the bird, then dropped his arm and began negotiating the steep slope of the decline.

CHAPTER X

He moved down the litter of small rock and shale, slick with mist from the thundering falls coating the entire area with a sheen of clean, cold water. The going was not treacherous. He discovered the natural curve of the debris allowed him to work easily back and forth as he went. The bottom, so many man-heights down that the boy could not even estimate how far it was when he stood and looked back the way he'd come, was cloaked in shadow and forbidding. The thrumming, constant beat of the falls, the swirling mist, and the deep, penetrating wetness all gave off a sense of foreboding that he found mildly uncomfortable, yet tolerable. The huge impact pool, where the water churned back and around, was almost invisible because of the huge clouds of spray. Only for the briefest time did it clear, but never enough to see where the water actually struck, or even the other side of the pool.

The boy moved along the flat bank, noticing how the plant life had been stripped away by the Great Flood. Willows that had been nearly full-grown, once near the areas next to the rapid water where it came rushing out and down from the seething impact basin, had been washed away like they had never existed in the first place.

There was no hesitation when he came to the area he wanted to climb. He looked up once, just to assure himself of the possibility of what he was about to attempt. The very top edge of the great escarpment was invisible from this close to its base, but it looked like the wall actually ran out over his head at an angle toward the river. He knew that wasn't so, as his perspective from the side of the falls had been much better, but it was another note of foreboding.

Working in through the spindly saplings, he reached the hard, vertical surface. It was solid and easy climbing at the base. He'd adjusted his throwing stick by strapping it across his back. Even his rock basket had been moved so it rode over the back of his left hip. The rearrangement of the wall had provided near perfect holds for his hands and feet. Only the coldness of being in dark shadow and the wetness everywhere bothered him at all. He did not look back or down, just up at the next in the seemingly never-ending network of cracks and crevices. The long days of carrying the heavy slate loads had built his arms and legs into thin, stringy bands of hard muscle. The memory of warriors filling his basket rapidly while he was required to face away from them, they not speaking to him, only among themselves, and then the same treatment from the women of the tribe when he stood facing away from them to unload, burned in his mind.

The boy's arms and legs pumped as emotion drove him upward at a fierce pace. Thighs burning, but never giving way, he moved like a serpent through the reeds of the old streambed, upward, always upward.

The bird did not make its presence known until he rested, crouched sideways on the first significant ledge he'd found. His chest had hitched in shock when he saw it sitting just above him on a small outcrop only an arm's length away. It had somehow flown and perched there without the boy hearing anything.

"Shoo," he yelled up at it, then waved his left hand right before its outthrust breast. The bird pecked the back of his hand soundly.

"Ow!" he said, quickly withdrawing the appendage and checking for damage, but there was only an irritated, red spot.

He looked up again. "Stupid bird. I'm sorry I told you where I was going." Then he thought about what he just said. "Well, who is the one talking to birds here?" he muttered, and then looked down.

The adjustment was so rapid that he teetered back, pressing himself into the hard rock wall, both hands bracing against the lip of the ledge. Then he breathed deeply and took in the wondrous sight beneath him.

The white mist was well below, as was the edge of the smaller cliff. Now he could see the cliff extending far out onto the plain before trailing away and becoming part of its flatness. The sun warmed him and a gentle wind blew his long, dark hair past his eyes. As other males of the tribe, he wore it flowing free unless engaged in hunting or work, at which times it was allowable to tie it back into one mass at the back of the head. He had forgotten to gather one of the smaller pieces of vine for that small chore, so he just brushed it out of his way. Refreshed by the wind and sun, and ignoring the ever-present bird, he resumed the climb.

From the edge of the falls, he had stood and seen a tiny pine sticking out from the very top of the cliff edge. Taking his second rest at another ledge, the boy caught a glimpse of it far above.

The reality of the height of the wall came to him with that sight. The pine was huge, many man-heights tall, and its trunk was as thick as he was long. The rest of the trip was short, for the boy would not make the mistake of looking down again.

The bird goaded him on with its frequent passes back and forth before coming to rest somewhere just to the side or just above. Its squawk seemed to get louder as the thunder of the falls receded, although he could still feel the deep, drumming sound right through the rock face.

"You are the noisiest, most irritating thing," he said disgustedly. His whole body hurt and his thighs burned furiously. He knew he had to press on because each stop caused his legs to not want to push him up anymore. There would be no going down, as he knew that he just did not have the strength for it. And with this awareness, fear gripped him. Not of the height. He no longer thought of it. *No,* he thought, *but what if there is a place between here and the top that doesn't have any place to grip?* The thought ate at him until he had to move again. This time, before he could go on, he had to ease himself up and down many times before his calves would relax. He could not stop again.

It was only within full view of the large roots of the outthrust pine that had been his target for most of the way that he came to the dreaded place. What had started out as a wide, traversing ledge that he could walk on narrowed away to nothing. He was forced to stop and consider, but this time he did not squat. His legs were weakening and tremors had developed in both thighs. Fear built up within his chest and bile rose up from his stomach to his throat. Where the sun had warmed him earlier, it now beat down with unceasing intensity. He was thirsty and tired. He also knew, from overhearing the warrior's conversations years before, that the two things ran closely together and their combination was very dangerous.

Behind him, the bird squawked loudly. They were so high up that the sound of the distant falls was just a minor thrum in the distance.

The boy turned and inclined his gaze back to the bird standing at the other end of the ledge. It squawked once again as it noted his attention.

"Gloating, are we?" the boy breathed out with a twisted smile.

The bird stepped back, as if at the poison in his tone. Then he stepped back a bit farther right near the sharp end of the ledge.

"You're going to fall right off," the boy said, but to himself softly, because just as the words died away, the bird appeared to walk right into the stone wall and disappear.

Quickly he turned around on the narrow outcrop and worked his way to the other end. Then he saw it: an inverted crack that ran up the rock vertically, but was almost impossible to see unless you stepped right to the very edge of the ledge. The bird squawked from above and then flew straight out from the face of the wall with a flurry of quick, strong wing-beats.

The boy wedged himself into the deep crack and slowly eased himself up, his legs reinvigorated with a surge of elation and adrenaline.

"Thank you," he yelled outward, although he knew the distant bird could not possibly hear him, or understand if he did. He climbed until his hands contacted the solid mass of a tree root, and he knew with a smile what tree stood high above that root.

He rapidly covered the last few man-heights and stood under the great, spreading branches of the huge pine. It was bigger by far than any of the puny, green-needled trees below. The wind whispered through the tree, and its shade was dark and complete. The boy rested, sitting just back from the edge of the deep precipice, and leaned forward against his drawn-up knees to take in the view.

He could see all the way up and down the long valley. Directly below was the falls, unheard over the wind and sighing pine, and from this distance was not much larger than his fist as he extended it out before him. But it was a thing of grand beauty. It took a few moments for him to look upriver and observe the new dwelling of his tribe.

When he had been helping in its construction, the structure had appeared just a rough and loosely held together complex of stone rooms. From his current vantage point it was clearly one great, flat building made up of many rooms, with a brown cloud of smoke that sat right atop it. The boy realized that one of his future jobs would be hauling wood. The idea of many cooking fires instead of the single, large one that had been such a fixture of cave life was hard to accept.

The fire had been where they had gathered, and where he had learned about most of what went on in the tribe. He wondered if the new change would be a good thing. Thinking about the recent changes made him uncomfortable, but then, just thinking of the tribe at all now made him uncomfortable, he realized.

Set upriver and out in the distant line of water was the island, and when the boy saw it, a pang of loneliness shot through him. He missed the Mur. It was the only creature he still considered a friend. With that thought came the now familiar squawk of the black bird. With its usual flair it dropped out of the sky, landed with a resounding plop on a branch just above the boy's head. It sat only an arm's length away, but appeared to share his interest in the view rather than look at him.

"And then there is you," the boy laughed aloud. "All right. Two friends then." He closely scanned the plumage of the bird for any more of the horrid bugs, but he saw nothing. The animal seemed to rest much more comfortably than it had before.

He looked out over the vast valley below and thought of life in general. There seemed to be the slightest tendril of smoke from downriver, but he discounted it. Nothing lived over there, according to the well-traveled warriors. His mind went back to the bird.

Twice he had helped damaged animals just as his mother helped injured and ill tribesmen, except for the warriors, who were Shaman Huslinth's domain. His mother had quietly stated to his father that this was why so many of the warriors died of their wounds. His father had heard the argument before, and discounted it by citing the code of the warrior. After that there was only silence.

The boy had helped two wild animals and they, in turn, had helped him. He could not understand why others in the tribe, who thought of themselves as superior to animals, were not like that at all. And he knew it was not just his own tribe. Many of the trading parties had come back either in triumph from cheating an upriver tribe or in anger over having been cheated themselves.

He sat holding his head with one hand, his hair blowing out over the lip of the escarpment wall, viewing the entire length and breadth of the world as he knew it. He could no more come to terms with his attempts at understanding the way men and women thought than he could understand how his actions during the catastrophe could have been so misunderstood and so severely punished.

He had only asked his father one question since the pronouncement of his sentence, and it had gone unanswered. In his life he had never heard the earth cry out before. He had never seen it move beneath his feet. And could not possibly have returned from the island to life back at the caves, the same as it had been. The memory of the water rushing by, filled with dirt, trees, boulders, and more, still haunted him when he was close to the river, and stared into it.

"How could this have happened to me?" he whispered, near tears for the first time since falling to the ground in the cave.

"Squawk," the bird replied from just above him.

The bird's response was so quick following the boy's soft, plaintive cry that he could not help but turn his head and laugh, wiping away tears not quite formed.

"You're right. Whatever you said. Nobody has ever climbed this wall before." The realization of the singular triumph energized his body in a way little else could have. Pushing himself up, he reslung the throwing stick and retied the rock basket at his waist. Then he surveyed the roof of the world. The surface was a light-colored rock, not nearly as dark as that of the great wall. Wherever the pines grew, only a small, round patch of brown needles lay under them. As far as he could see, the terrain was the same, and he immediately decided that he liked its strange features, so different from the world below. His tiredness and thirst dropped away as he surged forward, his direction straight in from the edge, where the great, green trees seemed to part before him in a never-ending series of natural paths.

CHAPTER XI

After his rest, the boy ran lightly, as he had done before on the path next to the river, not looking back for the bird, but knowing that it was gliding and flapping lightly behind. He smoothly wove around the whispering pines, the bottom branches of all so high that he ran right through beneath, atop the soft, needle-cushioned carpets covering the ground. His body had just begun to thrill with the pure beauty and fun of the workout when he suddenly pulled up in stunned surprise. He had run no more than three or four hundred man-lengths to encounter another escarpment lip, almost identical to the one he had just left.

The bird passed low over his right shoulder and wafted right into the draft blowing up from below. He soared up magnificently, with his great, wide wings spread, but the boy did not even notice. He stared out in shock, looking along the precipice first one way, then the other. Finally, he looked straight out, where the black bird soared back to catch still another updraft. He could not believe what he was looking at. It was another valley almost the exact same size as the one that the tribe inhabited.

The warriors of the tribe taught that nothing of any consequence existed beyond the valley. But, there before his eyes, beyond the valley that spread out below, was another distant escarpment. The only thing lacking was a river running down its center.

Gently the boy slid from his feet into a sitting position, his legs folded under him and crossed at the ankle. In just seconds the size of his world had been doubled.

Directly in front of him, the bird appeared from below. A strong current ran up the face of the escarpment, the opposite of the flow on the other side, the boy noted absently, staring at the near immobile bird. He was almost still in the air, able to balance the downward pull of his weight against the strength of the wind's upward thrust.

The bird seemed to be waiting for something, so the boy whistled. Sometimes, before the catastrophe, he had whistled to try and attract birds close enough to hit with a stone. He had never had any success, but this time the bird dropped out of the wind and landed on the lip not far from the boy's right knee. He whistled again to see if he might affect the animal a second time. Immediately the bird fluttered up and landed on his shoulder, striking his head with its left wing as it pivoted before setting down.

"Ow!" the boy hissed, in pain from the talons digging into his bare shoulder, but mostly from fright. The thick beak waved jerkily from side-to-side, no more than a hand's breadth from his right eye. The boy sat frozen, not knowing what to do. The bird squawked, the harsh sound deafening in the boy's right ear.

"Ah," was all he said, both shoulders pulling up as his eyes closed.

The bird just stood, as if it was quite used to the arrangement, while the boy rubbed the top of his hand where the hard beak had pecked at him. He took a deep breath.

"Looks like I am stuck with you, at least for awhile," he eyed the bird guardedly out of his squinted right eye, trying to keep his head turned slightly away to the left. "Maybe one day you will just disappear, like Murgatroyd," he said, but only received another raucous cry in return.

"Don't . . . talk," the boy managed, almost under his breath, wanting to hold his hurting ear. Not wanting to dislodge the bird, the boy slowly got up. As soon as he was standing, the bird dropped forward and down, as if it would strike the ground right at his feet, but no more than a hand above it the great wings extended, and the bird leveled until encountering the updraft. Then it soared once more and rolled to dive deep down into the canyon.

"Prideful bird!" the boy yelled after it, although he had enjoyed the performance. "My bird can certainly fly," he said with a smile.

He decided to move downriver, or to what would have been downriver on the other side of the high plateau. Initially he trotted as near to the rim as the haphazard growth of the trees would allow, working toward what he guessed to be the plateau's center. The trees were the largest there and he could run beneath most of them. The bird played in the air all around him, weaving and swooping among the pines as they went.

After walking for some time, the boy realized he was much farther away from the cave complex and the tribe than he had ever been alone. He wondered if anyone even thought of him, then banished the idea from his mind. He felt no sense of separation or loss with the growing distance, only a warm comfort to be running free among the trees and with the noisy, funny bird as a playful companion.

The boy did not stop until the sun was more than directly overhead, and when he did, he was not certain what had caught his attention at first.

He had just seen a long, high rock before him and instead of changing direction to avoid it, as he would have for a tree, he had simply picked up speed and vaulted the stone, lightly tapping it with one bare foot as he went over.

It was the stone, he realized standing in a small clearing. The boy looked back. There was something strange about it. He turned and walked back. The trees had thickened here so that the sun cast a dark green hue as it shone through the interwoven branches just above his head.

The bird landed on the flat surface of the rock just as the boy reached it. Pecking at a chunk of moss in one place and then a small pile of old brown needles in another, it walked along the length of the stone, while the boy stood and marveled. The stone was not a simple boulder at all, and he would never have been able to turn to avoid it.

It was a flat rock almost four man-heights long, hewn to form square corners and almost flat sides. He moved slowly along it, examining the surface carefully with his hands. Where the stone ended, another began, cut to the same dimensions as the one he had jumped over, and followed by another and another. Each of the strange monoliths had been butted tightly up against the next, forming almost a straight line at that.

At a fast run, the boy paralleled the row of stones. As he had suspected, he soon came to the far escarpment wall again. The cut rock wall ran from one side of the plateau to the other. He did not even attempt to run to the river escarpment to prove his theory. He just knew he was right, but he did not know what to make of it. Instantly, he was reminded of the carving that he had seen on the island . . . but who could carve in stone? It could be worked, as with the head of a granite hammer, or knapped, like when flint was heated and cooled to chip off pieces and form a spear point, but he had never heard of the carving of hard stone. *What could possibly be used that would be tough enough?* he wondered. It was a mystery he knew he could not solve, so he slowly continued his run. Although the bird flew with him again, he was lost in thought regarding what he had just seen, and ill prepared for what he ran into next.

"Oh," was audibly forced out of his lungs when he saw the fallen figure. The land had just opened into a broad clearing where only a few giant pines loomed, while the remainder of the foliage was very low brush, saplings, and a lush carpet of vine grass. There was very little snow here compared to the valley. He had loped into the open space and almost crossed it without heed. Only a glance to his right had revealed the unnatural lines, or he would have passed it without notice.

The figure stood upright and was not much higher than the boy himself. Covered in green moss and patches of other multicolored growth, it would have passed for a shaft of old pine trunk, stripped of all branches and left standing, if the only "branch" had not been holding a curved implement.

It was a man, but made of rock, and it, like the blocks of the wall and the symbol on the island, was carved. The boy circled the strange figure, maintaining a reverent distance from it. What could have been a broken bare branch was a stone arm extended, but the rest of the object was so covered in plant growth that he could not make out much detail, except he knew it was made to look exactly like a small human being.

The bird showed his irreverence by landing on the statue's head, squawking loudly, and then relieving itself down one side. The boy shook his head slowly from side to side and approached closer, the bird's familiarity lessening his fear.

"What is this?" he whispered, ignoring the bird. For the first time, he turned outward and examined the clearing. One structure after another appeared out of the surrounding bracken and under the overhanging pines. The clearing was actually the center area of a village of artificial dwellings. As he slowly turned to take it in, he marveled at his discovery. The stories around the cooking fires had mentioned different tribes living upriver, but it had never occurred to the boy that there might have been tribes that came before his people. He worked some of the algae off the "shoulder" of the statue with his thumbnail.

The surface underneath was of smooth whitish stone and it

rippled, as if the figure was covered in some strange flowing garment. The thought of old tribesmen from long ago bothered the boy. If only he had some warrior training. It had been said among the children that in warrior training, the Shaman taught all about what happened to the dead. Buried in the very rearmost caves of the old complex, the dead were never openly spoken of, except in passing at the most sacred of tribal ceremonies. The boy's shoulders dropped as he viewed the area and remembered that he was forever barred from training and even from the ceremonies.

The bird made one of its bad landings on his right shoulder and the pain brought the boy out of his reverie. Sharp talons dug into his skin once again.

"Would you stop that?" he hissed, trying to dislodge the creature by rolling his shoulder, but without success. He was afraid to do more, as he did not trust the bird's sharp, pointed beak and its closeness to his head. While trying to shoo the bird away, the boy's focus was drawn to the ground in front of him, and its unnatural flatness.

Stooping, he cleared away the nearby vine grass, which spread easily beneath his pushing hands. The bird stayed on his shoulder, squawking very quietly, as if in keeping with the boy's mood. The ground here was not dirt at all, he saw immediately. Flat stones, squared and of completely equal size, were laid one next to another. The boy was reminded of the slate floors of the new tribal structure, but those were nothing compared to what he was standing on. He noted that the vine grass spread across the surface from all sides. The creases between the stones were too small and too tight to allow any growth between. It was beyond his ability to comprehend such construction, and he simply stood and stared, trying to take it all in.

The more he looked around, the more the "village" took on a visual kind of logic. He stood at one end of a stone floor, only half as wide as it was long. The statue was at the same end, furthermost from the rumpled buildings under the pines. At the other end, near the ruins, was a pedestal of some kind. Just as he became aware of it, the bird dove off his shoulder in its characteristic swoop just above the ground and landed right on top of the object. Then he squawked once and waited. The boy twisted up one side of his lips and walked forward.

A flat, round piece of thick stone sat atop a much thinner column. The whole thing only came up to the boy's waist, but it was so solid that clearing some of the growth from it did not cause the top to even vibrate. He shooed the bird away, although the creature really only moved about the top, deftly avoiding the boy's batting hand.

Looking down on it, he saw that the top was a perfect circle. Carefully he cleared the moss away from the center. What he uncovered gave him even more unease. There was a short rod, no more than a hand-height tall, sticking straight up from the middle. He bent, and with his right index finger, scraped lightly near the spear-like point. Yellow metal gleamed at his touch, and the boy jerked back his hand and took two steps backward, staring first at his fingernail and then the revealed yellow tip.

"Metal. It's metal," he said quietly.

The tribe possessed no metal. It existed only well upriver, and then more in legend than anything else. The Shaman said it was bad fortune to have anything that was not natural to the earth itself, and had pronounced metal evil long ago. Yet, already at odds with the Shaman, he had nothing to lose, so he resolutely stepped back to the pedestal and cleaned as much of the rod as he could. It gleamed yellow in the sunlight, a bright glow that he found strangely pleasing. The metal was beautiful.

"I must tell my father . . ." his voice trailed away at the mere thought of what he had just said. His father, the proud senior warrior of the tribe, had only one shame in his life, and that was his youngest son. And the Shaman had pronounced metal as a great evil. Slowly, the boy moved to retrieve the covering carpet of bright green moss that he had cast aside.

There would be no telling anybody anything, the boy thought. His life was enough of a disaster. Not one member of the tribe knew, nor would now care about his experiences on the island, he knew, with the possible exception of his mother. But even she, his biggest supporter, had never asked a single question of his momentous day and night missing from the tribe.

The rumor among the warriors was that metal was the most valuable trading commodity of all. The boy smiled as he completed his work. He had a secret treasure that he did not have to share with a living soul. The bird squawked lightly. Having jumped about and avoided all of the boy's moves with the moss, it now stood on the green moss carpet, pecked once at the rod, then eyed the boy a bit more indignantly than usual.

"Well, one living soul, then," he said to the bird. "But you won't tell anybody, will you?"

The bird didn't answer this time, but only stared up at him with its dark, unblinking eye.

CHAPTER XII

The climb up the escarpment and the run through the trees along the top of the plateau had allowed the boy to think about the warrior training he intended to create for himself. He did not consider any of his experiences or discoveries since the catastrophe as proper preparation. Warriors were excellent trackers and hunters, and that was where he planned to concentrate his work. Without a spear, he had only his newly discovered throwing stick and, although it launched the special, round rocks at tremendous velocity, the mark of a warrior had everything to do with striking his target with accuracy.

He had left the tribal structure without a water skin and without food of any kind, so he first prowled through the ruins to see what he could find. While he searched the semi-erect buildings, he could not help but be amazed at the workmanship of a tribe that must have died—or left—many, many suns back. No craftsman of his own group could come close to making even one of the building stones unless he devoted all of his time to it, reflected the boy.

Food was plentiful among the shade of fallen rock, and water collected in many small natural bowls among the ruins. After eating all the small white and brown mushrooms he could hold and sipping the water from three small stone basins, he set to work with his equipment.

Not far from where he had discovered the pedestal was a large plate of roughly hewn slate. Puffing away, the boy managed to angle the heavy slab up against a near vertical pile of the building stones. Then he paced four of his longest paces across the floor between the pedestal and the strange carved figure.

Methodically, he went to work with the clawed stick and his special rocks. Loading, then throwing them toward the slate target, he experimented with different ways of holding the stick and various launch angles. Then he would collect the stones that had missed and lay among the carved rocks, trot back to his original standing place, reload, and do it all over again. The bird had settled on the soft carpet atop the pedestal to observe the unusual repetitive behavior. He squawked occasionally, but the boy paid him no mind.

The boy worked until the sun had made long shadows that fell from everything of size in the area. His body covered in perspiration, he decided to move half the distance to his target and let his last rocks fly from there. When he had started, only one stone out of the collection had hit the large slate from four paces, but near the end he was hitting with all but one. The bird had spent the afternoon departing from and then returning to the pedestal, but the boy's concentration was so great that he did not notice.

With his last rock, he reared back with the stick fully extended, bent so far backward that the claw almost touched the ground. Pulling his left leg into the air and then snapping it down while whipping his body forward, he launched the missile. It was by far his smoothest and most powerful throw of the day.

The stone flew true and struck the slate dead in its center. The sharp crack of the impact was followed by a thud as the slate fell to the ground in two pieces. The small explosion had been unbelievably loud, surprising the boy, and even the bird squawked loudly. . . . His follow-through had been so complete and unbalancing that the boy did not even know he had hit the target until he heard it. He ran to the slate pieces and examined them closely. The heavy flat chunk he had used as a target was almost a hand's breadth in thickness. It bore white scars and some minor chipping from the impacts of the stones that had been thrown from the farther distance.

"Can't be," the boy intoned, gently rubbing the indentation that was the contact point for the stone. Cracks radiated out with the grain of the slate and he saw immediately where the deepest line had been the actual breaking point. The power of the throwing stick at close range was unbelievable. It would have taken a large, granite hammer to do the same damage, and that would only work if the slate had been heated and quickly cooled in water.

"Wuh!" was the only expression he could think to say. The boy gathered his things and then sat with his back leaning against the mossy pillar of the pedestal. He held the last rock he'd thrown in his left hand and he massaged it slowly, watching the bird perform one of its clumsy approaches to land above his head on the round tabletop.

The gray-black stone was unmarred from its impacts on the slate. He realized he would need more than the small handful he possessed. While on the hunt, a warrior could not be expected to stop and find his missile after each missed attempt. No, he would need more and, as plentiful as they were on the island, he had not seen any even close in size or shape, anywhere since. He inserted the stone into the basket on his left hip.

The arrangement was uncomfortable and ungainly for running or climbing, so he sat back and envisioned a long, smooth tube, preferably one made of bearskin, that could be slung over the shoulder with the stick. But he discounted the idea then and there. He had no bearskin, nor any other animal skin for that matter, and his current status just about assured that he would never have it. Winter would be worsening, and he had managed to lose his shirt on the island. No mention of it had been made back at the tribe, but he could not survive the winter with only his makeshift breechcloth as covering. He dreaded having to ask his father for anything after what had happened.

The dour thought was shaken from his mind by the bird jumping from above his head. It landed on his pulled-up knee and bounced once, turning in midair to wind up standing next to him. Then it absently pecked at the ground around his foot, as if the entire aerial display was perfectly normal. The boy stared at the animal, large for a black bird, but small compared to most other creatures of the valley. At that moment he realized just how much it meant to him to have the bird's companionship, and also to have been chosen by the seemingly stupid creature. He held out his right arm and swept it about the ruins he could see.

"I claim these ruins for myself and this bird," he announced and then smiled grandly at the pecking animal. It promptly, and accidentally—or so it seemed—pecked his unprotected foot. Quickly, he pulled his left leg up.

"That's not food, and you know it!" he yelled. He massaged the wounded big toe. He was almost positive that the bird had a sense of humor, and he was equally positive that he didn't like it much at all.

"You have to have a name," he said after a moment's reflection. "Let's see, bird of the old village that you are. There was not a word he could remember of the language for "old" so he skipped it.

"Tagawan," he said, experimentally. "That's it. Tagawan," he yelled out and pointed with one finger at the same time. The bird looked up and then went right back to pecking away, between the tufts of vine grass in front of the boy's feet.

He looked down next to him where the sun's shadow was

getting longer and longer.

"C'mon, Tagawan, we have to get down before the sun does." He pushed up to a standing position and deftly slipped the last of the stones back into his small basket-pouch. He took off running back toward the cliff wall. The wall came up quickly and this time, instead of leaping over, he jumped atop the flat surface and stopped. The bird zoomed by overhead. The boy looked back toward the old ruins and thought for a moment.

"The other side," he yelled out to the disappearing bird. "I know why the wall is here." He was elated. The wall ran from one great escarpment to the other. It was a defensive barrier to keep warriors of other tribes out.

"So there has to be one on the other side of the ruins!" he cried in satisfaction, sorry that he didn't have time to prove his theory. He would, however, take the time to see if the wall extended right out toward the river valley of his tribe. He ran atop the flat, slippery surface, balancing easily because of his bare feet and his stable lope. He came to the cliff edge in just a few heartbeats, and it was just as he had surmised. He smiled, and then looked for the bird, only to find him flying far out over the valley. He looked back upriver. He had not run the wall just to prove that it went all the way to the lip, but to also be able to find the giant, outthrust pine. There it was, far up the wall, but unmistakable.

The short run to the base of the leaning trunk had not tired him. Even so, he sat on the edge, once again overlooking the wide, unchanged valley below. The falls still faintly drummed its insistent beat up through the solid rock and the smoke still hung lightly in a flat cloud over the new tribal structure. He dangled his lower legs over the edge and peered at the near invisible bank below. From his height, the thick, swollen water exiting the impact pool was no larger than his little finger. And everything, except a very few outward-jutting rocks on the face, was impossible to see.

He took several deep breaths as he realized he had been dreading the climb down since he had discovered the ancient ruins. He would now be going down blind to many of the hand-holds he had seen and made on the way up. He was afraid.

Tagawan flew in toward the cliff at high speed and it looked for a heartbeat like he would strike the rock, but instead flared his wings into the downdraft common to the river side of the plateau and braked to a halt at the boy's left knee. He pecked the skin there lightly, as if to say "let's get going." The boy smiled and moved to stroke the bird's shiny, black feathers, but the agile bird easily evaded his hand, backed off a few paces, and squawked loudly.

"Stupid bird," he whispered affectionately, then turned onto his stomach, feeling his way back under the tree's root system and down the rock chimney to the ledge.

All the way down, the bird made frequent forays onto nearby crevices or ledges to note the boy's progress. He was too intent at trying to figure out how he had negotiated his way up to pay any attention, other than to occasionally call out the bird's name when it came in too close.

It was easier and yet harder to descend than he had thought. Easier, because he didn't have to push his weight ever higher with each step, and also because if he came to a dead end, which happened frequently, he simply climbed back out and tried another route. The harder part was fatigue. His muscles were weakened and his mind seemed weakened too, especially as the light began to fail. For the top half of the descent, when he was sure he was on the "right" path, he had stopped every so often and scratched a small mark into the face with his flint knife. But, as he went lower, he had to give up the practice and simply hope that he could find his way back up the next time. That there would be a next time he did not even question. The plateau and what he had discovered was already calling him back, and he had not reached the side of the river.

Finally, he dropped exhausted into the brush and saplings at the bottom, not even sure if it was the exact place he had begun earlier that day. The thunder of the falls and the wet mist of water everywhere joined with the waning sunlight in making his trip back to the tribe a cold and difficult one.

The serpentine climb to the top of the falls was without incident, except that Tagawan was nowhere to be seen. The animal's abrupt disappearance bothered the boy more than he wanted to admit. He stopped frequently to search the sky, always expecting to have the strange bird fly out of nowhere and painfully land on him. But the bird was gone.

"The only thing you can trust wild animals to be is wild," his father had told him a few summers earlier, and up until the catastrophe, the boy had believed him utterly. Since that event he knew better. His interpretation of both the Mur and the bird could not be that far off. And the thought of his father's teachings being wrong bothered him greatly. The boy had been able to tell himself that his father simply had to support the orders of the Chief and Council, and likely even the Shaman, in his near banishment. He had not questioned directly his father's own beliefs about what had happened. But the animal experience brought it all back, and his chest hurt from the deep emotion.

"Squawk." Tagawan sat atop his old perch above the river side-pool.

The boy could not help but smile and the weight in his chest lifted. Covered with sweat and grime from his exertions, he plunged directly into the clear water. It was only waist deep, yet bitterly cold from its constant replenishment from the racing river. He dipped and washed himself for a long time, refreshing himself physically and inuring himself mentally for the short walk back to the tribe. Soaked to the bone he looked up and saw the bird still sitting on his rock pillar observing him, so he splashed it mightily. Tagawan burst off its perch with a wild beating of its wings so intense that the boy ducked into the water, laughing.

"Tagawan," he yelled, as the bird disappeared into the white mist of the falls, "I was just playing a joke." But the bird was gone. He hoped the bird did not attempt to fly near the structure. As a boy, and real member of the tribe, he had learned to throw small stones at any bird that looked like it might supplement the evening meal.

"Fly well, my friend," the boy called softly over his shoulder and then began the short hike up to the tribal dwelling.

Chapter XIII

The boy made his way upriver, staying to what remained of the old path from before the catastrophe. The late afternoon sun glowed a deep red against the pale trace of his travel. Just as he reached the nexus where the main trail ran up to the tribal structure, he saw a collection of the women near the bank, rubbing skins in the shallows and talking about whatever women talked about when they were alone.

He stopped briefly to see if his mother worked among them, but quickly ascertained that she did not. He was about to step off and regain his stride when he saw the girl. While the remainder of the women worked and talked, she simply stood by, straight and tall, her long, black hair upbraided, waving gently in the late afternoon breeze. She turned to look at him and their eyes met.

There was no gender division in the tribe among the children, so they all knew each other quite well. The boy stared at the Shaman's daughter, whom he had played with years before. As the children grew to maturity, they tended naturally to form small groups of the same gender and begin imitation of the elders. Prior to any training, there was a natural infusion and sharing of knowledge about what they would become and do in the tribe as they became adults. The bonds that might have formed between children were never strong, however, as so many did not survive the bitter cold of winter or the lack of food during the summer drought.

The girl stared back at him with large, luminous eyes, sparkling bright in the light of the low-angled sun. He noted her height. Although she was a female and the same number of summers as himself, she stood a good hand-width taller, and with a severe erectness that magnified that.

The Mur and the bird had given the boy a new sense of looking upon other living things and, as he looked upon the attractive features of the tall girl, he felt a magnetic longing. The developing feeling was crushed as it began, however, with the girl's turn to another female and then pointing and laughing. In the excitement of the day's events, and under the spell of the moment, he had forgotten his new status.

Before he could turn away, one of the older women motioned to him, and then pointed at a stack of dried skins. Instead of running or slinking away, the boy shifted the ungainly load to his back with a resigned sort of pleasure, much the same as he had done with the heavier burdens of slate. He was able to hide under the load and cast his thoughts back to the two most momentous days of his life, and what they might mean.

Bent over in order to balance the untied bundle, he did stop once, just as he began up the trail, to properly adjust the skins for the short haul. He glanced back.

The girl stood just as before, erect and staring at his departure. Quickly, he looked away and started out, only to stub the toes of his right foot into a low, flat rock. He went down so fast that he did not even have time to break his fall or protect his face.

Lacerated on the right cheek and feeling as if the throwing stick had been driven halfway through his back, the boy gathered the skins once more and, not looking back but hearing the laughs of derision, limped up the worn path to the tribal structure.

The structure took shape before him, and it was much easier

to imagine all the rooms with all the tribal members within because of the magnificent view from atop the plateau. The interior was an unexplored maze to him, although he had seen bands of children running in and out of the many doors during his hike up the slope. The great opening in the roof, which he had seen from above, was not visible from the ground, but he knew instinctively that it must be for tribal meetings and Council use. It was very likely that he would never see that chamber, the boy glumly realized.

He laid down the load as gently as he could before one of the unoccupied doors. The skins would have many owners and he was not about to try to match them all up with what was in the pile. The only enthusiasm he felt for anything was to discuss some of what he had discovered with his mother. There was so very much that he did not understand at all.

The boy stood next to the opening of the family room and looked within.

His mother was resettling a reed surface that had been laid over the cold slate floor stones. He turned and looked back down the trail toward the setting red sun, but failed to catch sight of the returning gaggle of women. Nor did he see Tagawan, and that relieved him considerably. He had so little left in his life that the bird had rapidly become his best and only friend. He thought of the Mur, but immediately dismissed the image. He couldn't ever expect to see that magical animal again.

The smell of food wafted out of the opening and caught the boy's nose. His mother was cooking and cleaning, something that took almost all of her days, or in time of celebrations, her nights as well.

He didn't have to hunch down to get through the opening as his father and brothers would have. The Chief had modified his mother's plans for the rooms so that the walls could be lower and therefore have less distance to fall in case of another catastrophe. He moved quietly to stand at her side, but she continued to kneel, working the braided reeds into a far corner of the room. He knew she was aware of his presence. She had a gift that way, and sometimes he wondered if it were a physical thing or something to do with how often she could just guess right, as with the idea for the artificial structure. After all, he reflected for a moment, examining the fitted rock wall nearest his hand, how could a woman know enough to be reasonably responsible for such a thing?

Prior to the earth and water event, he had experienced many discussions with her, and only in their absence did he realize they were among the most prized memories he carried. Since then, although much had transpired, they had not spoken except for the few words of general encouragement that she made from time to time in passing.

"Mother," he said quietly, and then waited. When she did not respond, he repeated the word three times, each with the same intonation and with the same spacing of time in between. He was prepared to continue in that manner for the entire evening, if necessary.

"Yes," she said finally, the word coming out like a sigh. She pulled up from her knees and turned to face him, then sat back on a square-shaped rock that had been set against the far wall near the corner. The boy noted how she had already turned the spaces between the stacked flat wall-rocks into small receptacles for her many small pouches of medicine. The entire far wall held her collection, each small leather bag set into a space with its twisted opening outward. Only she knew what was in each and what, of the many maladies suffered in the tribe, was cured by what.

She stared up at him with a gentle expression, but did not speak further.

"I'd like to tell you what happened . . ." the boy began, but his voice cracked and then trailed away. He bit the inside of his cheek in frustration. It had been so easy to put together exactly what he wanted to tell her when he had been walking back. But now he could not get the words out without tears. He tensed his body and hardened himself inside. She had not said a word, merely looking at him with her soul-penetrating look, something only she seemed to possess.

It took many deep breaths but he finally began. The story, from the moment he had awakened in terror and fled, through his encounter with the Mur, escape from the island, and even the swim back, all poured out of him, one event after another. Somehow, he managed to include the throwing stick and the strange rock carving. Running out of air, he stopped. What had been a coherent series of life-shaking events had somehow come out of his mouth as a series of never-ending wild stories, never even venturing into anything about the bird, the climb, or the ancient ruins atop the plateau.

Throughout his narrative, his mother maintained her silence. Nodding at the right times and smiling mildly at others, she had seemed to follow the helter-skelter presentation with some kind of coherent understanding. When he at last fell silent, fingering the sharp end of his unmentioned flint knife, he stood and awaited her reply.

She began to speak, and his hopeful expression of appeal rapidly turned to one of carved wood.

"In this life you will come to see that things are not the way you are seeing them right now. Your childhood dreams will fade quickly, and, maybe over time, your rash action . . ." she paused and looked down at the floor, obviously uncomfortable with her own words, "your very forgivable rash actions will be forgotten by all before you reach adulthood."

His shock was so great that he could not move a muscle in his body or his face. It was shock that was as sharp and deep as that he had felt from the events of the catastrophe. She went on.

"Your heart is good, but your imagination still carries the wonder of childhood, where every little experience is a grand adventure. Creatures of your dreams rise up to become real and places of fantasy have the solidness of reality." Her hand slapped the rock beneath her in emphasis at the last.

He stared into her sharp, intelligent eyes, and something deep within him changed. She instantly knew something had transpired, but could only look away in response. The boy did not, could not cry. He simply stared at her, unmoving in the center of the room, except for his thumb still tracing the end of the knife. He did not notice the drops of blood slowly falling to the reed-covered slate below.

His brain seemed to have split in half. One part of it knew, in detail, that his mother was saying things to him not necessarily of her own belief, but because they were the things she needed him to believe to survive in the tribe. He had not been banished, but his stature was so low that his very survival would be difficult, even were he to say nothing to anyone about anything.

The other part stared down at her. The depth of the mother-son betrayal so strongly delivered had opened an immense void between them. He could not look away, not even to blink, and she could not meet his stare.

She rose smoothly to her feet and moved to enclose him in one of her warm, loving hugs, but he backed away until she stopped, her arms still extended. His look did not change, nor did his eyes leave hers.

From his waist vine, he removed the bloodstained flint knife.

"My first omen," he said flatly, and then with his other hand, deftly unslung the throwing stick, revealing the claw formation at its head.

"My third omen," he waved the device forward marginally,

his eyes finally focusing on it instead of her. And then he spoke more to himself than to anyone.

"And the second omen," he breathed deeply, looking back to her widened eyes, "the second omen you shall meet in due time."

He did not know why he said what he did. It was like the real him was standing nearby, witnessing the exchange but not taking any part.

It almost appeared from her expression that she understood what he did not, and a tear rolled down from her left eye.

Emotion no longer choked him, but the boy could not think of anything else to say. The word "good-bye" had almost come forth except, in quickly turning it over in his mind, he realized the expression would simply be inaccurate. He had no place else to go and was completely dependent upon the tribe for food and shelter. The bitter realization also came to him that he did not want to reveal anything further of his innermost feelings. Open trust and sharing were lost to him.

The boy turned and stepped through the opening to the outside, where the sun was just going down, and the deep red glow left behind sat on the distant horizon.

The shaking of the earth and the rampaging waters had torn his life asunder, prying him loose from everything he had understood to be true, and from everyone close in his life. Then it had stepped in and provided unbelievable events and impossible creatures to replace them. The boy leaned his back against the rough laid stones of the structure wall, feeling the sharp points dig into his flesh, but not caring.

He stepped toward the sun and then looked back at the new tribal structure and the activity surrounding it. It was true. He had not been banished by the tribe, but he was an outcast all the same.

Chapter XIV

The boy left his mother and walked toward the river, thinking about nothing except the rush of the water under the dwindling rays of the sun.

His intentions were unclear, even to him, until he crossed the smaller winding path that paralleled the flow. The hunters stood grouped at the river's edge, while the women, whom the boy now realized must have been waiting for them, worked at skinning and washing the butchered meat and roughly cleaned skins of the kill. Single-edged flint knives, similar to but larger than the boy's, were used with a speed and dexterity that was mesmerizing to behold.

The normal hunt returned a varied selection of furred carcasses, most of which had perished attempting to avoid the line of ground beaters surrounding them. Rarely was any predator captured or killed in this fashion, however. Watching the efficient process, he noted that the animals had all grown their thickened winter coats. Summer coats were the preferred hide, as the winter fur was much thicker and tended to fall away from the skin with even the gentlest of use. It could be used for insulation between bare skins, however, so nothing of any animal, taken winter or summer, went to waste.

Two hunters stood patiently, a newly stripped sapling slung between them. They neither bowed nor gave any indication that their load was burdensome or heavy. A chunky animal was slung under the pole, tied tightly with a long strand of vine. The sleek blackness of its fur drew the boy's eyes.

The boy's father strode among the women, proudly issuing commands. It was obvious that the bear was his taking by the manner in which he paced, always returning to pat the side of the entwined dead animal.

A bear kill was uncommon among the hunters, so much so that the boy could remember each individual incident and the ensuing adventure story of each one's death. They were only ever deliberately hunted in the fall season, as the tremendous fat they stored for winter hibernation slowed their considerable speed and even made them less aggressive. It was the dream of every hunter to uncover one in its state of hibernation, slay it in its torpor, and then return to the tribe a hero for life.

It took only moments for the carcass to be lowered and cut away from the pole. The boy was ordered back to the structure with his first load of butchered meat. Upon his return, only the hide-wrapped meat of the bear remained. He slung it over his shoulder with an easy swing and began the journey back. His father walked at his side, but he did not speak, simply directing that the entire bundle be taken in to his mother. The boy complied, unwrapping the hide and placing the unevenly cut chunks on the hearth. He had been surprised by the lightness of the load on the trail up and now was even more surprised by the small volume of meat. Without saying anything to his occupied mother, he gathered the bearskin and moved outside. Unrolling it, he held it out before him.

"It's smaller than me," he whispered to himself, or so he thought.

"It's still a bear," his father's deep voice boomed from behind him, touched with anger.

The boy draped the hide out on the ground, fur side down, so his mother could begin tanning it when she was done inside. He had intended to talk to his father about what had happened to his life, but shook his head. It seemed everything he had done since the catastrophe angered those around him.

"I meant no disrespect," he began sincerely, but his father only looked away, the redness of his face belying any understanding or belief. The boy knew it was not a good time to discuss anything with the man, but he could not stop himself from trying.

"Father?" he said softly, and then waited long until finally his father's massive head turned to face him.

"I don't understand," he began, and then paused, choosing his words carefully, "I am being punished for something I didn't do. The tribe has never experienced anything like the Great Flood. I could not have known that the caves would fall, or that the water would rise, or that I would be trapped on that island. It is not fair to select me and me alone to pay this terrible price."

Silence was all the response he got. He had spoken quickly but evenly, and in a respectful tone, working hard to keep emotion from pitching his voice ever higher. But he felt it all and unconsciously leaned one shoulder against the structure wall for physical support. His father, who had met the boy's eyes evenly throughout his delivery, looked down and then knelt to work the wet side of the exposed hide with the long edge of his flint knife. The boy waited, unmoving, his eyes following his father's every move. Finally, the big man sat back on his heels, but did not look up when he spoke.

"You are measured upon your actions. No amount of discussion can change that. Admittedly, sometimes you are measured on the basis of what people think your actions are or were, as in this case. The Chief pronounced his sentence, in full agreement of the Shaman and the assembled warrior council. Whatever you think or feel does not matter. You must accept this decision as the correct one, as I myself have."

The great man would not look up at him, and the boy was reminded of his mother's inability to meet his eyes earlier. He could not let the issue drop.

"So the Chief and the Shaman, and even the full tribal council, do not want to know the truth," the boy said with great intensity, only barely able to keep from adding his father's name to the list.

The raw emotion reached his father this time and the man stood to face him. He stepped forward, his chin well above the boy's head, but canted down. His penetrating gaze met the boy's with a bleak coldness. "That is not what I said at all. The Chief's decision is not the truth. But once made, and fully supported, it is accepted and enforced as the truth." With that, he stepped forward around the boy to enter the room opening.

The boy had flinched, both physically and mentally. He stood confused.

"How can a decision make the truth and not the truth make the decision?" he whispered, the concept of such accepted injustice playing at the very edge of his ability of understanding.

As the time for the meal approached, the entire village gathered in the center of the great structure. Never before had there been the opportunity for all members of the band to meet in one formal place. The caves had been too segmented and poorly lit, while the area nearby under the escarpment too unprotected. The boy was not sure whether the ban placed upon him from attendance at tribal councils applied to general gatherings for the great meal of the day, but it mattered little as his appetite was nonexistent. He found a spot upon the reeds along the wall closest to the door and fell into a fitful sleep. He awoke several times to hear his father's snore, with the image of the Shaman's daughter at the forefront of his mind. The memory of her sideways stare and the languid look of her tall body would not leave him.

Automatically he arose just near the break of dawn, as had been his habit as long as he could remember. The light was so minimal that he could only tell the time by instinct. The early morning cold was upon the land, accentuated by the sound of the rushing river in the distance. The boy stood outside and worked the stiffness from his body. The tree on the island, its jointed perch filled with bird-collected debris, had been the softest sleeping accommodation he had known.

The ancient village atop the plateau was on his mind. Why had it been built atop something so high that nobody, nobody in his right mind, could climb to it? Then there was the island, where it had all begun, and it called to him. He needed a supply of the round rocks, but even more than that, he needed some resolution to the strong emotions roiling through his mind. He wasn't sure that an answer lay there or anywhere, but his return would be a necessary step in a direction he could not yet fully comprehend. He sensed that it was vitally important somehow. And it gave him a sense of meaning, which served to offset his sense of isolation, although he didn't think he would ever belong to any tribe or group again in his life.

The run down to the water's edge warmed him considerably. Instead of awaiting the first light of dawn in stillness, he turned and raced down the barely visible path toward the falls. He thought of the water while he ran. One day he would explore far upriver. There had to be an explanation for why the waters had risen and then never fallen again. There seemed to be no such curiosity within even the adventuring hearts of the warriors. The water's new vital presence in their midst was only discussed in terms of those things of the world that happened but could never be truly understood. No longer did he have the freedom to openly bring such subjects up with any of the warriors. Now their only acknowledgment that he even existed was that when they happened to see him, they avoided even walking or standing nearby. The boy increased speed, his bare feet seeming to hardly touch as they struck the softer clumps of tufted grass along the indistinct path's edges.

When he had awakened earlier in the structure, he had found an old, thin, leather garment next to him. The fit was loose and the absence of sleeves assured that it would never provide true warmth in the winter, but it was a great improvement over nakedness. The boy planned to turn into an advantage the fact that it was far too long for his body.

Reaching the small pool, with the sun still well below the cliff-top horizon, but providing a usable light, he sat with his back to one of the larger rocks surrounding it and went to work. He noticed nothing as he toiled with his own edged blade, deftly cutting the bottom from the garment and then working the sections to fit as unpadded wraps for both feet. The most difficult part was in the cutting of thin strips to cross and recross through the small holes he made with the very tip of the needle-sharp flint. There was even enough of the jerkin's remains to cut a proper, albeit thin, belt and thong for the throwing stick.

He stared glumly into the pool when he was done, comforted by his now passable attire, yet lost in thought about the situation with his parents and the tribe. He had never been close to either of his brothers, but now there was only a cold silence between them. The boy brought his gaze up, thinking about how wonderful it would be if the wild water, so crushing and thunderous nearby, could just wash his problems away. A movement in the water caught his attention, and he remembered that he had not eaten since the mushroom feast atop the plateau. He sharpened a stick with his flint knife, stepped into the pool, and became motionless. A form almost the same color as the bottom glided by his right leg and he struck sharply downward with his stick, pinning a foot-sized fish to the bottom. He knelt, holding the stick against the bottom and pulled the flopping fish to the surface. On the shore he sat and consumed the fish raw, relishing every bite.

Suddenly the bird struck his shoulder a glancing blow, seeming to stumble midair, beat its wings wildly above the small pool, and then landed clumsily on its now customary rock pedestal.

"Ahhh," yelled the boy, immediately grateful for the leather covering his upper body.

"Squawk!" screamed Tagawan in response.

"Stupid bird." The boy rubbed his right shoulder where the bird had hit him, but he did so with a smile. The cold had seeped back into him and he shivered. It would be a long, cold winter. Sticking his right hand back into the pool water to clean it, he felt again the temperature. As when he had made the swim from the island, the water was much colder than anything that surrounded it. Wherever it came from, it must be winter there.

"Come on," he yelled at the grooming bird, then rose quickly and took off at a run back in the direction he had come from. He did not have to look back for Tagawan as the animal swooped down, flapping back and forth before him as he ran. The early light of full dawn made the bird's feathers look shiny purple instead of black.

Although the sun showered the far side of the river in yellow warmth, there was no stir of activity as he crossed the intersecting trail that led back up to the structure. He continued on without even hesitating, his mind briefly thinking of the beautiful girl who had stood near the very spot they were passing. The path became a trace after only a short time, as only the warriors ventured upriver. The much discussed tribes of the upper valley region never ventured near the caves, and any interaction was best left to the warriors, or so the Chief had decreed.

The trace ended at a collection of boulders piled high before him. It was possible, even in the early morning light, to look into the shadow of the escarpment and see where they had calved, and then rolled to the river's edge. The boy stood and marveled once again at the power of such events and the great fortune he had experienced that fateful morning in simply surviving them.

The river doglegged back toward the cliff, just beyond the pile of boulders, and the sound of rapids came over and around the great rocks. With his new foot wraps, the boy was even quicker and more nimble than before. He went up, using the most minute of footholds and his momentum to scale the rocks, his right hand clutching the stick and his left barely touching here and there to stabilize himself.

From atop the highest point, he surveyed the river below. The rapids were caused by the squeezing of the river as it rounded the weak curve, channeled by the pile of boulders he stood on. From there it fanned out broadly until it was cleaved into two distinct channels by the prow of the great cliff face on the island. The boy stared at the small, isolated plat of rock and land. The huge tree flowered up behind the knife-edged rock in almost perfect symmetry. It was a beautiful sight to the boy, and he understood why he had to once more step upon the island's surface. Maybe there was an answer there, an explanation that he had missed, or maybe just a spot of warm comfort in a world that had grown cold and uncaring.

Chapter XV

The river rushed past beneath the boy's position atop the boulder as he thought about his passage to the island, and the risk of such a venture. Tagawan found a spot nearby just as the sun broke from above the escarpment to shine down on him.

His ability to reach the island was not in doubt. He stared at the rapids, which ended their whitewater run just past where the rocks jutted out beneath him. He would simply throw himself into the fast current and let it carry him downriver. There was plenty of distance and time for him to make sure that he could place himself to pass down one side of the island or the other. Either the reeds on the far side or the rocks and debris on the near side would allow him to leave the water.

It was getting off the island that gave him pause. Aside from the encounter with the snake, which he did not see as likely to repeat itself, the fear of going over the falls was anything but diminished from his first, nearly fatal crossing attempt. He looked up at the ever-present cloud visible down past the island. The thrum of the water's fall could be felt all the way up through the boulder he sat on.

"I'm not tired, sick, or hurt this time," he told the grooming bird.

Idly, he tossed pebble after pebble into the speeding water below. He had no intention of pushing a log on his departure from the island. He would carry the extra stones in the basket, except he would use his new thong to strap it across his back.

The emphasis would be speed, and this time he had a full knowledge of not only the falls' existence, but exactly how far it was downriver. He tossed another pebble that seemed to disappear without a splash in the heavy current.

"Once again," he said to Tagawan, "what have I got to lose?" The bird squawked in agreement, then plunged from the rocks straight down toward the water, extending his wings at the last possible instant and flaring out over the roiling river.

"I wish I could do that . . ." the boy's voice trailed away in admiration as Tagawan climbed and then banked back around.

His mind made up, the boy quickly scrambled back down the rock pile to a short, squat tree near the river's edge. Somehow neither the cascade of monstrous stones nor the initial wave of the catastrophic flood had destroyed it. Carefully, he placed his modified jerkin and weapons under some brush at the base of its thick, fat trunk. He kept only the leather belt and the empty rock basket he had woven from vines while still on the island.

He returned back up the rocks to sit next to Tagawan, the bird once again sunning himself and working his thick coat of feathers. The boy examined his newly fashioned foot wraps and tried to calculate just how much speed they might cost him in the water. With both arms to pull, his legs to kick, and no log to push, he thought they would not hamper nearly so much as they would help him to push off the boulder when he jumped, and to also grab the sharp, rocky bottom when he made landfall.

He stood preparing himself. Tagawan flew out and then back to hover, wings working furiously just before him. He had to smile.

"No, I'm not crazy," he laughed, then plunged out as far as his legs could propel him. When he hit, it was like splashing into liquid ice. The cold was so bad that even as he surfaced quickly, he could not pull in a breath before he went flying over an underwater boulder, smashing down into its swirling lee current. He didn't get any air until he was forcefully kicked out of the hole that the water's mad rush formed on the downwater side.

The boy kept bobbing up and down like a tortured piece of wood as he was swept through the last of the whitewater. He seemed to go from one big wave to the next, only having time to catch one breath in between. Calmness came, but no release from his fears, as the speed of the water was much greater than it had appeared.

He stroked for all he was worth toward the center, his hands surging forward under the water and then pulling powerfully back while his legs kicked with all his strength.

The plan worked so well he could not believe it. The water drew him down toward the cliff's edge, which he never even came close to before curving out and then down right next to the reed bank. Grabbing a handful of the tough plants, he was neatly deposited right onto the well-remembered surface of the slate rock.

The bird landed hard right at the boy's left elbow and walked in circles squawking quietly, as if acquainting himself with an interesting new domain. The water level here had dropped back down to the level of what it had been during his previous single day there. The mud was dry dirt and the brush had started to grow among the littered piles of debris. He laughed as he stood and looked around him. The entire area was spotted with the perfect round spheres of all sizes. It took only the shortest time to gather more than enough to fill his small basket.

The sun illuminated the entire open area that stood between the great tree and the stone cliff as the boy began his exploration. The conditions reminded him eerily of the morning of that day now long ago. He was thankful for the foot wrappings as the surface was rough, still holding the imprint of his own tracks, as well as deep impressions from those of the Mur.

Standing at the base of the tree, he peered up, but could not make out the perch where he had spent the night. Tagawan circled the huge trunk, occasionally diving down and whizzing by his head.

"Bird humor," the boy said to himself, all the while shaking his head at the animal's antics. He moved around the brush and approached the now hardened area of mud where he had fallen and then found the first omen. His fingers went to the spot where he normally carried it, but there was nothing. His omen lay beneath the tree along the far side of the bank with the remainder of his belongings.

His impression was still there, hardened into the mud. A spot of white caught the boy's attention. With his fingers he reached down and pried a massive chunk of the reddish-brown clay loose. As it came up, the area of white extended into a long, thick line. The boy rocked back on his heels, the clay falling from his grasp. It was a vein. A vein of white flint.

With excitement racing through him, the boy worked and pried until he had a sizable piece in his hand. The vein was all the same. Near the top it was as thick as the length of half his forefinger, but it narrowed to a natural, sharp edge at the bottom about two fingers down, almost as if it had been broken from a larger, thicker piece.

The chunk he held in his hand was nearly identical to the one he had left on the far shore. There was no decision to be made as he cleaned it off and carefully slid it into the special loops he had fashioned in the leather belt. Then he stopped to consider. The tribe was forced to trade at unfavorable rates for flint, as there were no known sources throughout the valley, and certainly not the highly prized white variety. The Shaman insisted that all flint came from the great earth entity, and that it was their proper due to pay dearly for such gifts. The pure whiteness of the flint glinted up at the boy. He had only seen the dull gray or black varieties

Carefully, he replaced the clay piece he had dislodged only moments before, then proceeded to tamp the area with his wrapped feet until it was as smooth as possible. With its location so near to the trunk of the huge tree and its very special nature to the boy, he knew there would be no difficulty finding it in the future. For now, it could stay in Nature's care. He no longer thought in terms of great discoveries that could be brought home for the benefit of his family and the tribe.

His last stop was at the base of the rock wall. He cleared the branches and brush as best he could and then simply gazed upon the hypnotic carving. It was beautiful, but no matter how much time he spent looking at it he could not imagine what it might signify. Tagawan squawked from high up atop the tip of the great stone.

"I'm coming," he whispered back, more to himself than to the obnoxious bird. Covering the design as best he could, the boy made his way quickly up to the top of the rock. They sat together, the boy checking the distance to shore but with frequent glances toward the cloud rising above the cataract, the bird working at his feathers with the sharp tip of his orange-yellow beak.

The boy's plan was simple. He would leave the same way that he had come, with a great leap out into the current and then a continuous, strong swim to the bank. It should have been simple except he could not get the image of the water going over that not-so-distant ledge and on down into the roiling caldron below.

The visit to the island had answered none of the gnawing questions that ate at him. It had only served to raise more questions and yielded new mysteries. He sat and wondered about his own mental state. Why had he overridden any sense of normal caution? Although he was in excellent physical condition from his hard work on the tribal structure and his own climbing and running, the task before him was unforgiving if he failed. The slightest cramp or muscle spasm would easily doom his efforts. That conclusion was not what bothered him, however. It was that he had considered every bit of the risk before he'd made the decision to attempt the island again.

He closed his eyes and sought strength from within, but only thoughts of his reception the last time he had departed the small piece of land came to him. His chin sank to his chest. Then a small smile began to play about his lips.

"I ran in terror and then did not return to help . . ." the boy verbalized the words of his father. He opened his eyes and looked out over the water and up toward the rising sun. Its warmth radiated from the rock beneath him and a fresh breeze blew up from the river below. Tagawan banked in close and squawked as he raced across the face of the massif.

"So, I lack courage, huh, my friend?" he spoke out to the bird as it passed, but his gaze turned toward the smoke rising from the tribal area. Then he rose, leaped off the cliff wall, and plummeted into the strong current below.

The water was again a great physical shock. Deep cold grabbed his tightened chest as he fought to the surface and then swung around to view his progress past the island. Fear at what he saw broke through the paralyzing numbness, and he began the long struggle toward the distant bank. Tagawan flitted in front of him, as if encouraging him to redouble his efforts.

A branch came out of nowhere and tangled itself around his chest. He panicked and went under, the thought of another snake bringing him to near hysteria. Surfacing again, he breathed deeply twice, the current drawing him inexorably toward the falls, the roar of it now a deep vibration running through his entire body. He carefully dislodged the clinging leaves and soggy, small branches and pushed the branch away.

With leaden legs, just as before, and eyes stinging from the cloudy water, he finally felt the first brush of the riverbed below. Two more strokes and he jammed both wrapped feet onto a large underwater rock and stopped his downriver plunge, but the current was still too strong. He managed to push off toward the bank as the water carried him off his perch, and then followed the same procedure three more times.

Exhausted, cold, but no longer frightened, the boy came to a stop flat on his stomach in the eddy that flowed into the bird's small side-pool. He knew exactly where he was because Tagawan sat on his usual perch and squawked at him, facing the river instead of the pool.

"I made it," the boy said, feeling a growing exhilaration at just being alive. Even the cold of the water no longer felt the same as he staggered out of the passing current, the thought of his foolishness in risking such a swim for a second time lessening.

He knelt and then canted back on his heels next to the pool to clean himself off. His face and chest were completely covered in the thick clay mud of the bank.

"You're awfully quiet," he said up to the bird before he noticed the girl. She stood three man-lengths away on the path, one hand held over her mouth to keep from laughing, but her mirth was more than evident from her sparkling eyes and heaving chest.

As soon as she noted his attention she turned and raced back upriver toward the tribal structure.

"Great," he whispered angrily to himself, trying to wipe the thick layer of mud from his face. Finally, he just plunged forward into the shallow pool.

"Thanks for the warning," he said toward the quietly squawking bird, but it paid him no mind, merely twisting and turning as it groomed itself.

The boy followed suit, scraping the layer of mud off, then rinsing himself with handfuls of water. Clean at last, he started upriver to recover his belongings. This time he loped lightly, without the spring he had evidenced earlier, his steps heavier from the gloomy thoughts on the low level of his social condition. He quickened his pace as he retraced the path that led up to the structure, but his anticipation that the girl might be working by the side of the river went unconfirmed. None of his tribesmen were anywhere to be seen.

Chapter XVI

The river flowed with its usual intensity, as the boy sat staring at the white of the rapids, wondering what caused those bits of water to change color. Such questions often arose in his mind, and he missed the closeness to his mother that had allowed for their discussion. She could almost never answer, but she always acted so very interested that he had even asked. That none of them, except possibly the Shaman—and he only spoke in terms that most could not understand at all—had a true grasp of what lay above, below, and around them always surprised the boy. The other perplexing fact was simply that none of the other members of the tribe seemed to care.

It was with those thoughts in mind that he sat beside the river at midday, waiting for his foot wraps to dry out following a good pounding on the nearby rocks. The special stones he had risked his life for were hidden behind the bird's pedestal back at the pool.

The return trip downriver was made with only one small incident. The women had regathered at the base of the intersecting trails to work on their daily load of skins. The girl was not among them, something he sensed that even before he was close enough for true identification. That, too, was a strange feeling as, following his mother's example and training, he didn't believe in, and shouldn't rely upon, anything he could not see or touch. The tribe needed a successful figure like the Shaman. Why, exactly, the boy did not understand, but it seemed it had to do with necessary historic beliefs that were required to hold a tribe together.

He would not have stopped at all, afraid of being assigned to another laborious and lowly task, but the women all stood as one and then a few pointed at him . . . no, at the bird. He was so accustomed to Tagawan's possessive nature that he had only absently noted it landing on his shoulder.

"Shoo!" he said, crossing his left hand up to dislodge the animal.

Tagawan took flight by surprise, batting his wings madly and then climbing upward at a steep angle. His squawks of complaint trailed back down behind him as they all stared for a moment. When the women directed their gaze back toward him, the boy felt distinctly uncomfortable, as if he'd done something else wrong, so he launched into a full run along the downriver path.

Stopping at the pool, he looked up to see the bird circling high above, barely visible to even the boy's keen vision. He surprised himself by hoping that the animal was not offended by his treatment in front of the women. Their collective look had been so strange that it had sent a shiver through him, one that he did not at all understand.

He recovered half of the stones, deciding to store the other half where they were for future use. His basket was crammed full and would be uncomfortable, even as it was, on his climb back up the escarpment. If he stored half the remainder on the plateau, it would make his normal load bearable, at least until he was able to procure enough leather to fashion his rock tube.

He climbed with his usual skill, having found his old point of entry quite easily below the falls. In passing the great cataract and the noisy caldron below, he had taken a personal oath not to tempt the Earth god again with more reckless abandon. The additional flint he made ready use of, carving a thin marking

next to the more subtle foot and handholds. His trip up the face
of the cliff went much faster than his first, but the bird did not
rejoin him until he was near the ledge below the large, angled
pine. It fluttered in, and then stared down from the ledge he
was about to ascend to.

"What?" the boy said, looking up the short distance between
them. "All right. I apologize." He shook his head and actually
looked around to make sure nobody was watching him talk to
an animal. The women of the tribe had no doubt made a decision about him in that regard anyway, he reflected ruefully. The
bird seemed to understand and squawked lightly in acceptance.

"Overbearing. That's what you are. I have to keep some kind
of control . . ." his voice trailed away as he joined Tagawan on
the ledge.

Inside, however, he smiled, as the bird had become a most
welcome fixture in his lonely life.

He readjusted his load before making the last assault. The
tube was a vital necessity, as climbing required the use of both
hands. It was a doubly difficult task if one was constantly fid-
dling with a poorly constructed container of stones, he mused.
But then running was equally affected, if one had to hold on to
one's supplies while trying to keep a good rhythm or avoid
obstacles.

The boy thought about the crippled boy with the crippled
arm and strange eyes. From time to time his mother had taken
weak or injured children into their family part of the caves, and
that had extended over into their single room within the tribal
structure. He had seen the crippled child several times, but had
simply moved around him. They had never spoken. His mother
had said that the boy would recover, but the falling rocks of the
cave roof had so damaged the shoulder bones of his right
shoulder that he would never have use of the arm or hand again.
He would be of little use to the tribe and, like the boy, could

never even hope to hunt or become a warrior. Such children usually perished in the harsher winter months, so he put all thought of the unfortunate child out of his mind. Reaching the top, he settled onto one of the huge roots that snaked over the rim. A high, bright sun illuminated all below and he stared into the beautiful, ever-shifting cloud of the falls. A thought came upon him so suddenly that he spoke it aloud.

"What was she doing all the way down at the falls alone?" The bird squawked nearby in response, as the boy sat and rubbed his chin. His brow furrowed as he considered.

"She came down to see me," he concluded, again to the bird's instant response and approval. Young women of the tribe never traveled that far without escort, and that was almost always made up of other women. Not that they were prevented. It was just not done. All of a sudden the valley below looked to be a better, more cheerful place.

"Yes, that has to be it." He made a fist and curved it back into his chest as he said the words. Then, with a renewed sense of energy and purpose, he leapt up and ran between the trees toward the valley side of the ancient wall.

When he reached the now familiar and sharply edged blocks, he vaulted atop the last one in the line and gazed briefly down-river. Again he thought he could see a thin wisp of smoke far, far down the valley, but he could not be sure. As nothing was in that direction, he assumed that the warriors on a hunt must have uncharacteristically gone over there.

The ruins beckoned as a stiff wind gusted through the whispering pines. Tagawan skipped forward in little flights from pine to pine. The bird seemed at its happiest within the confines located between the two lines of walls. Its attitude was contagious, and the boy soon found himself literally bouncing along on the thick, brown pine needles, running full out under the large, lower branches spread out only a hand's breadth above his head.

The remainder of the day was spent in practice with the throwing stick, taking frequent breaks to explore the ruins with the bird, and then back to more practice.

Days turned into weeks of the same routine. Early in the morning, just after dawn, he would climb to the plateau and not return to the tribe until nightfall. And nobody cared. He was not wanted or even given enough stature to be able to help the tribe. He had become an object of necessary responsibility because of his father's stature as a great hunter. He had figured out that nobody really cared if he returned from his adventures or not, possibly save only his family. Using the stone-carved statue of a man in the overgrown courtyard, he found that he could hit it consistently from over thirty man-lengths and not only that, he could vary the speed of his projectile without much affecting his accuracy.

It was after the delivery of one of his most powerful swings of the stick that the boy made a most profound discovery.

He wound back until the stick almost touched the ground behind him, and his body was tipped so far back he could only see the trees and the sky, then he whipped forward and let the stone fly at just the right instant as the stick came over and down. The swing itself caused him to pivot so far forward that the only time he really saw the target was just before the stone released and then just an instant in the middle of its rapid motion. The sound of the projectile striking the target usually came before he could get his eyes back up and fully focused.

The sound had returned all wrong. A miss made almost no noise at all, and was followed by long periods of disappointed searching. But he never quit until he had found the precious stone. A hit was a solid *whack*, deep and strong. The sound from this particular strike had been fractured and muted. He ran to the nicked and marred statue. He knew he had struck the statue somewhere near center, but the rock was not lying nearby, as usual. Not until he got up close did he see: it was there, but had shattered into several pieces.

The boy knelt in surprise, and then gathered together the pieces to receive a second shock.

"No wonder," he breathed. The stones were lighter than normal rocks of the same size because they were hollow. But that was just one part of it. The inside was made of bright, clear, and even-colored material. He stared, turning the largest curved piece over and over between his hands. The boy was astonished. He had never heard of hollow rocks before, not from his mother or even in the gossip told around the old cave cooking fires.

The inside of the rock was covered with clear crystals, some half as long and nearly as thick as one of his fingers. The base of each was of green stone. Holding the piece up to the sun it sparkled beautifully and the green seemed to suffuse through the clear of the crystals.

Tagawan landed on the top of the statue and promptly relieved himself on it, adding to the series of older white streaks already there. The boy scowled at him, as the mess tended to leave residue on his throwing stones. The bird ignored him and turned to squawk happily at the clearing all around.

The boy sat and worked the inside of the stone with one of his flint knives. He was able to break off several of the larger pieces before stopping to consider. He sat rolling the largest chunk over in his fingers, his back up against the gently flowing curves of the statue. The stone was amazing because the crystal shards had straight edges, and they met at the tip of the inward-pointing end. There was nothing that was truly straight in his life. The rocks of the ancient wall were roughly straight, and even some of the granite hammers of the tribe were worked to an almost straight edge, but nothing as perfect as what he held in his hand, and it had not been made by human beings.

Combing through the rest of the rock pieces, he pried out a handful of the green-based crystals. He sighed. Now he would need another pouch. Only days before he had been able to make his first kill with the throwing stick. A small fox that had stood and watched as he made his strange windup and delivery. The stone had struck the animal in the chest and it had just dropped where it was. In gutting and skinning the small beast, he had come to understand why. Almost every bone forward of its midback region was broken into one or more pieces. The power of the stick-thrown rocks was extraordinary.

He had stripped, scraped, and then dried the hide, but it was far from a fine piece of leather. The secret of the tanning was kept closely guarded by the women. He stayed up until almost too late in the afternoon to descend the cliff face. He'd sewn the cut pieces into a rough tube only to find that getting his throwing rocks out of such a soft leather container was difficult at best. The secret of the hardened, thick leather of warrior footskins was closely kept as well, but by the warriors. It was knowledge he was never likely to learn, and that thought depressed him.

There had been enough fox skin left over for a knife pouch, which he packed the crystals into for temporary storage. He had two hands' worth of throwing rocks up on the plateau, of which he could fit only one hand's worth into his new, ungainly tube. The other five he stored pressed under one edge of the statue with the five below at the pool. He tried to buoy himself up mentally with the knowledge that even without warrior training, or the assistance and companionship of that group, he was better equipped than any of them. But it didn't work. His thoughts kept returning to his strange, virtual outcast status.

The bird flew down to join him, landing roughly on his right shoulder. The boy ignored it only because a new idea had popped into his head.

In reality, he was not the only member of the tribe in such a circumstance. There was the crippled boy his mother had cared for. He too had to be considered almost like him, and even though he would not be construed to be a coward, he would have the same lowly non-laborer status, as his father was the most important worker in the tribe . . . he was the flint knapper . . . the boy wiped away the tears on his cheeks and got to his feet. Tagawan lifted off and flew to the nearest pine branch, waiting for the boy's next move.

"That's it, the cripple," he said as he assembled his gear. Although not easy to use, the new rock tube was a big improvement over the basket for storage. Slung across his back over the opposite shoulder the throwing stick was on, it freed both of his hands for running, climbing, or any other activity.

A smile lit his face, and he took off for the leaning pine at a run, while Tagawan flew into the air before he had covered half the distance to the tree line. Together they ran and flew among the pines, he laughing and the bird squawking until they reached the face. The boy did not even slow, but went right into the now practiced descent. The bird hopped and flew from ledge to crevice, seeming to point out the best of the hand and footholds.

Chapter XVII

He arrived back, at what had come to be termed simply "the village," in record time and much earlier in the day than usual. It was a beehive of activity while the sun was high. Winter brought shorter days, but also much shorter periods where real warmth was provided.

The sun of early morning and late afternoon was a cool sun. Winter's inexorable grip on the entire valley was well on its way. Preparations for the cold season were evident all about. Meat and skins were hung on wooden frames and even left to lie atop the structure roof for drying. Although there were few predators in the valley, it was loaded with small scavengers. Everything edible or vulnerable to small teeth had to be protected or suspended in the air. Young boys in warrior training, as he might have been one, guarded against threats from the air with their small throwing stones. Tagawan, fortunately, gave the entire area around the structure a wide birth, only occasionally flying over it at great altitude. As had become typical, no tribal member acknowledged either his departure or his return. Nobody, including both of his parents, ever inquired as to where he had been or why he might have been there. Even the ability to perform menial jobs nobody else usually wanted to do was generally denied him. One day he had tried to demonstrate his throwing stick to his father had been what he now considered the regular exhibition of attitude and treatment by all of the tribe. His father had scoffed and labeled the device a "child's toy" as he had fumbled to show the power of it. His father had merely watched the broken display with patience and then remarked that warriors were men of the spear and bound by the code of the spear.

His life had become one of mystery and wonder and yet none of that could be shared with anyone in his tribe, not even his family. His status, as lowly as he had feared it would be, was in actuality lower than he could have imagined. The boy had somehow almost ceased to exist in the tribe's mind.

That he could come and go as he wished, eat at the communal dinner in the great, open room, and receive shelter within the walls of his parents' room were accepted by all, but nothing else was given—no kind look, no confirmation of his very existence within the tribe. Only his mother reached out to communicate with him at all, and he could give her nothing back until he had somehow proven himself. The boy did not understand that either. He so missed her intelligent conversation, but it was her looks of sadness and deep concern that hurt him the most.

There was no one in the room when he arrived, his father was no doubt still out hunting and his mother probably searching the riverbanks for more of her special medicinal potions. The boy had seen his two brothers standing guard atop the sapling and mud roof of the structure, but they had either failed to recognize or simply refused to acknowledge him. He checked the fire coals of the cooking ring to find considerable heat under a thick coating of ash. He looked around the now familiar room and realized that he had come to truly appreciate the advantages of the structure over the old cave complex. It was warm and dry all over, except for the winds that somehow worked their way between even the thickly stacked stone walls. There had been talk of using the clay from the riverbank to fill in the spaces between all the stones, but no one had wanted to perform the major renovation it would have taken to accomplish the task. An attempt had been made to simply apply the clay to the outside of the stacked walls but the material simply washed away if it was struck by any moisture at all.

For some reason, the insects that had plagued them so badly in the cave complex mostly stayed out of the artificial structure, yet no one could say why. His father and the warriors in general frequently complained about what they considered a poor substitute for the old caves. It was unnatural to them, as it was to the Shaman. If the caves had survived in any size or condition, the boy knew that the structure would be abandoned overnight.

His father's senior warrior status had assured the family of an outside-facing room and one with a cooking fire and smoke tube. All the warriors wanted to be located in outside-facing rooms while the leaders of the tribe chose rooms close to the communal area and the interior of the structure. The hunters could not bear to be too far inside the complex. The crippled boy had only stayed with the family for a few nights and then had been moved back to one of the tiny, interior rooms. The boy worked his way from one room to another, with no one questioning or asking anything of him. Only rarely did anyone even look at him.

Stooping, the boy entered a darkened interior so dim that he stumbled across a small pile of something he didn't recognize. The boy felt the bundle move and stepped back. It was the crippled boy, he realized, lying upon an old mottled sleeping skin.

The boy looked up at him, but said nothing. A leather thong ran from a tied wrist back and forth between his belt and then over the left shoulder. His identity, even in the dim light, was obvious.

"You, crippled boy," he said, but the youngster made no reply.

He just stared back with his hard eyes.

"Can you come to the river?" he asked, his tone flat and rough even to his own hearing. At the same time, he stepped back through the opening and waited. If the child could not walk, then his idea and his trip back were both wasted. He felt no sense of sympathy. He had been long taught that a useless human was a burden to the tribe, unless he had important parents, and should be allowed to pass back to the Earth god as quickly and painlessly as possible. In truth, however, injured or crippled members of the tribe were pretty much tolerated except at birth. For some reason, there seemed to be many more female babies born with defects than males. The boy had once asked his mother about why that was, but she had simply replied that females were weaker than men. But the boy had watched her eyes closely and their expression had not supported her words. Only a few male children were present in the tribe who did not participate in the normal functions of the tribe.

There was a lengthy pause while the boy waited, looking the other one over. Suddenly the cripple stood, coming up almost exactly to the boy's height. Instead of large, blue eyes, the cripple's gaze was dark and more intense. His blond hair was shorn almost to his scalp, while the boy's was long and flowing in the warrior style.

The boy turned and led them out, hiding his surprise. He remembered the cripple as being smaller, although he had not seen much of him either before or after the catastrophe, and he had always been lying down or leaning against something, either in the caves or somewhere close to the new tribal structure.

They worked their way silently back through the maze of interior rooms. Even though all the rooms with fire pits had smoke tubes, still the overpowering smell was of burning wood. The Chief had assigned the warriors in training the task of hauling firewood from the river and coal from a thick, black, upriver vein in the escarpment wall. The boy wondered if they would get around to him for that chore, as their consumption of fire materials was so much greater than it had been in the caves. He hoped they would as he wanted to show that he could do the job better than anyone else. When they reached the outside, both breathed in deeply for some time. Finally, the boy spoke.

"Can you climb?" he asked in a clearly dispirited voice. He had quickly examined the cripple's noticeably withered arm and hand and his entire drooping shoulder.

The blond cripple nodded vigorously, but the boy grimaced and shook his head. Without another word, he turned and trotted for the river. He didn't even look to see if the crippled boy followed, his disappointment so deep.

The bird sat on its perch and regarded their approach. The boy stopped at the edge of the pool and noted the hesitation behind him. The blond cripple had stopped several paces back.

"That's a strange-looking bird," he said uncertainly, pointing with his good hand.

The boy looked back at him, then turned to the bird. He whistled and then clapped both hands together. Tagawan obligingly beat his wings, jumped off his perch, crossed the pond, and alighted on the boy's shoulder. He squawked loudly once to receive maximum attention, and then studied the blond cripple with his left eye.

The blond boy backed up a full step. "I've never seen a bird do something like this before. Not like what he just did, anyway," he finished.

"He's a bird all right and a smart one, as well." The boy said it with a smile. "And my bird," he added. "I have been whistling to get him to come, and now, well, sometimes he does."

The cripple reached out with a tentative finger to touch the animal, but did not pull it back in time. He sucked on the small wound where he had been pecked by the sharp, fat beak, and stared silently. At that, Tagawan squawked once more, and began cleaning the roots of his body feathers.

The boy smiled again and shrugged. "I think he's happy now," he said, then pushed against the bird's body until it leaped back across the pool to the top of the pedestal. He turned to the younger boy.

"I can't call you 'cripple' all the time. We won't be given names until adulthood, but we have to call each other something." He said the words in a flat, resigned voice, knowing that since they were the only two of their status in the tribe, their association together was almost unavoidable. The boy was not comfortable, however, with having someone around who was seen as useless to the tribe. He still thought of his own situation as somehow retrievable.

"What will you be called?" the blond cripple asked, still absently massaging his pecked hand and watching the bird without expression.

The boy didn't know if he meant what names they would give one another or what he might be called by the tribe upon adulthood designation, so he waited, but the cripple merely watched the preening bird.

"Ah!" he finally said in exasperation. The cripple was impossible. "My father is the senior hunter so I will be son-of-hunter. Da-ga-ryl. You know that already," he added acidly. Still the blond boy said nothing.

"Daryl, then, it sounds better. I formally name myself Daryl." He watched the blond cripple for any reaction at the uncommon customization of his future given name. Names in the tribe were extremely sensitive descriptions of a person, particularly a warrior. Usually, a name was directly related to what value the person provided to the tribe. Daryl knew that he had only added the "you know already" because he could never now follow in his father's footsteps.

"Well?" he finally asked, wondering at the same time why he was seeking the cripple's approval at all. He had, after all, invited the blond out to his domain, and he was not the cripple.

"Daryl it is," concluded the blond, not even looking in the boy's direction, instead watching the ever-changing cloud of white mist.

"I'll be Nado," he whispered, more to the passing water than to the boy.

"Nado? What is Nado?" Daryl inquired, perplexed.

"I don't know, I just like the sound," answered the crippled boy.

Daryl could only shake his head. He'd never heard of anything like it. "Where do you get ideas like that?" he inquired. "Nobody gets to name themselves something that has no meaning at all."

For the first time Nado smiled, and it was a radiant smile from such a serious and intense face.

"Well, you just named yourself Daryl, didn't you? . . . Daryl did not laugh, only shook his head and looked into the other boy's deep brown eyes with dark eyebrows hanging over them. He followed Nado as the other boy, still laughing, moved closer to the edge of the falls to take it all in.

"Beautiful. It's beautiful. I didn't think it would be this grand."

The tribe could not avoid being influenced by the constant thunder of the falls, but very few of the villagers ventured down to examine it closer. Obviously, Nado had been one of the ones whom had not. He stood gaping.

Daryl waited a full hundred breaths, but the other boy did not move. When he could restrain himself no longer, he set off down the steep trail.

"C'mon," he said loudly over one shoulder, nearly deafened by the cacophony below. He nimbly broke into a run, the bird preceding him, using every feature of the switchback he had become so quick at negotiating. At the bottom he turned back to see the barefooted Nado only halfway down. Daryl sighed. *The cripple will need foot wraps before long,* he thought. He then followed the thought with a smile. It was fun to have someone to compete with other than the bird.

Daryl waited impatiently for Nado to reach the bottom. When he did, however, he turned to peer at the great cauldron of beating, swirling water where the falls impacted the riverbed. Speech was not even possible here. Again Daryl waited until he could wait no longer. He touched the boy on the shoulder, noting his stunned look of wonder at what he was seeing, then pointed downriver. It was hard for Daryl to remember how he had stood with just the same expression the first time he had encountered the brutal action within the pool.

They ran lightly but quickly down the makeshift trail, Daryl taking the lead to give direction where necessary, around a stand of trees here or a pile of rocks there. When he reached the almost invisible break in the thick saplings lining the base of the escarpment wall, he stopped abruptly. Nado ran on a good few man-lengths beyond and then he too stopped and turned to follow Daryl's eyes up the near inverted face of the cliff. "We climb," Daryl said, not moving, his stare still straight up. Tagawan had landed on one of the branches of a sapling almost too small to support his weight. "Fat bird," the boy whispered, now far enough from the falls to be heard. Tagawan squawked in seemingly obvious disagreement.

"Climb what?" Nado said, a great frown wrinkling his forehead.

The boy merely pointed straight up. Nado's expression changed completely as the skin of his face pulled flat and expressionless. Daryl watched closely out of the corner of his eye to see how the cripple would take to the idea. He almost smiled at

Nado's now white complexion and stunned expression.

"Can you do it?" he inquired mildly, still not breaking his gaze from the seemingly impossible surface. The first hand and footholds were among the most difficult to figure out of the entire experience, he knew, but said nothing. He expected Nado to voice his disapproval.

"Of course," Nado replied, as if they were merely setting out on another running path. That surprised the boy enough to swing his head around. Many questions sprang to his mind, but he decided to follow along with the cripple's decision and say nothing further about the climb until the next day.

"Tomorrow, then, we will climb." Daryl and Nado both craned their heads back to look up the imposing face of the cliff.

Chapter XVIII

Both boys rose early and met near the water to catch breakfast and prepare for the day. The sun was low, well before its midpoint, when they began the actual climb. The boy pointed out every small hold and how he had marked them. Surprise and vague unease were the emotions that ran through Daryl's mind as he watched the cripple follow behind him. Nado took directions silently and well, but that was not nearly so surprising as his ability to climb with only one good arm and hand.

Nado had significant leg strength, greater than Daryl's. When the boy needed hands and feet alternately working to move up the face, Nado accomplished the task by pushing up strongly on the footholds while guiding his body with the single arm. Daryl also noticed that the crippled arm was not completely useless, as he had at first believed. The hand could grasp, but it could not extend because of the shoulder joint injury.

They reached the last ledge where the hidden chimney ran up to the bottom of the pine root system. Without that feature, the overhang would have been impossible to negotiate. The climb had taken nearly as long as Daryl's first time, when he had known none of the special holds or grasping surfaces. Part of the reason was simply that he had paused often to point out each important place as they had gone up. Also, in the back of his mind he had worried about what he might do if the crippled boy fell. Finally, he had just stopped thinking about it, but the delay meant that their visit to the ruins would be short. He could not expect Nado to make it back down without full sunlight.

The bird was already squawking from his perch on the big tree, impatient and impudent as usual. Daryl watched Nado glance down. He had never looked down until the summit was reached, but for some reason the other boy was not bothered by the height. He had paused to look below them all the way up the cliff. Still, the exit from the chimney onto the lip of the escarpment wall was a difficult feat.

The boy sighed and then edged over to reveal the protruding lip of the chimney near the end of the ledge. That feature assured that the vital secret to the climb would not be discovered by accident. Nado smiled in pleasant surprise.

"I wondered," was all the tight-lipped boy said.

They went up with Daryl in the lead, talking Nado through the movements, although the pressure of the climber's back against the curved side of the chimney was pretty automatic. If one pressed hard with their feet against the other rough surface, you could slowly work your way up. Daryl remembered how difficult it might be without a leather jerkin to protect his back and slowed his ascent. But Nado pushed up against him and they picked up speed again. The conversion from stretched out to grasp the edge of the lip and one of the large roots would be difficult, however.

Daryl's technique was to reach up with one hand, push off with both feet, and then grab the root with his other hand. Then he simply levered himself up using his feet to scrape and push for whatever assistance they could provide. When he reached the top he turned to see immediately that Nado would not be able to use that method. He had no other arm to toss over the root and help pull his body up. Daryl had no ideas so he lay and breathed, staring down at the boy. Nado was wedged tightly and had stopped to rest, as well. Daryl's forehead wrinkled with a frown as he contemplated the cripple's position. Then Nado suddenly reached up above his head to the lip where it curved out, dropped his legs, and twisted in to face the wall. Scrabbling with both bare feet, he found enough purchase to push his agile upper body right up over the edge. He had not had to use the root on the other side of the chimney at all. Standing and massaging his good hand with his bad, he leaped across the narrow cut and stood next to Daryl, looking out over the great valley below.

Daryl knew his own legs did not have that power, but he also saw a certain advantage to climbing with bare feet. His own thin wraps would not allow for that kind of gripping power, and he tucked that fact away for the time when Nado wore leathers similar to his own. Like the climb up, the climb down would be harder the first time as well. But it would not involve so much of the unknown, and the fear of climbing at such heights would be much less.

"Well?" Nado said, as the boy rose to join him. The wind now blew from their back as it eased its way over the lip and down into the valley below. At first he thought Nado was talking about the unbelievable view, but then the boy spoke again.

"How did I do?" and all doubt was removed.

"Not too bad," was all Daryl could think to reply. He pushed away the worries that still played through his mind about the climb back down. Daryl thought Nado's climbing was one of the most impressive feats he had ever witnessed. In a way, he felt proud of the crippled youth, as if his success was something that Daryl had been partially responsible for. He smiled as they both stared up and down the valley.

"Yes, it's so beautiful . . ." Nado's voice trailed away, misinterpreting the boy's grin. Tagawan squawked from his nearby tree branch.

"He wants us to get moving," Daryl said. He noted Nado's

eyes examining the equipment tightly strapped to his body and prepared to explain each piece, but again the strange boy asked nothing. He simply waited for what would come next.

Daryl took off in his ground-eating light lope, with Nado following. Tagawan immediately raced out front, bobbing, hopping, and flitting from pine to pine.

"Does that bird go everywhere with you?" Nado asked.

"Yes," Daryl responded, with no expression in his voice, annoyed by the other boy's apparent lack of interest in his things. The worry of the return climb also weighed heavily on him. Without wanting to, after all, it was partnering him with another tribal reject, he liked the cripple and he did not want to be responsible if the unusual boy was killed.

"I've never seen him at the village," Nado said, suddenly willing to talk, but only about things of little consequence. Daryl could not believe that the boy was not overcome with the awe of being atop the plateau for the first time. If the warriors had ever found a way to venture up the escarpment, they had never spoken of it.

"He doesn't go to the village," Daryl said, letting some of his exasperation show in his tone. There was a dignity of silence required in what they were doing, although he could not explain why he felt that way. And he could not think of any way to require it of Nado.

The wall appeared before them as a horizontal line. Daryl leaped up onto its surface without pausing in stride and looked back. He had brought Nado along the same central winding way as he had first traversed with the bird. Tagawan joined him on the rock slab, also watching the other boy. Nado had stopped in his tracks two full man-lengths from the wall.

"What is this?" he breathed in a stunned whisper, his eyes flitting up and down the long line of fitted monolithic stones. Daryl smiled and looked down as if to bring the bird in on his triumph. Finally something had taken the crippled boy completely by surprise, and it felt good to stand above and enjoy his awe.

"It's nothing," the boy responded, "nothing next to the other things you are about to see." He laughed. Nado moved slowly up to the near neck-high edge of the wall. Slowly he brushed the surface and then tried to run his fingernails into the almost invisible line that separated one huge stone from another. Tagawan had not moved and his head bent down to allow his left eye to follow the boy's movement.

"Hello bird," Nado said absently, still examining the joint intently. Tagawan pecked his outstretched hand right above the center knuckle.

"Ow!" Nado brought the back of his hand right to his mouth. The bird squawked contentedly, but did not move away. "The bird is mean," Nado said, between bouts of sucking on the small wound. Then he went back to examining the surface of the rock.

"Actually, I think he likes you," Daryl said, although the idea filled him with unease. It was unlikely that the bird would allow the other boy into such close vicinity so soon after just coming into contact with him. He worried that maybe the animal was becoming too friendly with humans and would soon turn up at the community supper . . . in the stew pot.

Daryl ran along the top of the flat surface, heading toward the end that hung out over the valley on the other side of the plateau. Nado backed a few paces and vaulted to the top of the wall while Tagawan hopped quickly away.

"Come on bird," Nado yelled back, "we must keep up with our master," and he was off in pursuit of Daryl.

They seemed to reach the end in no time at all. Daryl stood near the edge and looked out over the barren valley, marveling at how dry and desolate it looked without the vibrant noise and rush and the great river. Nado pulled up next to his right shoulder and just stood there, looking slowly up and down the great wide expanse of land. Daryl waited patiently as the time dragged by, while Tagawan cruised along, riding the updrafts just out in front of them.

"Another valley," Nado finally said, his voice giving away his shock. "And another beyond that," he added, pointing across at the far distant escarpment as he spoke.

"What?" was all Daryl could think to say, as he tried to see what the other boy was talking about. "I do not see anything." But all Nado did was laugh.

"What do you find funny?" Daryl asked, stung over the comment.

"You cannot see it, but it must be there. I always have wondered about the far wall of our own valley. Did you ever wonder if there was another valley beyond that wall?"

Daryl looked over and met Nado's eyes. He had never even considered that such a thing might exist.

"Ours is there," and Nado pointed back, "and now this is here." His arm swept out to where the bird played. "It has to be that there are more. It just has to be."

Daryl believed him utterly. He could not understand why he had not seen it himself until Nado had mentioned it. He watched the crippled boy take in the new territory below, the wind ruffling his short hair back, and his expression of deep, satisfied wonder. This time Daryl was impressed.

"Thank you," he said, the words coming out unbidden. He hadn't meant to say them aloud. But Nado just smiled and nodded.

"You were right. The view from the other side is nothing compared to this one, well, except for the falls anyway." Nado swung his good arm up and down the valley.

Daryl smiled back at him, and then shook his head slowly, realizing then just how much he had missed companionship since the catastrophe. "No, I wasn't talking about this. Come on." He caught Nado's mystified look and then took off along the top of the wall toward the center trail.

Somehow Tagawan was already perched on a nearby branch as he leaped to the pine needle floor and ran, heedless of whether Nado was following or not. His smile was for even more than the great feeling that running among the plateau pines gave him. He circled past, well away from the beginning of the ruins, instead racing through the pines until he neared an area that led right to one corner of the flat-laid stone clearing. He stopped behind the thick trunk of a tall, high-branched pine.

Nado pulled up behind him and the squawk of the bird could be heard from out in the clearing. The cripple moved to peek out, but the boy held him back.

"Careful. Just take a quick look." Daryl whispered, holding Nado's good arm near his shoulder.

Nado leaned slightly outward, looking around the trunk and into the clearing just beyond. He jerked his head back in.

"There's somebody there!" he hissed. Daryl laughed at his fearful expression. Nado's brow furrowed, but he made no move to look again. Daryl laughed so hard that tears came to his eyes. Nado's expression darkened, and he looked at the other boy like he had gone crazy. Finally, still holding Nado by the arm, Daryl dragged him out from behind the trunk and toward the waiting bird. They got halfway to the statue before Nado shrugged his hold off when he saw the effigy that had fooled him.

"What is it?" Nado asked, his head slanting as he tried to discern what it was.

Daryl walked up to the effigy and turned back. "I do not know. I have never seen anything like it. It is a small human made of stone." Before the words were out of Daryl's mouth, Nado ran to the statue. He batted the bird away as if it was a mere cobweb. Tagawan leaped to Daryl's shoulder and squawked angrily. Nado's good hand worked over the surface of the stone, peeling moss and scraping dirt and the bird's dried messes off the surface. Then he stood back.

"It's magnificent," he said in awe. Daryl looked from the statue to the boy and then back again. He had never seen such a thing either on his first visit, but his reaction had not been anything like Nado's. He would have laughed again but he remembered what the crippled boy had said at the edge of the new valley. There was something in his heart or mind that was different. But it was a difference Daryl liked.

Chapter XIX

"What do you think it is?" Nado asked, stepping back, but Daryl did not know what to answer. Instead he just looked at the statue and remained silent, finally understanding that the crippled boy was not really talking to him at all. Nado leaned closer to examine the stone figure. "These scratches are pretty fresh."

"Oh, those are from my new throwing stick," Daryl said, unlimbering the device and working a single round stone from his leather tube.

Nado turned his head to briefly examine the device and its projectile. Then he raised one eyebrow.

"I use it for training. You know . . . target practice," and he made a motion of throwing the rock but then quickly dropped the stick arm, still holding the rock in his other hand. Nado's face had suddenly turned ferocious.

"No. Never again," his good arm swung out as if to protect the statue. "This is a treasure for all of our tribe—for all tribes everywhere. Can't you see that?"

Daryl stood mute. He felt chastised, but could not understand why.

"What is she wearing?" Nado asked, his attention focused back to the object itself.

"She? Wearing?" Daryl asked. He had never considered any of the object's details once he had recognized it as some human-made representation, no matter how impossible it would have been for his own tribe to duplicate.

"Look at the way they carved the stone, how it seems to flow. It's a female wearing some sort of material. Not even our finest worked leathers would hang so smoothly and without seams." Nado's hand caressed the surface as he talked.

"What if it was the skin of a really big animal?" Daryl offered. When the other boy looked back at him, his expression was so derisive that Daryl decided he would comment no further.

"This may be the greatest thing in all the world," Nado said, then swept his overdeveloped right arm around the open area to illustrate. He never completed the swing. His attention had been so drawn to the statue and his absorption so complete that he had not yet seen what lay just beneath the brush, needles, and moss at the edges of the clearing.

"What is it?" Nado asked breathlessly, turning around and around in his attempt to take in all of the old crumbling buildings.

"An ancient village. Long before what our tribe has built by the river." Daryl watched Nado take it all in, again surprised by the other boy's reaction. Where he had first known fear when he had found the wall and the ruins, Nado seemed to show only a stunned sort of joy and intense interest.

Suddenly the blond cripple ran toward the closest part of the ruins. Tagawan followed, swooping and playing much as he did every time they ran through the pines. Daryl could not help but smile at the other boy's exuberance, as he came after them.

Nado would stop to roll over an old carved stone or peer under a leaning slab, and then run on to another part of the ruins. There was pile after pile, each one representing some sort of individual building, or so Daryl thought. He watched the growing shadows closely when it seemed that the youth would never tire of his endless examination. The day was passing at what seemed an accelerated pace, and the gnawing concerns over their climb back down would not leave him.

He withheld himself until he could no longer. "Come, we have to get back . . ." he began, but Nado cut him off.

"Does anyone know?" the question was accompanied by Nado's turn toward him with his usual penetrating, brown-eyed stare. As with most of the questions posed by the crippled boy, this one took Daryl completely by surprise.

"Ah, well, I guess not."

"Why?" Nado crossed his arms as he spoke.

"I don't know," the boy got out truthfully, then thought about it briefly. "Nobody would believe me if I told them."

His conclusion was met by a growing smile on Nado's face. He shook his head slowly from side to side. "I would say that's an understatement." He relaxed his arms and swung completely around in his agreement. "I have never even imagined something like all this could exist."

"Well, there is one more thing . . ." The boy trailed off before he loped back to the open area at the far end from the statue. He stopped when he reached the pedestal, still buried under the thick coat of moss and lichen, just as he'd left it from his first visit. He waited just long enough for Nado to reach him, then unceremoniously pulled away the moss.

"What is it?" whispered Nado, his hands caressing the round basin before examining the shiny yellow tube sticking up from its center.

"Metal," Daryl answered, as if it was a commonplace substance and not one that neither of them had only ever heard of, and certainly never expected to see.

"Metal," breathed the crippled boy, so quietly that Daryl leaned toward him. Tagawan flew in and landed on his angled shoulder blade, then hopped up as he straightened. A quiet squawk accompanied his clumsy landing, but both boys ignored him. Nado kept feeling the thin coldness of the erect cylinder, then used the same hand to clear all debris from the indented circle, bending down to examine the stone surface.

"What are you doing?" Daryl asked.

"There are grooves around the top," the other boy breathed, his eyes no more than half a hand's breadth from the surface.

"Good. Fine. Great. We have to go. The climb down is much more difficult, and we will lose the light." Daryl didn't even want to imagine what that would mean if they were caught halfway down the face without the sun to guide them. The thought sent a shiver through his thin frame.

"You worry too much," but his words came out with a resigned sigh as Nado stood, then without instruction gently replaced the layers of moss just as Daryl had removed them. A slender sapling edged up and over the lip of the pedestal top. Nado pushed it out of the way, but it bent right back to interfere with his final effort.

"Here," Daryl said in a clipped tone, handing the cripple the second of the white flint blades he had found on the island. Nado tentatively accepted the knife, but stopped to study the fine natural edge.

"I'm not even going to ask this time." He shook his head in amazement and easily severed the irritating limb at its base. He held out the small flint knife in his good hand.

"Keep it," Daryl said, again matter-of-factly. "It's an omen." He reached down and took his own similar blade from its leather pouch, then shoved it back into the scabbard-like container. "This was my first," he allowed, then met the other boy's wide eyes.

"Omen?" and there was a slight delay of time. "How many 'omens' do you have?" He said the word omen in a reverential tone. A warrior was issued such a necessary tool only after successfully completing the training and then the secret initiation as well. No mere boy carried such a thing, the value was incalculable.

"We have to go!" Daryl replied, then set off on the trail toward the wall.

"But, but, there is so much . . ." Nado yelled after him, then followed, watching the crazy bird, as he secretly thought of the creature, swinging out back and forth before the running figure.

This time Daryl vaulted the wall, touching only lightly the top center stone with his right foot. Nado, with feet bare and trying to be careful, could only vault up and then gingerly select a soft pile of old brown needles for his landing. It seemed that they arrived at the base of the great pine in no time at all. Nado could not help voicing his feelings.

"This was wonderful. I have never had such a run in my life."

The two boys sat on the lip, taking in the tremendous view up and down the valley. The bird perched nearby, grooming and appearing to wait for their attempt at a descent.

"So, you have told no one of this place, or anything up here?" Nado asked again.

"No," Daryl replied, wondering what the strange-thinking boy was getting at.

"Not even your father or mother?" Nado continued, his voice casual.

"I said no," Daryl bit back, beginning to grow impatient.

"Good," the crippled boy whispered.

"What?" Daryl was shocked. Part of his impatience at the questions was his belief that Nado would find him disloyal to the tribe. His father was the most senior warrior, while Nado's was the master flint-knapper, as well as the Chief's brother. Within the tribe all members were always to think of the band first. Always first. Nothing was held to oneself except in cases where courting was in progress or the secrets of the warriors and some women's rituals. But Daryl knew that he was not really a member of the tribe anymore. He was accepted only as an obligation. A necessary burden. He no longer felt any sense of loyalty, other than to do what he was told.

They descended together, Daryl's confidence growing in the crippled youth's ability to use the different holds as they moved down. Coming out of the chimney onto the ledge under the tree was made easy by Nado being second. Daryl simply grabbed his good arm and pulled him physically onto the small protruding shelf of stone. From there they worked back and forth in the system of almost accidental switchbacks Daryl had felt his way through on his first ascent.

During a rest, while both of them stood braced with their faces pressed into the wall, Daryl asked the question that had been on his mind since the top. "Why did you say good?"

Nado did not respond, instead poking at Tagawan, who had sat on a small rock outcropping nearby. The bird pecked him, but not hard.

"Well?" Daryl demanded.

"Well what? Can't you figure it out for yourself?" Nado smiled his cynical, derisive smile that so infuriated Daryl. But the boy contained himself and waited.

"If the Shaman finds out what is up there, we'll both be sacrificed to the Earth god, that's why! Don't you ever listen? He is forever running around claiming that we are the special and only real tribe in the world. And that world is the valley, if you haven't—and you obviously haven't—figured it out." He spoke quickly, his words containing an acidic bite. They impacted Daryl so powerfully, however, that he was not even upset with the delivery. He thought long and deep before he replied.

"Oh."

"Oh . . . ? Oh? . . . ? Is that it? You amaze me. How can you be so dumb and so smart all at the same time?" Nado's exasperation was obvious on his face.

"Smart?" Daryl was surprised. He did not think of himself as smart. In fact, he thought of Nado as much smarter, and he was surprised the cripple would use the word to describe him at all.

"No, smart stupid!" Nado replied, laughing openly.

"Why do you say that?" Daryl said, irritated that he could not understand the other boy better. Then he was angry at himself for sounding so weak and upset. His image of himself was anything but any of that, but somehow Nado seemed to draw feelings and thoughts out of him that he had never entertained before.

They climbed in silence the rest of the way down, except for short, clipped comments from Daryl on where Nado might place his hand or feet for the best hold. At the bottom, they sat tucked deep within the bases of the saplings to rest before the hike back up to the tribal structure.

"I'm sorry," Nado said, both of them staring through the branches and leaves at the water pumping wildly out of the nearby cauldron. While his voice was a shout against the thunderous noise, it came across as more of half-whisper, both because of its tone and because of the constant mist that fell as well.

Daryl did not reply, still sulking.

"Sometimes you just don't seem to get things that are obvious to me. That is all I meant by calling you stupid. But then, look at all we saw today. All of it. And your throwing stick, whether it works or not, who else would have thought of it? In one day, you have expanded my knowledge of the world more than in all the time I have been in it. You are the smartest person I have ever known."

Daryl was unused to Nado's only very occasional lengthy comments, and he had never been so complimented in his life.

Embarrassed by his earlier thoughts, he looked out of the side of his right eye, but did not for a moment doubt the crippled boy's sincerity. Instead, he just shrugged. "What is it that I miss? Nobody can tell what the Shaman might do. I just stay away from him."

"Oh, really," Nado said, but he did not pronounce the word as a question. He shook his head and thought while neither of them spoke. Tagawan rushed out of the great gray cloud and nearly splattered into the saplings, finding one too weak for his weight, but sitting on the bent-over branch anyway.

"All right. I will give you a different example," Nado said. "You really do not know what went on about that whole thing of your being punished, just short of outcasting, do you?"

Daryl's face registered his utter surprised shock at the statement.

"See, I thought not," Nado said triumphantly, but sadly. When he did not immediately continue, Daryl had to speak.

"What are you talking about?" his voice rose with confusion and anger, but he didn't notice.

"The punishment for your supposed cowardice. That had little or nothing to do with what you did or did not do with respect to the great catastrophe." Nado then waited for the expected answer, and got it.

"It didn't?" Daryl was beside himself, both hands digging into his bent knees in frustrated shock.

"You are the senior warrior's son. And you are the fastest runner, and the smartest, best-looking child in the tribe. Your brother will follow in your father's footsteps, since you are such a little thing." Nado stopped briefly to laugh before continuing. "So you are a candidate."

Daryl could not get it no matter how hard he tried.

"Candidate for what?" he said, his frown so deep that his forehead hurt.

160

"Candidate for Chief some day. You are a threat . . . or at least you were. The Chief has a son too, you know." Nado got a stick and poked at the overly quiet bird, while Daryl just sat there and thought, no longer frustrated, but still in shock.

His mind raced back and forth over all the events since that fateful day on the island. He had agonized over the injustice of it, over the fact that no one in the tribe was willing to listen to the truth, or listen at all. And until Nado had spoken, using what was so obvious to him merely as an example, Daryl could not have guessed. But the sense of it, the logic, was all there. The Chief ruled the tribe almost completely. Only very, very rarely did the council of warriors ever not agree to whatever the Chief wanted.

They broke through the bushes together, neither boy saying anything and with Daryl still mulling over what he knew. As they made their way up the rip-rap next to the falls, he glanced at the crippled boy's profile. The sound of the nearby falls drowned out his words when he spoke.

"You're right. I'm stupid when it comes to people, I guess. I'm glad I have you around now."

Chapter XX

They reached the small pool where Tagawan was already ensconced upon his stone perch and well into his never-ending chore of grooming. Daryl had not spoken for the remainder of their climb, but his thoughts had gone into areas he had never consciously considered before.

While growing up in the cave complex and the area around it, he had seen and known Nado all of his life, but they had almost never spoken. Daryl had remained remote from almost all contact with the other children. His only real relationship had been with his mother. He had never felt any need to become a part of the small, ever-changing children's groups, not even those of his brother. What had changed inside him? As they sat on large stones at the pool's edge, his right hand moved to the center of his chest. It was an unconscious gesture that he was not even aware of. Nado noted the movement and looked over, but said nothing.

"Was it for survival?" Daryl suddenly asked, whether to himself or Nado, he wasn't sure. The other boy looked at him again, his frown expressing his inability to understand the question.

"That I don't . . . that I haven't known you . . . or any of them?" Daryl's hand moved from his chest to wave toward the tribal structure as he continued, "But it's all changed. And I don't understand." He shook his head, sadness coming over his features. "It was the great catastrophe, I just know it." Daryl was thinking aloud more than actually speaking. "Nothing is the same for me."

There was a silence before Nado spoke. "It changed for everyone. It's just that most cannot even discuss it. And I, for that matter, never bothered to try to know you either. I just thought I was another of those that would just wither and die in some very cold winter." The boys looked at one another. Neither had ever spoken such words to anyone nor heard any member of the tribe discuss the subject. Silence ensued while each of them examined the water gently swirling in the small, cold pool. The bird squawked and clucked happily above them.

"Have you explored further down the plateau?" Nado asked, more to break the tension than to change the subject.

"There is another finely constructed wall the same distance from the ruins in the other direction." Daryl answered. "I don't know what lies beyond."

"As I thought. We must find out. What were they afraid of . . . those that lived there?" Nado looked back in the downriver direction as he spoke.

"It was a long time ago," Daryl said, "and there is nothing down the valley, anyway."

"How do you know?" Nado's voice was innocent, but the question was anything but. The question bothered Daryl much more than it might have if he had not seen what he thought was smoke from that same direction more than once. He was not imagining it. He knew that. So what could it be if the valley was uninhabited down its vast length? Might there be some natural phenomena brought on by the great earth shaking? The smoke must be something from inside the earth, but what?

Nado continued when it became obvious that Daryl was not going to say anymore. "And what of the valley beyond? We have to explore it." And the boy had no answer for that statement either. He could only sit and think to himself. Nado was the strangest creature he had ever encountered, even stranger than the bird or the Mur.

"If Tagawan wasn't right here, you wouldn't believe in him either," whispered the boy.

"What are you talking about?" Nado said, affronted, while the bird squawked at the mention of his name.

"You wouldn't believe in anything. Not anything I've told you, not about the island, or any of it, except what you can see and touch yourself," Daryl said in unexpected vehemence. He could not stop himself. "Where do you think I got that white flint blade to give you?" Daryl made believe he was looking all over around the pool and between them. "In fact, I'll bet you don't even believe in the Earth god, do you?"

Nado drew in a long, deep breath while Daryl looked down into the water, a bit sheepish about his accusations. He would have apologized, but once again the crippled boy surprised and shocked him.

"You're right. I don't believe in all that stuff. The Shaman just keeps gaining more and more power. The Chief is a good man, but past his prime. He is becoming a sick, doddering fool while the Shaman plots to be Chief." Nado stopped talking, but did not meet Daryl's eyes.

"What?" Daryl whispered. He could not believe what he had heard. The statement, all by itself, was sufficient to provoke an almost guaranteed vote of banishment, if any in the tribe had overheard him. He looked around in actual fear. Daryl had not really meant to question Nado that closely. He'd merely been stung by his own lack of credibility with the youth.

"Your mother doesn't believe in any of it either." Nado's comment cut off any further response from Daryl.

He was angry and didn't know why, as he listened to the crippled boy relate details of conversations Nado had had with Daryl's mother while he had lay in recovery. Nado looked over at him. "You're angry because you don't understand. Come on, it's almost dark." Nado rose and headed toward the village, but he stopped and swung back to wave at the departing bird.

Daryl followed, but could not help smiling as they made their way upriver. His thoughts were first twisted one way by the strange boy's comments, and then another. He was impossible to predict. They walked in silence until they were near the juncture of trails. Daryl realized that he had just experienced the happiest day of his life.

"Wait," he said suddenly, placing his left hand on Nado's shoulder to stop him. Daryl squatted down near a large rock and surveyed the area around them, making sure no one else was nearby.

"It's late and they've all gone on," Nado said, joining the boy by the side of the trail, a quizzical expression on his face. "Why have we stopped?"

Daryl loosened his flint knife from its pouch-like leather sheath. Squeezing the container, he gently brought forth a clear, sparkling object and held it in his closed fist.

"The special stones that I use with the stick. Some of them are hollow and one broke on that statue." He opened his hand. In the late afternoon light the crystal glistened as if wet, its finger-long sharp surfaces throwing off golden glints and its base almost glowing a mild, beautiful green.

"What is it?" Nado whispered, moving his face downward until his eyes were only a hand's breadth from Daryl's palm, but the boy did not answer. Nado's hand moved toward the object until Daryl grabbed it with his own free hand. Then he opened the other boy's palm by squeezing and dropped the crystal into it.

"It's yours."

Nado looked at his open hand, turning the beautiful stone between his fingers, staring at it. "What for?" he finally asked.

"Today," Daryl answered, "for today," not expecting the crippled youth to understand.

Nado said nothing, then slowly nodded, surprising Daryl. "Thank you. You were not bad yourself." They both smiled huge smiles, until Nado frowned and looked back down at the object.

"I have seen something like this once before." Nado's brow furrowed as he talked, thinking deeply. "My father. He has a crystal in his special pouch." Both of the boys thought of the special, secret contents of warrior's necklace pouches that neither of them would ever wear.

"How . . . ?" began Daryl, and then they both smiled guiltily. "Oh," he finished, but only after a moment. The revelation was another of those things Daryl had never expected to hear anyone admit. It was simply unheard of to attempt to break into a warrior's secret pouch. The punishment for getting caught was unthinkable. Daryl studied Nado while he examined his new gift. The crippled boy, Daryl decided, was easily the most astounding of all the events that happened to him since the catastrophe.

They walked together up the short path to the tribal structure, moving slowly. Nado examined the stone while Daryl tried to make sense out of what the odd boy had told him. Tagawan, uncharacteristically, flew far above both of them, banking in tight circles.

Nado kept rolling the crystal between his fingers. "Thank you. It's my first present from a friend—from a brother."

Daryl stopped at the words, looking in amazement at Nado, who finally stopped and turned, a quizzical expression on his face. Only warriors were entitled to refer to one another as brother. Even Daryl's real brothers were never spoken of in that specific way. Children were merely sons or daughters of the mother and father, individually or collectively. It sometimes made conversation within the family units, or the tribe itself, lengthy or laborious but the alternative was to dilute the value of the warriors, and that could not be considered.

Daryl stared into the crippled boy's eyes. If days could be omens, then this one must be another, he thought to himself and then smiled openly.

"All right. Brother . . ." the two boys clasped each other hand to forearm, solidly but briefly, in the warrior tradition. They broke and continued their journey, the structure in sight. Red hues were cast everywhere as the sun sank below the horizon, turning from a full disk to a last, tiny flash. The walls of the light brownish rock had turned a deep blood red to their eyes.

Nado finally slipped the small crystal into a carefully cut slot in the top of his leather belt, making sure that nothing but the green unremarkable base could be seen by any but the most careful observer. Just before they reached the village, he stopped and turned to Daryl, speaking in a tone that seemed to impart that he was giving the boy a gift in return.

"Look around you. Maybe for the first time." Nado's good arm whirled as he rotated in a quick circle. "Those old boulders over there," he pointed upriver, "or that riverbed, which was wide and deep even when the stream was but a trickle," and they both faced the now distant water, its rush still heard as well as the distant thunder of its passage over the falls. "Don't you think that this, the great catastrophe, has not happened many times before? You, who has been atop the plateau to see yet another plateau in the distance?"

Daryl understood everything that the crippled boy had said, but could not figure out what he was trying to conclude.

"Ah, yes," was all he could think to reply, but his raised eyebrows and the lines on his forehead gave away confusion.

Nado laughed long and hard. "What I mean is simple. Up until you climbed that wall, you thought the world was all in this valley. The warriors know better, but, along with the Chief and the Shaman, they say nothing. What you have learned since the catastrophe has changed everything you know, and the same is true for them," he waved at the structure, and then paused.

"Yes?" Daryl said, when the silence had lasted a near unbearable time.

"Don't you see? It's all so simple. The Earth god, the water god, the rock god, the valley, the valley beyond," Nado spoke fast, his eyes penetrating into Daryl's very mind. "It all means that we know nothing really. We know almost nothing, and they, the leaders of our tribe, are making it all up as they go."

The boy stood and thought about what Nado had said. His eyes pulled away from Nado's deep brown pools and went out to the tribe's building. There was little activity outside, as the families within stoked fires and prepared to congregate in the central cooking and meal area.

"Then what of what happened to me?" he whispered, more to himself than to Nado.

"It is the same. They make it up as they go along, but they deliver the made-up message as if it is as hard and firm as that statue of yours."

Daryl had not thought of the statue, or any of what he had found, except the things he carried, as his own.

"Then what do I do?" he asked, not really expecting an answer.

"What do you do?" Nado almost jumped up and down in his incredulity. "Why do you think I have made you my brother?" Daryl searched the immediate vicinity, fearful of any tribesman overhearing the incautious cripple. "You should have died. Anybody else would have died. Even the tribe tried to kill you. But no, what did you do?"

Daryl looked at Nado in silence, nothing coming into his mind at all, while the other boy stood, arm extended and his bright eyes wide open, waiting for the answer. When it did not come, he sighed deeply, dropping his arm as his shoulders slumped.

"You. You who have created his own special weapon, tamed the wildest of strange birds, and discovered a whole new world above . . . and you, the one who has done this, can't even see the greatest thing of all." Nado finished, then shook his head slowly from side to side. "You made yourself."

The sentence fell between them and Daryl considered it. He wanted to smile at what Nado had said, but he knew the other boy was much too serious to accept any humor whatsoever. Tagawan was anything but tame, although he was certainly strange, and the ruins above—*well*, he thought, *I did discover those*, but in truth he had merely been running away from the tribe, himself, and maybe even life.

Daryl couldn't think of a reply, so he nodded, smiled, and then walked over and into the opening to the family room, leaving Nado standing at the end of the path.

CHAPTER XXI

The winter grew colder and the valley prepared itself for the onset of a hard winter. After their initial climb, the boys had become inseparable, but were together at the compound only when it came to their very few community-assigned chores. No resistance was made to either their bonding or the fact that they simply disappeared for most of each day. Only Daryl's mother, who inquired from time to time what he was doing, and Nado's father, following a similar line of questioning, said anything. The remainder of the tribe seemed more than happy not to have to deal with either boy at all.

Together Daryl and Nado devised ways to shorten what few early morning tasks they had, and to enjoy them. This allowed them to spend as little time as possible within the area of the tribal structure. One of their schemes, however, caught the attention of the Shaman one morning.

From watching the warriors return from their hunting with larger game, Daryl had adapted the concept of hauling a heavy, center-mounted load on a long, stripped sapling. The water jugs were all made of fire-baked clay, and all had been shaped along the same basic design. A single handle ran from midway up the side to the lip. Daryl and Nado strung a series of jugs on a sapling pole, and then made only a few trips to the river. They would sink the pole and all the jugs into the water until they were full. Supporting the load on their shoulders, they hauled an entire day's water supply by making only one hand of runs down the path and back to the storage pool.

The Shaman had not been pleased when he had encountered them one early cold morning. "Stop," he commanded, surprising both boys while they were sinking the pole and pots into the cold water. Daryl looked at Nado in terror, then experienced a bit more fear when the boy merely looked up at the imposing Shaman and smiled.

"Yes, sir!" the crippled boy said. The Shaman carried a long, ornate staff, decorated at its top with the tribe's meager supply of eagle feathers. The wizened, old man tapped the staff methodically upon the hard clay under his feet, until Nado's smile faded.

"What have you done with the water jugs?" His voice sounded a bit like a combination of falling gravel and the distant thrum of the falls, Daryl decided. Too afraid to come out of the icy water, even though the pots were long full.

"We are filling and carrying them, as is our work," Nado said, carefully but with a touch of belligerence. Daryl cringed, trying not to look at the powerful figure above.

The thumping of the staff started again, and there was a lengthy silence, until it stopped. Then he spoke again.

"The jugs were made to be used in the traditional manner. To be carried. You have no work," the Shaman grimaced as he said the word 'you,' "but what work is assigned to you is to be conducted in the proper manner. As it was meant." He thumped his staff heavily and nodded. Staring at Nado, he waited for his acquiescence.

"I'm sure you're right," Nado replied, returning the older man with his own unblinking gaze. "It truly is not work at all. We conduct ourselves in the manner you describe, and we are told. We help them when we are assigned."

The Shaman stood perfectly still for a full hand of breaths, Daryl counted. On the last breath, as Daryl breathed it out, the old man thumped the staff once, then abruptly turned and stalked back up the path toward the village.

Daryl sighed deeply, collapsing out of the water onto the cold mud bank. "You are going to get us banished. What thoughts go through your mind?" he asked. Nado fidgeted with the pole, making sure they lost no jugs as they jiggled just under the water from the current's eddy and pull. Daryl noted that he no longer needed the thong to support his weak arm. It could be used, but it would always remain withered and near useless for anything requiring strength.

"That crafty old goat was trying to make our job harder. It is his nature," Nado said as he stared up the path with a frown at the Shaman's disappearing back. The eagle feathers blew brilliant atop Huslinth's staff, even at a distance.

"But you did not need to provoke him," Daryl said, reclaiming his end of the pole. They hauled it out of the water together and began the short journey back to the village.

"Provoke him? Ha!" Nado exclaimed with a laugh. "He did not understand that part at all. That is why he stood there so long. He left confused, not angry."

"I do not think I understood either," Daryl said, shaking his head. "But then, I do not understand half of the things you say . . . although they sound good."

Nado frowned, casting a black look over his shoulder toward his friend. Most of their conversations focused on the ruins at the top of the plateau, although they also frequently discussed the throwing sticks. It had taken Daryl a long time to find the right wooden "cup" to fashion a weapon for Nado. The cold, and increased preparations for winter, kept them from climbing the face every day. While they could not risk being caught atop the escarpment by the ever-shortening sun, Daryl was no longer afraid of the elements. They had found plenty of cover among all the old, broken walls of the ancient village, but Nado had well schooled him in the necessity for secrecy.

It was the same for the throwing sticks and any mention of the island. Instead of trying to prove anything new to the tribe, Nado encouraged Daryl to keep everything they had and knew to himself. As the Shaman had voiced criticism of their simple water-carrying method, so might he or the Chief limit or prevent their visitations.

Nado quickly became proficient at heaving the stones with his new weapon, but he would never equal Daryl's powerful throw. With the ability to wind all the way back while perfectly balancing the release with a strong left arm, his long range was uncanny. They practiced only at the flat site where the statue stood, although it was never again used for target practice. Nado had spent much of their days there cleaning and working it with the point of sharp, wooden sticks. It, and the metal-tipped pedestal at the other end, had become part of their personal treasure chest.

Nado's cynical philosophy had worked into Daryl's mind, but he still found such critical thinking foreign to him. They generally talked while they threw, having decided earlier that they would not continue their exploration along the plateau until winter had gone. Already, they had to take longer rests on the climb up to warm their hands. They had hunted enough small, furry animals, the only kind they ever saw above the escarpment wall, to fashion a rough jerkin for Nado, or they would have to stop their trips even earlier in the fall.

It was at one such throwing practice session that the subject of their low status was brought up by Nado.

"I'm going to make a pouch out of this." He showed Daryl a small piece of worked leather he'd managed to cut from one of the loads they carried for the tribe.

"You can't wear a pouch. Only warriors can wear a pouch, you know that." Daryl let go with one of his hardest throws as he spoke, the rock whistling through the air before striking the wooden wall they had built of old fallen pine trunks. Nado had decided the stones were just too rare to risk any more damage and the hollow ones had been retired altogether to a secret spot under the base of the statue. They now threw smaller, more dense stones to similar effect.

"Ah my brother, once more you assume, and therefore miss what I really said." Nado prepared his own missile and then reared back, less than half as far as Daryl's wind-up.

"Arrogant. That's what you are," Daryl said acidly as the crippled boy threw.

"The truth is not arrogance," huffed Nado, having missed the circle they'd laboriously carved on the vine-tied logs. They both walked to the target. Daryl noted that the wood also did not create the deflection problem he had when throwing at the slate or even the statue. They no longer had to look for stones that had rebounded into the brush. The wood absorbed the impact, causing the stones to fall right at the target's base.

"I said I was going to make a pouch. Not wear it. I will wear it when I am made a warrior." His confidence was so overpowering that at first Daryl could not even laugh. He simply stared into the boy's deep brown eyes, his forehead creasing into a deep frown.

"Do you not understand? We will never be warriors. The Chief, the council, the Shaman, and even my father and your father have sentenced us to nothingness."

"Ha. We will be warriors soon enough, and great ones too, I might add." He ground the cup a bit with the rounded surface of his recently thrown stone, as if to lay the cause of his miss off on the stick.

"You know the Chief is supreme, and once the council has backed him there has never been a time when his decision was changed," Daryl finished, out of breath more with the finality of what he had stated then anything else.

"A warrior is in here." Nado thumped his chest with his fist. "Not out there." His good arm waved at the ruins. "The Chief and the council can only decide what the people think about us, not what we think of ourselves. And Chiefs and Shamans come and go . . . and with new ones come new rules." He looked up from his grinding to meet Daryl's puzzled gaze. "You are what you are because you want to be. What are you?" He pushed Daryl's chest hard with the rounded knob of the throwing stick. The boy backed up from the heavy thump and his own sense of consternation. It was another of Nado's impossible questions that almost literally hurt his head to think about.

"I don't know," he answered, after scouring his mind for anything that would make sense to the other boy. How could he be a warrior in his heart? He had never been through warrior training. He could not be initiated by the council or designated one afterward. And no matter how hard he tried, he could not imagine being anything without the approval of the whole tribe.

"You're afraid. That's what you are. You're afraid to do anything against the wishes of the tribe, even though everything you already do would be against those wishes . . . except they don't know." Nado watched the boy carefully for a moment and then went on. "But I think fear is good. It means you're thinking. Only an idiot wouldn't be afraid of the falls, or even the fast, deep water of the river. I know you were afraid when you swam from the island, but you did it anyway. That's what makes a warrior . . . and it's in there."

He tapped Daryl on the chest as he pronounced "there," and the boy looked down, then rubbed his breastbone. Then he smiled and hesitantly whispered a question.

"Is there enough leather for two pouches?"

And they both laughed.

Chapter XXII

Midwinter brought an assortment of problems with which the boys, as well as the tribe, were ill equipped to deal. The decision to build the great tribal structure without any clay mortar or attempt a fix later in the fall compounded the problems of an abnormally cold winter. The wind was strong in the mornings and evenings, even when a blizzard was not blowing, and that terrible icy wind blew through the unmortared walls with a constant whistling howl. The outermost rooms were affected the most, and sleep could only be found if the fires in those rooms burned the day and the night. Many members of the tribe had moved inward, but the rooms that walled the exposed center area were not much warmer. The Chief and the Shaman occupied several of the larger central rooms each, but in those areas the fires burned bright and unceasing.

In early winter, both Daryl and Nado had exhausted themselves daily with the water chores, and then in packing the storage rooms with dried skins and food of every variety. But the long winter brought the most serious problem of all. Wood became scarce. The larger timbers were too difficult to work with flint knives, and even hand axes took inordinate amounts of time and energy to make even old, fallen logs transportable. The deep vein of exposed coal was increasingly difficult to draw from, as the crack iced over and the cold sucked all energy out of their whitened fingers.

But it was the mist of the falls that made daily life even

harsher. It settled onto every exposed surface and then froze into a clear, slippery trap for the unwary. The boy's thin foot wraps were no match for the cold, bare ground, and held no purchase at all on the icy mist layers. Many times they were forced to sit throughout the days and nights, drawing food from the storage rooms, and hoping the weather and the mist would clear enough so that they could restock their dwindling supplies of fuel.

There was no climbing in the winter, and Daryl's plan to walk across the frozen river right onto the island never materialized. The rapid rush of the water stayed with them throughout the long season, and the center of the fast-moving mass never came close to freezing over.

The first heavy snowfall on an early winter day had seen the last of the bird. Each day, weather permitting, Daryl would take the treacherous downriver path to the falls and sit on the iced rock across from Tagawan's pedestal. Nado would often accompany him, complaining of the idiocy of their ritual trip.

"The bird is gone, wherever birds go when they winter. It is their way." Nado spoke harshly, pacing up and down on the slippery, mist-covered surface of the frozen pool. He beat his hands together and then placed them under his arms, never quite successful at warming the bad one. He paced and repeated his movements endlessly, while Daryl sat unmoving, occasionally turning to look into the mist cloud, recalling how the bird would rush right out of it to land on his shoulder or the nearby perch.

"You don't understand," he told Nado simply, his voice a sigh.

"I don't understand," Nado flapped his hands, then replaced them, and went on, "I don't understand." His voice was pure amazement in its expression. Finally, he stopped and faced

Daryl directly.

"I do understand. The bird has gone . . . and it has taken part of your heart with it." He yelled so as not to be misunderstood over the nearby thunder of the falls.

The boy leaned back, having received the words almost physically. His hands slipped between his thighs and his head bent down, nodding slightly.

"And I'm sorry. I liked the damned thing too." Nado's voice had softened to the point that Daryl would not have heard except the crippled boy had clasped his shoulder and leaned close in toward his ear.

Few worked during the deepest period of the winter. The women tended the fires, cooking or doing related activities. The only work among the men was the continued winter hunts by the warriors and the water and fuel supply work performed by the two classless boys. The water had become by far the most difficult for Daryl and Nado. They could not maintain their pole system of transport on the icy treacherous trail, thereby increasing the risk of a bad fall by the repeated number of trips down and back that they had to make, carrying only two jugs each.

The water had become a black, moving pool of evil. Ice crusted along the banks, extending out almost half a man-length into the current, made refilling the pots extremely treacherous, and neither boy would have survived without the addition of Daryl's safety vines. At least once a day, on the days when they could even get to the river, one of them would have to pull himself back to the bank after breaking through the jagged ice.

"How can water cut you?" Nado asked one day, nursing a bruised slice he had taken on his palm in a recent fall. Daryl had no answer. The mystery of how water turned hard in the cold and then back into liquid in the warm was an unsolved one among all of the tribe, even to his mother. And how it could come out of the sky in its white fluffiness was an even greater mystery. His mother said that the greatest mystery of all, however, was how water could be held over a fire and return back to the sky. The Shaman held that it was all part of the living blood of the Earth god, and it was the only thing the man said that Nado felt made any sense at all.

Above all, winter meant waiting. Both Nado and Daryl were both thankful that their infrequent chores did not include taking the dead to be placed in the burial cairns at the back of the old cave complex. The many winter fatalities were stored there, to be encased into hammered depressions when the spring began its thaw.

In the winter, the tribesmen died in only three ways. They were hurt on one of the hunts and either froze to death being hauled back to the village tied to a pole or died from the injury itself. If they survived the injury or trip back, then when they warmed by the fires, any part of the body that was frozen usually turned black. Then it was only a matter of time until the black sickness consumed them completely. The second scourge was winter sickness. Almost any sickness at all caused wasting away and death, which was not seen in the warmer parts of the year. Finally, and so rare as to be almost nonexistent, was dying from living too long. The tribe was not a place where really old people lasted very long at all.

Even though it was the worst winter in tribal memory, only one in five would be lost. Normally such a winter would have consumed one-third to one-half of the entire population. Daryl's mother attributed it to the building of the tribal structure and the free-flowing cold wind that blew readily through its interiors, thereby preventing serious illness. But the warriors, including Daryl's father, attributed it to the solid supply of fat-laced meat they had brought in on their summer hunts. Even the Shaman got into it with his version of the special offerings he had made, and the sacrifice the Earth god had claimed in taking so many in the caves during the catastrophe. Daryl tried to make some rational sense out of which might be the correct explanation, but could not get Nado to comment. The boy would only laugh, as if there was something important that Daryl was missing.

Nado's father had once told him that the deaths of the weak were an absolute necessity for the tribe's survival, or else they would have to be cared for. Life was such that the tribe rewarded, with family, space, and honor, those who provided the most back to the whole. The tribe took care of all, without respect of position or the work they did, but usually there were few if any rewards for those that did or were only allowed to do the least. Daryl thought that this theory, only once expounded upon by the other boy, made more sense than either of the others, but he could not figure out why he felt that way.

When not working and especially on the days when the wind and snow made it impossible to venture out, the boys spent their time sleeping under as many of the hides and furs as they could assemble. Both were sons of important fathers, so neither suffered unduly, although their low status affected them intensely in other ways, when cooped up in the confines of the structure. Their only defense against the coldness, to which they were subjected by almost everyone else, was to huddle in one corner of Daryl's parent's room and consider their lot. They also discussed with great, hushed enthusiasm the earliest days of spring and their exploits up- and downriver, as well as the continuing exploration of the plateau and its ruins. Near the end of winter two subjects began to occupy a great part of their time: the bird, with the possibility of its return in the spring, and quite miserably for Daryl, the Shaman's daughter.

"You were right and wrong, all at the same time, about the bird, I mean," Daryl said to Nado one early afternoon. Both boys had cloaked themselves in the only two trophy bear skins in the village. The small one, normally used by his mother for sleeping, was draped over Nado's shoulders while both of them sat cross-legged, bent in toward the still hot coals from the fire of the night before.

"What did I say?" Nado asked with a sideways grin. Daryl looked at him for a few breaths before responding. Secretly he believed that Nado never forgot a single thing, but he could not get the boy to admit it. He wasn't at all sure that he liked the affectation of poor remembrance that Nado so often struck.

"You know very well . . . about how hurt I was over the bird's departure."

"Oh yes," Nado responded, forcing his expression to change to one of deep thought. "That he left with a portion of your heart." Nado smiled, while Daryl briefly grimaced.

"Tagawan is a bird, not a person. And animals are different. We can't understand what they think, or how they think, or even if they think at all, but I have figured out why I have felt badly about the loss." Daryl stopped at Nado's attentive reaction. The cripple's frown was real, but tinged with an expression that seemed to question Daryl's very sanity.

"The bird picked me. I do not know why. And it was a very difficult time." Daryl did not mention that his first real climb of the escarpment wall had been made possible only by his complete lack of concern about whether he survived the feat.

"But he saw something in me that was special to him. And that made me feel special. I do not know why. And when he left, well, I seemed to have lost some of that." Daryl finished, but did not want to leave the subject with a silence. "What do you think?" He watched Nado carefully.

"I think a lot," and his friend grinned broadly when he said it. "I think you are special. I think we do not know if Tagawan is a 'he' at all. I think the bird will be back in the spring, like most other birds. I think you will be no more nor less special when he shows up." Nado poked the fire in conclusion.

"You do?" Daryl replied immediately, but then was not sure of which comment he was answering, especially when Nado did not reply.

The Shaman's daughter entered their conversation quite by accident. The openings between rooms were thick, especially those near the inner open area wall, where Nado's room was located. His father had selected a room straight out from the Shaman's interior room quarters. Daryl was making one of his usual trips back to awaken the late-sleeping Nado when he ran right into the girl in the near darkness. They had to both squeeze through the opening just outside of where Nado's family lived.

"Sorry," Daryl murmured as they contacted one another, face to face, their chests touching in the center of the opening. For a brief moment they looked into each other's eyes, then she broke free and squeezed past him. He stood speechless, breathing deep and slow while he watched her disappear. Nado spoke so closely to his right ear that he jumped, striking his head against the side of the fitted rock wall.

"I should have guessed," Nado said, laughing as Daryl recovered from his startlement.

"What?" answered the boy, defensively, while rubbing the small knot above his ear.

"I just should have known," continued Nado, staring in the direction that the girl had disappeared. Daryl followed his gaze, remembering the liquidity of her eyes and the cooking fire coal warmth of her touch. His hand absently felt his own chest where it had been, for an instant, pressed to hers.

"Yes, she's beautiful," he whispered, slowly. But Nado laughed immediately, breaking the spell.

"I mean only that you can find trouble anywhere, at any time. That's the Shaman's daughter. That's trouble."

Daryl looked away, his brow furrowed. He didn't know how to respond, so he tucked his head and started through the labyrinth toward the outer room openings.

"Don't be angry," Nado hissed toward his back as he caught up. Both of them moved expertly among the personal belongings and sleeping piles, as they made their way along. The etiquette of the structure had automatically adjusted to the need for almost constant movement, day and night. Rooms opened onto other rooms directly, some having more than two openings, although most had the obligatory two, except for the Shamans' and Chief's quarters. In those multiple-room areas there were several rooms with only one door, but very few saw or ever entered them.

"I'm not angry," the boy threw over his shoulder, as he quietly avoided a small, silent child sitting near one of the openings.

"Yes, you are," continued Nado. "You didn't want me to know you want that girl—" Nado did not get a chance to finish the sentence. Daryl had stopped so fast that they collided in the very center of a family room.

"Ah," he exclaimed, intending to say more, but the family members had awakened to their clumsy thumping and hissed at them. It was the only accepted complaint allowed within the structure and they quickly fled out into the cold winter wind. Even though it was near dark, Daryl knew it was not snowing. Both boys had become used to the blowing crystals that were gathered from the ground and then swirled, in never-ending patterns, through the air around them.

Daryl had hoped that the discussion regarding the girl would end there, but Nado was persistent, and the winter's end left little of present substance while holding out the hope of much to yearn for ahead. And it made Nado full of impish behavior. Daryl was determined not to talk about the girl no matter what Nado might say. He proved it by remaining mute in the face of frequent provocations during their chores, although Nado never mentioned the dangerous subject within the rumor-filled complex of the village again.

"I know her name," Nado said quietly, waist-deep in the freezing cold of the rushing river. They would take turns and remain in the water until it was impossible to tolerate the cold any longer. The boy on the shore fed the bottles, one at a time, to the boy in the water.

Daryl dropped a filled jug, spilling the water down his foot wraps and up his breechcloth. The cold was so cutting and vicious, all he could do was inhale sharply. Then he turned his fierce glare on Nado's back. But, hardening his stomach muscles, he still remained silent.

"You know, the Shaman's daughter, she has a name," Nado went on, wrestling a jug up out of the water with his one powerful arm.

Daryl could take it no more. He slogged the container ashore by gripping its body and coasting it along the short stretch of ice, deliberately jerking Nado's safety vine as he did so. Nado reacted with a most satisfying start, and the boy smiled.

"All right. You just have to talk about this. But that's impossible and you know it. The name of a woman is given at ceremony, and that will not be until the summer following this coming one." Daryl had learned the tribal rule early in his years, as they all had, but he had paid particular attention since first encountering the girl as a woman by the side of the river. Upon receiving her name she would immediately become eligible for marriage to a warrior, and could be so claimed with the permission of her father. Nado did not reply, and they changed places, carefully knotting the safety vine about Daryl's waist. He shivered as he waded right into the current, but managed not to make any sound.

"Her father is Huslinth, as well you know. Daughter of Huslinth, or Sagalinth, is all that is allowed and that only by her family. What are you up to?" With a pot fully submerged and bubbling away, Daryl craned back to look up at Nado's unabashed yet knowing smile.

"You know very well that her parents recommend the name, and that tradition is almost always followed. Her mother spoke of it to her father, who spoke of it to my father." A long, deliberate pause ensued, until Daryl thought it would never end.

"Well?" he could literally not contain himself. The pot sat in the water fully filled, but the boy made no move to withdraw it. For some reason he thought of his mother's words to his father long ago. Everyone in the tribe always thought his or her own secrets were kept, yet they knew all the secrets of everyone else.

For a moment, Daryl thought that Nado's sense of humor would drag the moment of the secret's revelation on and on. The other boy must have seen something in his expression, however, as he merely said the word.

"Pargalon. It's Pargalon. The woman of the mist." Then he shrugged. "Of course, to you that will be shortened to Parlon, no doubt.

Daryl dragged the heavy, filled jug from the icy water, a great smile playing across his face. He whispered the name over and over as he worked while Nado stood on the bank, shaking his head slowly.

Chapter XXIII

High above the great billowing clouds of white vapor, Tagawan flew, his sleek black wings tautly extended with muscles relaxed, the notches at the bone end of each joint rigidly locked into place. He could ply the cold currents and warm rising thermals endlessly if he needed. Slowly he circled the huge basin below, the clouds of spray rising in ever changing forms and then falling back as the tiny drops of moisture joined one another and grew heavier.

Occasionally, his head would cock to one side in order to watch a small area at the very top of the falls, close to the escarpment wall. He had flown almost nonstop, day and night, from his foraging pastures in the south. The cold of winter did not drive him, as neither cold nor water penetrated his thick, well-oiled plumage.

But with winter's bite came a scarcity of available food, to the point that some genetic switch was thrown and his departure to warmer climates became automatic. The summer past had changed everything, however.

The boy was strong in his mind as he flew. In his five previous summers, he had not pair-bonded until meeting the boy. Now he flew in endless high circles, waiting for his return. The small, black pool of water, little more than a dot below, remained unchanged, with the stones surrounding it and even the perch he favored visible from even this great height. Smoke still issued from the place of the human beings, as always, and the bird frequently flicked his eye in that direction. It was the place of origin for the boy, but also a place to be avoided.

Tagawan never considered that his selection of such a strange being to pair-bond with, from a species so utterly different as to defy all logic and imagination, was in any way abnormal. It was right, and he did what felt right. Even the addition of the second boy had only meant a slight increase in the size of his flock.

The bird's razor-sharp vision caught a moving image and he reacted instantly, his right wing snapping into the side of his body. He dropped immediately over and down, pulling in the left wing tightly, and then fell like a spear down through the ever swirling mist. The cold vapor condensed into ice water and his body was covered in fast-streaming rivulets of liquid. But nothing reached his sensitive skin.

Just above the roiling cauldron of water was a thin layer of clear air. Tagawan flared into that air, both wings bent forward and with tips well back, converting the speed of the plunge into level and then rising flight. He was propelled back up into the mist, then out and above smooth, rushing water, just where it curved over the edge. The combination of lift and speed was exhilarating as he approached the perch, flaring too late in his excitement and only at the last instant was he able to avoid hitting the boy in the center of his chest. Instead, he struck hard into the left collarbone of the boy's shoulder.

Daryl almost went over backward from the impact, but regained his balance before he fell. He could not suppress a deep grunt of shock and surprise. Nado laughed loudly at the performance.

"He's back, as I thought," he said, moving forward to welcome the bird. Daryl had never gotten comfortable with the bird's close proximity to his face, or its ear-piercing squawks when it was on his shoulder, and the fact that the bird really never stopped moving around. The thin, worn leather of the boy's jerkin provided woefully inadequate protection from its needle-sharp claws.

"Yes," Daryl squeezed out in a disgusted tone, but his smile was impossible to disguise or hide. He poked the bird's chest and received the accustomed hard peck on the back of his hand.

"He's bigger," Nado noted, peering at the animal from only a hand's breadth away, "but other than that . . ." and his voice trailed away. Then the bird feigned a peck with its wide, sharp beak and Nado pulled back. "Nasty bird," he whispered, but his tone carried no conviction.

The winter had been a hard one, and the tribe had suffered, although not as badly as it would have if it had still been huddled in the cold, wet caves. Midway through the worst of the snows, Daryl had come up with the idea of doubling the layers of their simply constructed footskins. Between the layers, he had packed in a thick sheaf of tiny twigs and crushed leaves from the bottom of one of the storage rooms. Nado had worried for days over whether they would be held accountable for cutting up one of the stored skins for the extra leather. But the winter was so cold that all anyone cared about was the never-ending supply of wood and coal the boys provided. Nobody cared that they were too low in stature to even be allowed the work. The thicker wraps they wore were much clumsier, and they could never use them to climb or run far, but they provided enough insulation to allow them to forage farther from the structure and stay outside longer.

"This would work for full warrior's leathers, you know," Daryl said as they loaded coal into their open pots. Once the foot problem had been solved, they were only limited by the cold that seeped into their bodies. Loading coal was the hardest chore because they had to work within the confines of the stone crack and could not move much. Gathering wood could be done almost at a run.

"What?" Nado said peevishly, his hands black from the coal, but also his lower face where he had been constantly blowing on his hands to warm them. "And where do we get the leather? It's bad enough that we will probably be banished for your thieving."

"Your feet aren't cold, are they?" Daryl shot back.

"Yes, I don't doubt that the new leather foot covers would work," Nado said, ignoring Daryl's response entirely. "And it might save some of the wounded warriors when they can't move or when they slept out there." He waved one arm upriver as he stood just outside the crack in the blowing snow. They worked all day long in the coldest of the winter days, loading, gathering, and then returning to warm before the fire of Nado's father, before heading back into the bitter chill.

Nado shook his head. "Brilliant. How do you do it? Just when I think you do not have a real brain in your head, you think up stuff that is so impossible, and it works. And another thing, the full skins would never work because the warriors would all look like short little Murs." They both laughed at the idea, Daryl going so far as to imagine his huge ferocious-looking father all wrapped in thick, padded hides.

The coming of spring had changed everything. And it had come like none other in memory. One day it was winter, and then the next morning it was warm and the ice was gone. Day after day they waited for a return of the cold, until it was obvious that spring had descended upon them in full bloom and all at once.

Daryl's infatuation with Parlon had grown as the months had passed, and she had grown as well. There was no question that, even at her young age, she was the tallest woman in the tribe.

Several days into the spring weather had returned the women to the riverbank for the washing and cleaning of skins dirtied from a full winter's use. Loyally, Daryl and Nado had trudged out to the bird's perch every morning. He had not been seen since the first day of his return. Both had agreed that Tagawan's regular arrival in spring would signal the beginning of their travels and adventures. He sat perched, waiting for their approach.

On their walk back, Tagawan flew swooping circles about them, taking them past the working women. They stopped for a moment to appraise the bird's antics out over the water. Parlon stood, then raised one hand to shield her eyes as she watched the bird.

"You know, she's taller than either of us," Nado said, studying the girl in full profile. "And maybe she likes brown eyes instead of blue," he added lightly. Daryl's head swiveled so fast that Nado raised his good arm, almost in defense. "Just talking, that's all," he tried to get out without laughing.

Both boys had hardened considerably during the long season, and under the heavy burden of constant work. Neither thought of themselves in any light as potential suitors for the tribe's claiming process, however. Their low status had been driven into them no matter how resistant Nado was to the process or to its finality. With the coming of the next summer, Parlon would be named, and then any warrior could stake a claim. If that claim was honored by the girl, her father, and then approved by the Chief, then she would be wed the following solstice. Both boys had been very sensitive to even the slightest discussion that might mention the tall girl as a woman to be claimed, but they had heard nothing throughout the winter.

"She's too beautiful," Daryl said one day. "All the warriors are afraid of her beauty."

Nado just looked at him in reply, his head moving from side to side. "Too tall. Too big. Remember, the warriors like small game, like your father's bear." Daryl looked up. He had not thought that Nado was so observant as to note the puny size of his father's much-celebrated kill from the summer before.

"She has such big, round eyes," Daryl went on, but Nado would have no more of it.

"Enough. What does it matter? Soon she will be the wife of another warrior. We cannot claim her." His harsh words cut Daryl visibly, and his shoulders slumped a fraction. "Well, we can't claim her right this minute, anyway. There is a span of seasons to consider."

At that Daryl picked up a bit. In his heart he had dreamed for some opportunity to change the Chief's heart toward him. Nado called him Old Bagestone when far from the tribal area, even though the family name of the Chief was not supposed to be used at all unless in a warrior's ceremony.

Daryl had not mentioned his remaining great secret to Nado. It was the one he was hoping to use to win Parlon, or at least use for the opportunity to try to win her: the secret supply of white flint on the island. That treasure might hold the secret to great wealth for the entire tribe. Only such a tremendous discovery might ever lift the sentence that had been placed upon his shoulders. He thought of Nado, with whom he shared the same shameful status, but Nado's was because of an unchangeable physical infirmity. How could he share his plan with him when it would certainly, if successful, elevate Daryl into the class of warriors while leaving the cripple to fend for himself? The thought process involved, along with the impossibility of the dilemma, caused his head to physically ache. He massaged the front of his head with the knuckles of his right hand while staring up at the bending form of the girl.

"You massage your head," Nado said quietly. "In looking at her, I'm thinking that it's not the part of your body that's aching right now," Nado finished the words, let out a brief laugh and then ran toward the structure as Daryl pursued him.

191

Chapter XXIV

Their plan to climb the escarpment wall on the day of Tagawan's return could not be implemented until half a moon had passed, and the warmth of full summer was being felt at midday. The council had met and made a decision to apply riverbank clay to all outside walls of the structure, although this time the clay would be worked between the already laid stones with small slivers of wood, and both boys were once more thrown into their old roles of heavy material transporters. The activity of spring went on around them as they plied the path, up and back, to and from the river, carrying skin sacks of wet clay loaded to capacity.

Tagawan flew high above them, but no contact was made with the bird, except for the early morning pilgrimage both boys made to the pool on a daily basis. Finally, the day dawned when their work was done. The structure had taken on a more solid appearance, yet it blended in so nearly with the cliff wall just beyond that it would not have been easily noticeable from the river without the constant cloud of smoke that hung above its center.

The first climb up the escarpment was an exercise in familiarity and social interchange. Nado led all the way, seeming to have an instinctive touch that Daryl obviously lacked. They talked while they climbed, their progress and communication monitored at close range by the ever-present bird.

Tagawan could not contain his pleasure and fluttered about,

squawking and cooing at each new change in direction or pause for rest, while they, in turn, included the bird in their discourse, as if it understood their every word.

"What if the Chief changes his mind?" Nado said during one of the infrequent breaks. Both of them stared down at the beautiful valley, neither having fully remembered the drama of the falls and the view in general. Daryl tore his gaze away to stare at the other boy.

"What do you mean?" he said. "The Chief never changes his mind."

"Right," Nado replied, but without conviction. "What about what we just had to do?" He let that question sink into the silence, then went on.

"We just spent all that time hauling clay to put on the walls. The Chief was the one that overruled your mother, remember? So he changed his mind, and decided she was right."

Daryl thought deeply. Nado was right. It was a valid example, and he was uncomfortable that, once again, he could never seem to win an argument with the blond cripple. Even worse, Nado had a habit of thinking about things for the longest periods of time and then bringing the subject up as if they had been discussing it only moments earlier, leaving Daryl struggling to catch up to him.

"I don't know," he finally answered, unwilling to completely concede his earlier point. It was somehow more comfortable to think of the Chief as never changing about anything, even something so vividly painful as his own low tribal status.

"What if he made you a warrior? He changed his mind once, he can do it again," Nado said. Daryl had become uncomfortable with the conversation, but he could not understand why. His answer was guarded, and hesitant.

"Yes?" Daryl said.

Nado finally pulled his own gaze from the panorama below

and returned Daryl's stare at the answer. "If you are made warrior, then I will be alone. We will not talk or spend the days doing what we do." His face turned as he completed the statement, his gaze once again slowly sweeping up and down the valley.

Neither boy spoke into the ensuing silence. In unspoken agreement, they resumed the climb, now conducted without discussion. Daryl's mind raced. It was as if the other boy had seen his thoughts earlier regarding the flint supply, and a possible approach to Old Bagestone. It was the only way that he could ever hope to claim Parlon. He had not considered that it would require him to give up not only his relationship with Nado, but their trips to the plateau as well. The bird squawked.

"And even you. What would I do with you?" he whispered at the nearby hovering animal.

They ascended up through the chimney, then over the lip and onto their usual places atop the great root of the now familiar pine tree. The bird landed above, and once again, Nado uncannily seemed to read Daryl's thoughts.

"And what of the stupid bird?" he said, pointing at the overloaded branch. As if understanding that he was the subject of conversation, Tagawan released his hold and dropped onto Nado's shoulder. It was the first time since being shooed away by the boy the previous summer that he had done so. Nado leaned his head as far away from the sharp beak as he could, but he made no effort to remove the bird. Daryl reached over and poked at its chest, and received the customary hard peck in return.

"Ow!" he said, overly loud. For some reason that reaction seemed to give the animal no end of pleasure.

"Think about it," Nado said. Daryl stared at the softly squawking bird as it carefully performed its grooming chores. There had never been a return of the parasites that had been the cause of their first meeting. He could not give up Tagawan or Nado. Covertly, he looked at his friend, and thought about his strange, short haircut. The crippled boy claimed that it was cooler and cleaner than the warrior's long flowing locks Daryl wore. *Cooler in the winter,* wondered Daryl, *or cleaner than their daily swims in the river backwater or submergence while filling water pots?*

No, he thought he knew perfectly well what the real reason was. Nado thought he looked better with his hair short, and that was it. But the boy would never admit that. Daryl smiled. Nado was so completely different from himself. How was it that he could like him so much?

They left the lip to make their way among the pines to the ancient ruins, both of them crisscrossing back and forth as they ran while Tagawan flitted first above one and then the other, sometimes taking the lead and avoiding the branches at their own level.

Nothing had changed, except for an accumulation of dirt on the statue, which Nado carefully removed with his flint blade and some small pieces of wood. Near the end of the previous fall Daryl had invented a new practice game. They spent much of the day playing it. Both loaded small pebbles into the cups of their throwing sticks and hunted one another among the fallen walls and stones of the ruins. The smaller projectiles did not fly as true or nearly as far as the special throwing rocks, and they only stung when they struck. When hitting the mark, after the initial yelp of the wounded party, both boys broke into gales of laughter.

Early afternoon brought them back to the clearing where Daryl brought out some of the dried meat he claimed from the winter storage area. In spite of the harsh winter, the tribe had not used up its entire store of food. The outside tribal structure had somehow contributed to a complete lack of spoilage, which had been common when it had been kept in the cave complex. The Shaman had grudgingly allowed that the Earth god preserved the food as a sign that their move to the artificial caves was approved, but Daryl's mother had quietly scoffed, saying that it was due to the simple fact that the caves had oozed moisture through the floor rocks.

They consumed the hard, stringy food without water, leaning against the solid pedestal while Tagawan perched on its lip and seemed to hang right over their heads. Nado threw the bird a chunk of stone-hard meat, which he swallowed with one loud gulp.

"Notice the shadow?" Nado pointed toward the short, angled darkness next to him, where the sun did not strike because of the pedestal's bulk. Daryl nodded.

"I think this thing," he pointed up with the chunk of meat in his good hand, "is for that." Daryl unconsciously looked up where the bird groomed and cooed. His look alone was so questioning that Nado went right on while chewing the last of the food supply.

"It measures the sun's movement." He stood and rolled back the heavy moss while the bird protested but did not leave, simply stepping around to avoid the boy's efforts. "Look."

Daryl stood unwillingly, then peered down where Nado had set his finger. The shadow from the sun slanted down from the yellow metal tube in a short, straight line, but went nowhere.

"I don't know," he said, shaking his head.

"Look. See all the characters around the edge? They are wearing the same outfit the statue wears," Nado said. Daryl's stare went out to the figure in the distance, unchanged since the day he had found it. Then his gaze went back and forth, from the pedestal to the figure and back.

"I think the figures are for measuring the sun's progress from when it rises to when it sets." Nado's finger touched the tip of the shadow and then ran out to one of the groups of figures near the edge.

"Ah, okay," Daryl said slowly, his hand massaging his chin. "So? What difference does it make? We get up when the sun rises and sleep when it sets."

Nado let out a sigh and then a laugh. "Yes, that's true. But with this, well, you could, or they could, use it to measure things. How long does it take to climb the wall, for example?

"The sun moves so far, but how far?" A glimmer of understanding appeared in Daryl's eyes as he caught the concept. He had seen his father measure the sun's path with his fingers extended out to arm's length, but that method was only taught in warrior training and he had not really understood his father's offhand response to his inquiry at the time.

"Yes," Daryl said. "I see it." Then he became more enthusiastic, his fingers running over the small, carved groups near the edge of the circle. "How do we prove it? How will we be sure?" he breathed, then looked up as Nado laughed. "What?" he said in consternation, standing back straight.

"The sun, you idiot, comes up every day and always moves at the same speed."

Daryl thought hard on the other boy's words. "It wouldn't work at night," he said, almost to himself. Nado laughed so hard he bent over, and then Daryl joined him, finally realizing what he had said.

They replaced the moss on the device once they had recovered.

"This is wonderful. We'll experiment later. This would be so much better than how we do it now," Nado looked up at Daryl's questioning stare. "You know, better than just using breaths and heartbeats, but not for short things, of course."

Daryl was not nearly so interested in what the result of the "experiment" would be as the experiment itself. One time near the start of winter, when the cold was closing in, Nado had decided to drop a huge rock from the top of the escarpment and time with heartbeats how long it took the rock to impact on the valley floor below. The descending rock had struck an outcrop, which started a small avalanche. The climb back down had been undertaken with much nervousness on the part of both boys, for fear that one of their vital hand or footholds might have been dislodged with the rest. They had not spoken of the incident, and it had turned out that the climbing holds had not been damaged.

"Another grand experiment. Not like the last, I hope," Daryl said a little worriedly, not sure himself whether he was being serious or not.

"Humph," was all Nado would reply.

The wild, playful run back to the lip of the wall happened without incident. Tagawan landed on his perch atop the usual, overstressed pine branch and squawked as they pulled up, laughing but not out of breath. The village labors of winter and then the reconstruction at the beginning of spring had hardened their bodies to a taut stringiness.

The sun was not near to the point, above the far escarpment, where they would have to begin the climb down. Nado sat farthest out on the thick, gnarled root, ready to lead the descent, as had become the custom between them. There was no longer any doubt whom the better climber was between the two, and Nado's arm was no longer even discussed. Only the fashioning of an especially high-throwing stone tube that was angled under the arm and steadied by the withered limb revealed any consideration for the disability at all.

"We must plan the summer," Nado said once they were both comfortable. Both stared out over the river, the view below impossible to ignore.

Daryl thought about the summer ahead, his primary concern

getting a chance to meet Parlon. "Okay," he murmured, without enthusiasm.

"We must explore up and down the river, and more of on plateau. I have not even seen the wall on the far side of the ruins. And then there is the island." Nado pointed out the small speck in the far distance upriver. They had discussed a return to the place where Daryl considered his own new life to have begun. The need for even more of the special stones was even greater than it had been when he had chanced the second trip, especially in light of what he had found inside the hollowed ones. If balanced and weighed in the hand, the hollow ones could be separated from the others. And there was the flint mine he had not informed Nado of. All of a sudden he shook his head and slapped the root between them with his right hand. Nado quickly turned his head.

"I forgot to tell you of the carving," Daryl said, his mouth pursed in disapproval at his own failure. The mystery of the carving had worried away at the back of his mind for the entire winter, even appearing in his dreams. Nado thought differently from him, as he had so blatantly proved with his analysis of the pedestal. The crippled boy might not be right, but he always had an interesting and engaging opinion.

"What carving?" Nado asked, waiting out the silence as long as he could.

"On the island—" began Daryl, but Nado interrupted, his voice filled with pleased surprise.

"A carving? On the island?" Nado's eyes went out to the speck of land, where, in reality, only the huge tree standing before the great stone mountain was visible from their position.

Daryl described the design that had been worked in the stone. They had to move off the root when he finished, as Nado demanded that he use a stick to draw it as best he could in the dirt nearby.

Nado ran his finger around the circle at the top of Daryl's drawing, then slowly traced each line down, his concentration so great that Daryl didn't feel he should say anything.

"A sign . . ." Nado breathed, very quietly.

"Sign," Daryl said, his head angling from side to side as he tried to see what Nado was seeing in the design. "The round circle is the sun. And the lines are the rays of the sun shining down. The bottom represents stairs, I think." Nado touched each part, as he spoke. Then he looked up, meeting Daryl's eyes for a brief moment.

"It's connected to the ruins. It has to be. There is an answer there somewhere," Nado went on, his eyes dropping back to his slow tracing finger.

"To what question?" Daryl could not understand what the other boy was getting at.

"The question, idiot, is obvious." Nado delayed for just a few breaths before he went on, "What is all that? Where did it come from? Who put it there? Why there? How is any of it possible? Our tribe is the most advanced people in the world and these ruins just can't be."

Daryl physically retreated half a man-length at the ferocity with which Nado's words were delivered. Although he had had similar thoughts all along, until that moment, the enormity of the ruins' very existence had never really hit home.

"I don't know," he said finally, knowing he had answered none of the questions, but also knowing that Nado had not expected any real insights anyway.

"Tomorrow we'll explore the plateau. We have to know what is there before we go to the island." Nado had risen to stare first in the direction of the ruins and then down upon the ever-swirling mist rising up from the falls. "And we don't want to go over that thing, ever." His eyes went to Daryl, his expression one of mild disbelief, then he shook his head and shrugged briefly. "Come on, let's climb down."

Chapter XXV

They returned in time for the initial gathering in the roofless center room, where preparations were underway for the single village meal, always served in the evening just after the sun set on the far horizon.

The area was in the shape of an oval with the cooking fire pit in the center, ringed by large stones rolled from the base of the escarpment wall. The fire itself burned low, radiating just enough heat to warm the open-air enclosure but not so hot that the first row of seated villagers was uncomfortable.

The inhabitants streamed through the many openings in the walls to the family rooms beyond. As usual, Daryl and Nado had stripped off all their specialized equipment and deposited it under brush not far from the bird's favorite pool. Tagawan had departed with a loud squawk, but only after they had turned up the path to the structure.

"Where does he go at night?" Nado asked, but Daryl had no answer, as no one in the village had ever entertained the question as far as he knew. "And does he sleep?"

At that Daryl could not keep silent. "Where do you get the never-ending questions from? Go ask the Shaman!"

Nado grew coldly silent, and they made their way to the structure without further comment.

The circles around the fire were very carefully laid out with respect to status. The most important families sat in the first row, with the Chief and his family in the very center, facing the fire and with their backs to the thinnest wall to the outside. The wall nearest the cliff had been built with only storage rooms within and there were only two openings in its entirety. Both Nado and Daryl had places in the front row, simply because of their fathers' respective importance. Daryl's family sat to the right of the Chief while Nado's occupied the immediate left.

Directly across the circle from the Chief sat the Shaman's family.

Daryl's eyes casually sought out Parlon's position through the flickering flames of the low fire. Her duties required that she perform the work of preparation and cooking. Only the married women served the meal, so he found her sitting to her father's right. If Huslinth had sired a son, then that would have been his position, but the family consisted of only the Shaman, his wife, Parlon, and her three younger sisters. They all sat on his left while his wife worked in the usual meal service. Only the Chief's wife was exempted from such duties, although it was under her supervision that they all performed their functions.

Daryl, as was his custom, never looked directly into the girl's eyes, although she seemed to have no trouble whatsoever staring directly into his. He tried never to let her catch him looking at her, but he knew that he frequently failed. Sometimes, he felt her stare so strongly that he would surreptitiously look behind him to see if she was really looking at someone in one of the lesser rows.

To Daryl's left sat his two brothers, custom dictating that the elder sit at the right hand of his father. It was a measure of great pride to his father that he had married a woman who only gave birth to sons, while the Shaman was cursed with a wife that could only deliver daughters. As women were the birth source, they were also properly assigned the responsibility for the gender of their children. Marriage was for life in the tribe, although a woman who could only bear children of a female gender usually died of sickness at a young age. Huslinth's fortune had not changed when his first wife had sickened following the birth of her fourth daughter. Only two of the four female children had survived sickness themselves. His current wife also could only deliver females, and that subject was quietly discussed with humor among the women of the tribe.

The meal of boiled, multimeat stew was served from great bowls, carried by one married woman and served by another. The order of serving was the same as the order of seating. Highest rank was served first and the analytical care with which that was done was not even noted by any of the tribal members, save Nado, who had cynical comments to make even about the eating habits of the people.

The food was eaten with the lip of the bowl and fingers to assist. When a meal was finished, the bowl was placed on the ground and the person left without ceremony. Only a single rule was rigidly applied to the order of departure. No tribal member left before the Chief, who left first, and then the Shaman. Daryl spent as little time in the great open room as possible, eating quickly, waiting for the Chief and Shaman to leave, and then departing immediately thereafter.

He was about to leave, and was placing his empty bowl before him when he noted Parlon rising. He caught a slight gleam that emanated from just above and between her breasts. Daryl froze, his hands holding his bowl only a hand's breadth above the ground in front of him. It was the crystal. The very crystal he had given Nado hung on a short thong of leather encircling her neck. There was no mistaking it. She noticed his frozen stare. Her fingers went up to replace the bauble within her leather tunic, as he tore his stunned gaze away and placed the bowl gently down.

He made no move to leave as Parlon's departing figure disappeared from his peripheral view, his eyes coldly centered upon the small flames rising from the fire ring. His mind was far from thoughts of the fire, however. Questions without answer poured through his mind.

What had Nado been thinking? Did he harbor secret feelings for Parlon that he had never shared? Was there communication going on between Parlon and Nado that he was unaware of? At that, he broke from his concentrated spell.

"Obviously," he whispered, but only to himself.

It was near dark by the time he had worked his way through the busy maze of the structure's interior. The evening was cool, but with all the promise of warmth that a late spring brought. Daryl breathed in deeply and then started down the path to the river, deep in thought. In no time he squatted by the bird's pool, where he bathed his hands, having no recollection at all of what he might have seen along the trail.

He felt Nado's approach before he heard the boy's tread. The growing sensitivity of his hunting instincts surprised him, but for the first time he did not get a warm feeling from the other boy's presence.

Nado knelt by his side and began his own washing ritual.

"The bird has retired," he said, looking up to the bare pedestal.

Daryl said nothing.

"I assume we are down here for more than an after-meal washing?" Nado continued, as Daryl maintained the silence. Both boys rocked back into crouches that either could maintain for the full course of a day or night. When it appeared that neither would move and Nado was not going to speak again, Daryl could not contain himself any longer.

"How could you?"

"How could I what?" Nado replied, his voice betraying nothing.

Daryl tried to peer at him from the corner of his left eye, but the light was fast disappearing and he could make out no expression on the other boy's face.

"The crystal," he forced out, more as a hiss than a phrase.

"Oh, that . . ." began Nado, his voice still giving away nothing.

"Yes, that!" Daryl's anger was barely contained. "You are supposed to be my friend. My only friend, except for . . ." and his emotion was so great that he could not remember the name, "that bird," he finally exploded out.

"Ah, I should have guessed," Nado said, then rushed into the small silence, "You assume I gave her the stone to gain her favor, huh?"

Daryl turned slightly, a puzzled look on his face from Nado's words, but also because of his tone. He nodded, but did not expect that Nado saw.

"Do you know why I call you idiot all the time?" He didn't pause for Daryl to answer. "You just don't get some of the simplest things in this world. Not even when they are right in front of your face. Do you really think that I would go after Parlon? After all we have been through?" Daryl shook his head, but knew his movement was unseen. He now wished he had said nothing at all.

"You were the only one in the tribe to come to me as a human being after the injury. Everyone treated me as dead or invisible. I could never pursue Parlon. I owe you my life. You are my brother."

Daryl did not know what to say. He wondered how he could make so many wrong decisions about people. The logic that Nado had laid out was unshakable, and so very easy to grasp, and yet he had missed it entirely.

"I'm sorry. I am an idiot," Daryl said miserably. "Brother." He added the forbidden word that had so much meaning between them. Nado did not reply, merely shaking his head in the dark.

"What does she think then?" Daryl asked, afraid to approach the issue in a more direct manner.

"I think she likes it," Nado replied, but his tone had changed and Daryl knew the other boy was toying with him.

"You know what I mean," his voice grated out.

Nado laughed. "She thinks it's from you. Idiot. I told her I was a messenger from you," he said with obvious relish.

Daryl was embarrassed and contrite at the same time. Then, when he thought about it for a few heartbeats, he was stunned.

"What have you done? What must she think?" He was so agitated that he stood and almost began to pace. Nado's hand grabbed his biceps and pulled him back.

"Oh sit down. She's wearing it, isn't she? What do you think she thinks?" Nado was scolding in his expression and delivery. Daryl crouched once more. "She touched the stone as if it was from the Earth god himself."

Daryl vividly recalled the image of Parlon's departure from the meal area, where she had touched the stone just as Nado said.

Nado started to laugh.

"What's so funny?" Daryl asked, miserable.

"You are. Did you really think I was after Parlon? Not that either of us has a chance." Nado laughed again, before going on, "You are the only one in the tribe that thinks she is a goddess, anyway. She is too big, too tall, and too everything . . . and the Shaman's daughter." His laughing voice subsided. "Too much trouble," he concluded.

"Why did you do it?" Daryl asked, finally thinking rationally.

"Oh, out of boredom. And, I guess to help you help yourself. You would die before you would ever approach her, so I did it for you."

"You should have asked me. I gave you the stone," Daryl shot back.

"It was my stone to do with what I wanted," Nado replied, and for that Daryl had no answer.

"Come on, the light is gone and it is getting cold." Nado stood, brushing off his leather jerkin.

"How am I going to face her tomorrow night at the meal?" Daryl had not moved, the idea of the next night paralyzing in its potential for embarrassment.

"Oh get up. You already have. I gave it to her almost a full moon ago."

Chapter XXVI

The following morning both boys were snared by Daryl's mother before they could escape the structure. They were forced to search the cold riverbank for some of her special roots and sprouts that could only be found in the early days of spring. The softened brown mud of the reed bank was already alive with yellow-green sprouts no more than a hand's breadth high. They talked while they worked. Daryl's mother, happy to be relieved of working in the cold, ankle-deep mud, sat nearby on top of a flat, sun-warmed rock. There she separated and bagged what they brought to her.

Tagawan remained close by, Daryl noted, flying low over the water and then landing to watch them from one of the massive boulders at the river's edge. He occasionally looked at Daryl's mother, but her attention was so focused on separating the special stems, shoots, and leaves that she took no notice of the bird.

The island was in full view from their position on the bank, and they discussed the trip that was now a part of their special summer plan. Daryl mentioned his narrow escape when he had encountered the snake in midriver.

"Snake?" Nado froze, repeating the word in a terrified voice.

No snakes had ever been found near the tribe's area, but the warriors brought back stories that had become legend. The bite of almost any of the long, sinuous creatures, no matter their size, was lethal. The tribe had lost several warriors to the reptiles, but only in conjunction with hunting within the deeper forest of the upper river regions.

Daryl described the snake in great detail, right up to its mysterious disappearance below the waters. Nado unconsciously moved a few feet back from the passing current, standing to get a better view of the thick and bunched bases of the reeds.

"You said nothing of a snake," Nado said, as he turned his head to view the intervening water between their position and that of the island. His face no longer showed the excited enthusiasm it had earlier. Daryl continued to work, hiding his small smile.

It took less than half the morning for them to complete their task, and eager to avoid being assigned other, more demeaning jobs around the structure, they headed downriver toward the climbing point below the falls. Tagawan squawked as they passed, neither boy stopping, knowing the bird would be up and after them without delay. Once atop the cliff, Daryl nodded and both boys headed downriver, running wildly among the pines toward a better resting place along the top of the escarpment, which they had decided upon the previous summer. When they stood at the very bottom of the wall, they had noticed a portion of the high rim that extended out from the lip, its narrow, flat tip seeming to point directly toward the cliff, which could be seen beyond the fast, rushing river across the great valley.

In no time, they had cleared a bit of brush from around the end of the wall, revealing that the last long stone of that same wall stuck out into the air, as if the edge of the cliff had given way under it. Tagawan was the first to claim the flat, open area as his own once they had cleared enough debris to bare the surface.

"I suppose if the bird thinks it is safe, it must be okay," Nado said hesitantly, as they stood trying to analyze whether the huge, long stone was solidly grounded enough to allow for their weight upon its extended tip.

"Ah, he can fly, if you will recall," Daryl said, not using the word "idiot," as Nado might have, but instead cocking his head and raising one eyebrow in an exaggerated manner. Nado merely sniffed at the insult before jumping up to take a place next to Tagawan. The bird cooed happily, and only attempted to peck the boy's extended hand once. Daryl joined them, easing slowly outward, both boys careful to place themselves right in the center of the stone.

Each of the three sides dropped off sharply to nothing below, or at least to a floor of the valley that was so far below that the man-heights could not even be calculated.

Nothing was said for many heartbeats. The view was greatly enhanced by their extension out into the open air above the canyon, and it seemed to draw them right into it. Daryl attempted to make sense of the downriver region of the valley, especially in light of the discovery they had made when they ventured to the plateau's far side.

The valley spread out so far, it was lost into the distance. The great river turned and moved away from the escarpment wall to reach its center, before also disappearing into the far distance. For the first time, although the rising shimmer interfered, Daryl noted that the distant cliff appeared gradually to slant downward as it trailed downriver. He wondered if the plateau they sat on did the same thing. He looked up and then down the vertical face. It was the first time he had ever considered that the wall did not just go on forever. If it did not, then it had to begin and end somewhere. He was about to discuss his new thoughts with Nado when the other boy spoke.

"What's that?" He pointed far downriver to a distant place between the river and the cliff face. They concentrated, both holding hands to their brows to block the high sun overhead.

"A cloud?" Nado ventured.

"That small and narrow?" Daryl asked. A brownish-gray cloud seemed to have formed so far down the river that it almost looked like it was an small, intruding finger coming right out of the horizon. It moved so slowly that it was easier to detect by looking away for a moment then looking back, rather than staring directly at it.

"Smoke," Nado tried again.

"No, I don't think so. Dust," Daryl concluded. At the word, they turned toward each other at the same instant, their eyes wide. Both boys had paid a heavy price the last time a great dust cloud had been a part of their lives. They never spoke of the catastrophe, no one in the village did, but it was never far from their minds.

They stood as one, intently examining the strange phenomena well down the valley. Daryl was the first to spot the moving dot.

"Something," he began, pointing down, but at a steeper angle this time.

"A man," Nado concluded. "Running," he observed. The dot weaved back and forth as it paralleled the waters of the river.

Both events were almost mind-numbing. Neither boy had ever observed either a great cloud of dust moving toward them, or any being downriver from the falls. The figure seemed pursued by the cloud.

"Down," Daryl said, and Nado nodded without question. Tagawan launched himself out over the valley, then dived steeply, as if Daryl had been talking to him.

They ran, this time neither twisting in and out of the pines, nor making any sound other than the soft padding of their leathers upon the brown needle bed. Nado took the lead in their climb, but both boys stopped only once to observe the approach of the fast-moving figure, now identifiable as human. Near the bottom, Daryl looked for a proper place to hide or prepare an ambush. There was no doubt that the moving man would have to pass between themselves and the river. No warrior expedition had yet found a passage across the treacherous waters, at least not one that they were willing to discuss.

They had never made the descent faster or in such complete silence. Nado's total attention on the climb had not even allowed for discussion of any plan, so Daryl decided that they would simply hide within the sapling row, backed up against the rubble pile, and try to calculate what to do when the being approached. That it was a stranger did not even need to be mentioned. Tribal members never ventured downriver. It had been declared completely barren long before either boy had been born.

Once down, Daryl and Nado immediately loaded their throwing sticks with the special rocks they had preselected for such an encounter. They crouched down and waited.

"Who and what could he be?" Nado whispered, but Daryl remained silent, his concentration on the downriver area unwavering. "And the cloud . . ." Daryl turned at the word, but just slightly, his eyes never moving from their darting examination beyond. "A catastrophe . . . maybe . . . I don't know . . ." his voice trailed away, not exactly sure why they had both rushed down to confront the running human's passage. Unspoken between them, however, was an innate fear of being trapped high on the plateau, should the earth and water move once again. And the running figure had to be a clue of some sort.

"Downriver . . . how could he be from downriver. Nothing is downriver," Nado said in his quiet, shushing tone. Daryl remembered only then that he had never shared with the other boy the suspected smoke plumes he had seen from time to time.

"What do we do?" Nado said when he didn't answer. Daryl glanced at the boy, surprised that Nado seemed to think that he had any idea of what to do at all. Running back to the tribe would have been his first response, except following what had happened after the last catastrophe, he wanted nothing to do with anyone until he was sure of what they might be dealing with.

He reflected on their hiding place, well hidden within dense clusters of sapling branches, covered with their new, bright green growth and next to boulders covered in lichen. The running figure would pass right by them, with almost no chance of spotting them. Daryl stood, then began to pry his way clear of the wooded protection.

"What are you doing?" hissed Nado.

"Come on," Daryl replied in his normal voice, knowing that under any other circumstances he would have laughed aloud at Nado's expression. "We have to find out what's happening, and whoever's coming is our only chance." He prepared his stick, knowing he could deliver at least one rock well before even the fastest runner might break cover from downriver and reach their position.

Nado silently joined him while the bird descended to a nearby rock, its normal billing and cooing silenced. Tagawan appeared to study the open area downriver with its left eye, walking slowly back and forth atop the boulder near which the boys hid.

It was only a few heartbeats before the running figure appeared. Daryl stretched back in preparation for his throw, but held his position as the figure stopped.

The figure was like no other person they had ever seen.

The intake of Nado's breath was audible in Daryl's left ear. The four of them stood frozen, staring at each other, until Tagawan broke the silence with a great squawk of what Nado would later say was open disgust.

The creature was shorter than any tribal adult, and broader, with only a worn breechcloth to cover its black-haired exterior.

The sloping shoulders led up to a massive head, jaw jutting forward and sagging down, but its nose was the most peculiar and ugly feature of its countenance. It was so flat and wide it lacked description, and it drooped in concert with the massive, sagging chin. Small, dark eyes were set in deep sockets of heavy, ridged bone. What appeared to be hair from its head simply did not end, and seemed to grow all the way down the body, occasionally giving way to bare patches, with one notable patch at the very top of the thing's head. It stood there unmoving, except for its heaving chest. *Its massive heaving chest,* Daryl thought. He had released the stone from his throwing stick simply from a natural revulsion.

"Throw?" Nado whispered. Then the thing spoke.

"Dongha," rasped strongly out of its throat, the great hairy lips barely moving. It uttered the word for friend.

"Friend," Nado said reflexively, unable to withhold the traditional greeting of strangers meeting one another from different tribes. "It speaks."

Slowly, with Daryl leading, they approached the creature, each boy dragging his stick behind him until they stood only a man-length from it. Although terribly ugly in every respect, Daryl noted that it seemed to present no threat at all. Its primary attention was divided between wild-eyed glances at them and then longer looks over its shoulder toward the down-river area.

It carried no weapon or implements of any kind. That the creature spoke at all was surprising to both boys, but that they were able to understand it was not. All the tribes of the valley spoke the same tongue, and understood one another, although some of the tribes, only encountered by the hunters, were said to be very difficult to understand.

The same fear that had driven the being from wherever it had come from had also been instilled into Daryl and Nado by their sighting of the dust cloud.

"What comes?" Daryl spoke as directly and clearly as he could, sensing that whatever kind of intellect the creature might have, with its appearance considered, it could not be greater than that of a young child. He waved the throwing stick down-river, and the beast's eyes followed it.

"Earth-move. Earth-move . . ." it replied, becoming even more agitated and starting to ease past them. Neither boy moved to stop it. Once it had edged closer to the saplings lining the base of the cliff, it launched itself into a broken run upriver toward the winding path that led up to the top of the falls. They watched it encounter the angled pile of debris and climb up. Its speed seemed to actually increase once it could use both hands to pull itself up through the mud and over the imbedded boulders.

"What was that?" Nado asked, when the creature had finally disappeared over the rim.

"I don't know," Daryl responded, his head shaking, then turning to once again consider the potential of the downriver threat.

Chapter XXVII

No words were necessary. Quickly, Daryl and Nado restrapped their sticks, slung them low, and left at a run for the village. The strange being had preceded them, but even his terrible visage was fading from their minds. The safety of the tribe was at stake, and they now had one simple mission, providing as much advance warning as possible.

The run from the rubble pile was only a blur, the sounds of the river's thunder fading into a surreal distance when they reached the flat, open area just before the structure.

Daryl's father sat on a long, flat stone just outside the opening to the family room, his back against the wall's dried clay exterior. The great spring hunt was less than a half moon's time away, and he was preparing his equipment. His hunter's instincts had gauged the boys' approach before he had even witnessed their expressions or heard their words. His attention sharply focused, he rose slowly.

"What is it?" he asked softly, his hands gripping the long hunter's spear in a diagonal guard position across his chest. His calmness was belied only by his steely grip on the spear's thick wooden shaft.

The boys stopped just short of him, both leaning forward and breathing heavily from the continuous sprint.

"Dust," Daryl pointed in the direction of the falls. "Great clouds of dust approaching." He panted several times, before going on. "A stranger," and he hesitated only a second to reflect on how badly the term described the bizarre, almost-but-not-human creature they had encountered. "He was running up-river. He said that another catastrophe is coming."

Daryl's father did not wait for further explanation. He simply turned and slipped into the opening. Daryl and Nado stood waiting, both glancing toward the river from time to time. Although nothing could be heard and the dust was not visible beyond and below the clouds of the fall's mist, a faint vibration could be felt coming from the earth itself. The hairs on the back of Daryl's neck stood fully erect.

Heartbeats later, the Chief stepped through the opening. The Chief's old, craggy face was a mass of bunched wrinkles. Warriors flowed out of the other front openings in the structure and clots of men collected, all intently gazing down the path toward the river.

No one spoke as stillness reigned over the scene. The sun was well past its high point, yet warmth was felt by none of the gathered men, all of whom, with the exception of Daryl and Nado, had taken up their warrior's spears, which had been left in parallel rows along the structure's outside wall. The Chief raised his spear and held it high and horizontal over his head. Then he pointed it back toward the escarpment wall.

"Back. Bring the women and children to the old cave entrance. But do not go in. We must remain back within the brush, but not too close to the wall," he motioned with his spear, and the area became a beehive of activity. "We don't know what this threat is," the Chief yelled out, then he turned to Daryl, his gaze glacial and penetrating.

"What comes?" he asked, his tone unfriendly and remote. The tip of the spear pointed at the boy's chest, as if whatever was coming was somehow related to something the boy had done.

Daryl missed none of the unspoken hostility, moving only

slightly away from Nado, so as to take the full brunt of the Chief's attitude himself. He tried to reflect on the question. The catastrophe had been nothing like what they were experiencing. There had been almost no time at all, and the sounds had all been different. The dust had come from everywhere, and not from a singular direction. He gave the only answer he could.

"I don't know, but it comes from downriver. You can feel it through the ground." He looked down after speaking.

The Chief and the boy's father did the same, but only for an instant. "We must go," the old man turned and bellowed to all about him, then struck out around the corner of the structure toward their old cave dwellings.

Nado started after the Chief and Daryl's father, almost running into Daryl's mother emerging from the family room at a run, her arms laden with leather sacks of special curatives. The boy stopped and turned when he saw that Daryl had not moved.

"Well?" he said, his head turning first toward the direction of the departing villagers and then back to Daryl.

"It's not a catastrophe. Not like last time," the boy replied flatly.

"Huh?" was all that Nado could think to say, at first. After only a few heartbeats of silence, he went on, "Then what is it?"

"I really don't know. But it is not that. The catastrophe passed like a wave in the river, except it was in the earth itself," Daryl said, as his arm swept the area from down- to upriver. "It passed in only a few blinks of a man's eye, all that distance . . . and the noise . . . it was terrible, and it came out of the earth from beneath our feet. And then there were great bolts of light." Daryl stopped, staring at Nado's open mouth.

Nado had been trapped in the cave, coming from sleep into a buried, painful wakefulness. He had witnessed only the after-effects of the event.

"No, whatever it is we must face it as men. It is a thing of man."

"What?" Nado replied. Daryl ignored him, noting that the vibration, which was just on the edge of detection, was increasing.

"What do we do?" Nado finally asked, looking around to see the last of his tribesmen head toward the cliff face.

"Fight. It is what warriors are supposed to do?" Daryl stepped several paces toward the river when he finished the sentence.

"Fight? With the warriors?" Nado looked toward the caves. "But we are not warriors. The warriors are in the caves. And what is there to fight?" The words came out broken, in a tone of extreme exasperation.

"That," Daryl said, pointing downriver in the direction from which they knew the dust to be forming. "Whatever is making the dust billow and move is what we fight."

"Oh, great. Of course." Nado shook his head in scorned resignation. "What else? We fight a dust cloud. Why did I not guess? Is there anything in your life, and now mine," he thumped his chest loudly with his strong arm, "that is normal?" Even under the circumstances, Daryl could not help but smile.

"C'mon. We will meet whatever it is in the opening down near the river. At the edge of the falls it narrows, and the ground is steep from there down." He was already moving as he spoke, trusting Nado to follow his lead.

They ran to where Tagawan sat, working on his feather coat as if there was not something terribly amiss in the world around him. The boys loped easily instead of sprinting, unlimbering their throwing sticks and smoothly loading stones from their leather carrying tubes as they went.

They waited close to the small pool, both staring down the steep slope of rubble toward where the escarpment jutted out toward the river's outflow from the great cauldron below.

Whatever was coming upriver would have to pass between that sharp face and edge of the waters. The mist parted and then closed with annoying regularity. Their attention was fully concentrated on the small area. The bird squawked at them occasionally, but neither boy paid it any mind.

Nado looked at Daryl standing next to him, and wondered if he felt the rise of bile in his throat that he felt in his. Daryl had been right about the terrible earth and water move that had so changed their lives. The growing vibration was nothing like that, but it was so strange and so powerful that he did everything he could to keep his limbs from shaking visibly.

"What do you suppose she thinks?" Daryl asked casually, his attention unwavering from the point down below.

Nado turned his head to look at him in surprise. "Who?" he asked, wondering if Daryl had gone insane with terror.

"Who?" Daryl replied. "Who do you think? Parlon."

"You're thinking about that girl at a time like this? What does it matter? We're both going to be killed anyway. She can watch!" Nado gestured behind them. From their vantage point just above and behind the tribal structure, the villagers would be able to just make out the two of them standing at the river, waiting.

"Oh?" Daryl's head whipped back, but he could not see anyone in the thick brush at the bottom of the escarpment wall. But he straightened up a bit. "We'll have to die well then." He did not look over at Nado when he said the words, and the other boy did not see the small, concealed smile that touched his lips.

As he spoke, however, Daryl reflected on the different way in which each of them appeared to respond to danger, Nado with a nervous, cynical, yet determined attitude, while he himself felt a slightly elated humor, although his stomach muscles hurt, cramping with rock-hard tension.

"There's little doubt of that," Nado shot back acidly. The words were no more than out of his mouth, however, when the cause of the great moving dust cloud rounded the wedge of escarpment rock downriver.

"The Mur," Daryl said, after staring for several heartbeats in complete shocked silence. In only a very short time the number of fast-approaching creatures that had become visible was greater than the entire population of the tribe itself.

The Mur moved like no other animal. Individually, each wide beast ranged slightly to one side and then back to the other as it ran, but the running itself was a sinuous, smooth, twisting affair. Built wide and heavy across the shoulders, the Mur eased forward with deceptive speed, more like a huge, heavy cat than the giant bear shapes they resembled. As a group, the herd surged forward in a spreading wave, the places that were narrowed seemed only to increase their speed as the animals pressed against one another, shoulder to shoulder. They did not stop to eat or inspect. They just came on. A single large Mur stayed just ahead of the others, always in front of the very center of the herd's mass.

Neither boy had moved since Daryl had identified the threat, but as the animals closed on the base of the rubble pile, they both began easing backward, holding their throwing sticks out to the side. A different sound could be heard over the thunder of the falls and the vibration felt through their feet. It was a never-ending series of animal trumpets. A high, shrill sound, that didn't seem to fit the great, menacing creatures at all, yet somehow added to the terrifying experience.

The elation Daryl had felt at finally being able to confront the unknown enemy had evaporated, along with the saliva in his mouth. The steep slope next to the falls would be no challenge at all for the Mur, as he had at first hoped. But after seeing the feral way they moved, and the intent of their advance, he knew that they would crest the lip of the falls very shortly. And there was no place to escape to, not for them and not for the tribe.

"We'll make our stand before the structure," he said quickly to Nado. The area just before the village was wide, flat, and slanted gently toward the river. They would have a perfectly clear field of fire for their throwing sticks. But he was sick inside. It had only taken a brief glimpse of the herd to realize fully that nothing their hunters or warriors possessed, or had ever heard of, would serve as any kind of weapon at all against the overwhelming mass of charging Mur.

But still they ran, their sticks tucked at their sides, their foot skins barely touching the surface of the ground.

Chapter XXVIII

The Mur spread out before them, as both boys slowly backed up until they could press no deeper into the rough, clay exterior of the tribal structure. A single Mur stepped from the renewed cloud of dust and debris that surrounded the mass of ever-moving bodies. The beasts no longer ran, but simply seemed to flow out along the river, some venturing into the fast-flowing waters, inhaling the liquid through their short trunks, and then expelling it in round, brief clouds above their heads. The leading Mur grew larger as it neared, until they looked up to see its eyes. It let out a great, hissing roar, the dust on the ground blowing out from the force of its breath.

Nado stepped forward, cocked his stick back, then released his stone at point-blank range into the Mur's blunt forehead. The missile struck at the point where the thick snout of the beast began its sinuous protrusion, and a small puff of dust appeared at the point of its impact. The animal raised its snout high then lowered it back to the ground, turning its head as it did so to view them with one large, unblinking eye, its two great tusks sweeping upward in a perfect curve.

"It did not even feel it!" Nado's voice was a frightened squeak as he retreated, making no attempt to reload a second stone. The sound of the rock's impact had been such a solid heavy *thunk* that he knew his weapon was useless.

Daryl's own throwing stick lay at his feet, only the holding end supported by his right hand, the rock having rolled half a man-length away. He stood unmoving, supported only by the structure wall, as he breathed deeply and stared.

Nado tore his eyes from the great beast before him to glance at the surrounding herd. Just behind the lead Mur were two even larger animals, with four tusks instead of just the two. After them, many others swept the area from side to side, while the entire mass appeared to be slowly easing forward.

"Why does it have only the two smaller tusks?" Nado whispered to Daryl, expecting the unmoving Mur before him to attack at any moment. The larger Mur had tusks that curved first inward and then out and back around, forming almost complete crooked circles. The smaller tusks protruded from just below their mouths, while the lone animal confronting them had only the upper two.

"The leg, look at the leg." Daryl pointed with his left hand. The left foreleg of the Mur was not covered with the thick, shiny fur that cloaked the rest of the animal. From its shoulder to just above its knee joint was a hand-width wide line of gray.

"It must have been injured at one time," Nado replied, peering at the area indicated. "Not that it matters."

"And that left eye . . . I would know it anywhere. Murgatroyd." The last word came out as a whisper, even difficult for Nado to hear.

"That Mur you found on the island?" Nado said in disbelief. "We are to be killed by the same animal you helped?" Nado pointed to its leg this time, his voice raising a full octave.

"Murgatroyd," the boy said louder, ignoring Nado, dropping his throwing stick entirely and stepping away from the wall.

The Mur raised its trunk and trumpeted loudly, then turned once more to regard the boy.

"You made it," Daryl said, his voice filled with pleasure and a great smile on his face. "And you brought all your friends," he waved to take in the ever pressing mass of the herd. "That is wonderful." He moved toward the animal, not stopping until he stood beside the creature's great head, reaching up to pat the beast solidly under the now blinking left eye.

Nado stood in shock. "This is the baby Mur from your story?" he asked, his tone revealing just how little of Daryl's island tale he had believed. "Well, it is not a baby anymore," was all he could think to add. He hesitantly approached until his chest was only half a man-length from Murgatroyd's gently swaying trunk.

"Murgatroyd . . . meet Nado, my friend," Daryl said as he patted the soft fur just beneath the Mur's eye. The animal's trunk-tip reached out to touch the other boy's forehead. Nado batted the thick appendage away, flinching and ducking his head.

"Ugh?" he cried, his face screwed up.

Daryl laughed, "It is okay, really. He did that to me all the time. You get used to it," he said, knowing full well that Nado would never get used to it. He had an aversion to the touch of animals, even Tagawan, that Daryl found mystifying and not a little humorous. "Here, pat him here," and Daryl demonstrated again by stroking the soft fur.

"I do not want to touch it," Nado said, his expression still sour.

Daryl was still so elated to have escaped immediate death and, at the same time, to be reunited with the mystical animal of his island adventure, that he could only beam and occasionally laugh. He stroked the Mur's great head, remembering how, only the summer before, he had not had to reach nearly so high to touch the same spot. The Mur had grown considerably.

"He knows that, but I think it is required," Daryl answered, his voice playful but insistent. Nado grudgingly stepped closer, reached upward, and set his good hand against the side of the Mur's head, then quickly dropped it and stepped back.

"He is filthy," he murmured, wiping the hand on his leather jerkin.

The Mur seemed to sense the boy's aversion, yet extended its trunk to touch the boy's head lightly once again. This time Nado did not push the soft tip away, only snorted quietly. "I suppose we must endure this sort of thing, in return for our lives."

Daryl stepped back at the words, scanning the herd beyond. "And what I do not understand," his voice more serious, "Murgatroyd seems to be the leader, but he's not old enough, at least I wouldn't think so. Look at the size of those two." He nodded at the two giant monsters that stood well back from Murgatroyd's flank. "And the rest. I have heard the warriors talk of great cats. These move more like cats than anything else I could have imagined."

Both boys watched the creatures weaving and wandering about, smelling everything with their sweeping trunks, never standing still for long. Some curled their trunks about tufts of low-lying brush and pulled the mass into their mouths, munching loudly. They never stopped milling slowly about, although the press toward the structure seemed to have eased a bit.

"And I do not think it is just our lives that, for whatever reason, have been spared. I think they would have crushed our village, and the tribe with it, out of existence. I do not understand," Daryl shook his head as he tried to take it all in. Nado simply nodded, his expression just as puzzled. Daryl looked back at Murgatroyd, focusing on a single part of his large body.

"Look," he said, pointing. Nado followed the boy's pointing finger. High on the Mur's shoulder, just above where the leg joined the back, a jagged piece of wood stuck out through the fur, its roughly splintered end no more than a hand's breadth from the surface.

"What is it?" Nado whispered, his brow wrinkled in thought. His conclusion was only a heartbeat in coming, however. "It's the broken shaft of a warrior's spear." The boys looked at one another, then Daryl spoke.

"Kneel down and I'll try to get it out." The shaft protruded just above arm's reach.

"Of course," Nado said, some of his old derisive attitude returning. "Maybe your calling is the fixing of broken animals." But he knelt on all fours next to the substantial front leg of the Mur, laying aside his empty throwing stick and tube of rocks. His willowy back tilted as he favored his damaged limb. Daryl pulled himself up, using Murgatroyd's thick fur as handholds. Standing on Nado's thin back, he grasped the short shaft and worked it gently back and forth, not stopping when the Mur let out a mewling series of roars. The beast did not move away from him, however.

Daryl felt the light touch of the Mur's exploring trunk-tip, but kept working the shaft back and forth. "Sorry Murgatroyd, but this has to come out and there's only one way." He did not feel the resistance lessen until both the Mur and Nado were both complaining. "It's coming. I'm getting it." The fluted flint tip came loose as he spoke, sliding out with a faint, liquid *plop*.

"Got it?" Nado asked, not waiting to hear the answer as he rolled, dumping Daryl to one side. They ended up in a heap, the fluted spear point landing between Nado's legs. Recovering before Daryl, he examined the fire-blackened piece.

"It didn't even penetrate his skin. There's no blood." They both looked up at the damaged area, although it was no longer visible in the shaggy fur. Murgatroyd's trunk-tip explored back and forth over the general area. But it had ceased crying.

"Do you suppose—" Nado held the needle-pointed blade in the air, the clear, glistening liquid from the Mur's thick skin still coating the surface, "—this had anything to do with his return?"

He gestured at the animal.

"I don't know," Daryl replied, looking out again over the herd, "We know nothing about them." He shrugged in frustration. "I don't think anyone has been this close to one without becoming a meal." The legend of the predatory nature of the Mur was embedded into every member of the tribe. The Mur were one of the reasons that most tribes of humans lived in caves with small openings. To be caught in the open and spotted by even a single hunting Mur was an almost certain death sentence. The only warrior defense was to split and run in every direction, with the fortunate survivors meeting up only later, always a few numbers short of the original group.

"I can understand why this," Nado again gestured at Murgatroyd as he rose to stand beside Daryl, "this . . . animal . . . has not attacked. But them . . ." His good arm swept out over the vast number of moving beasts below, ". . . why they have not attacked us?" He shook his head.

The Mur were slowly but surely clearing every bit of soft foliage from the area between the structure and the river, Daryl observed. They appeared to sample and eat whatever was at hand, or trunk. A few of the smaller ones even attempted to try some of the embedded reeds sticking out of the sides of the structure's rooftop, but then they turned and headed for the water.

A great squawk came from above, and Daryl had only an instant to look up before Tagawan collided with his right shoulder, knocking him against the Mur's flank. Murgatroyd's massive head turned, his huge eye blinking once as he took in the noisy, new arrival. The bird squawked so mightily at the beast that Daryl held up his left hand to cover Murgatroyd's right ear. At the same time, a great bellow came from the two giant males that seemed to follow Murgatroyd everywhere. They turned toward the main body of the herd and started walking toward the river. Daryl realized he could not have matched their speed even in his most rapid sprint.

Murgatroyd stared at them for several more heartbeats longer. Slowly he turned, first his head and then the remainder of his body, toward the rest of the mighty herd. He let out a single bellow, then walked toward the river.

Chapter XXIX

The Mur drifted toward the river, almost as if they had been commanded to do so by some unseen force. But they did not move directly toward the water, and again Daryl was reminded of what the warriors had said about cats. Unless specifically attacking, those elusive predators slunk about in a fashion that was impossible for a watching human to understand. And so it was with the Mur. They just seemed to gravitate toward the water, their short, little sniffing runs and snuffling asides drawing them all together. Daryl and Nado watched the back of Murgatroyd disappear into the reddish-brown mass. The waning sun shone just above the red, furry field moving below, while the water was almost gray-black in its spring flow.

Tagawan squawked loudly after the departing animals, finally leaving the relative safety of Daryl's shoulder for a low-lying boulder.

"Oh great warbird, I see you have returned." Nado's welcome to the bird was given with his usual snide tone. The bird squawked loudly back, apparently missing the boy's sardonic delivery, and then ignored them both to attend to necessary grooming. "Stupid bird," growled Nado, as Daryl retrieved his fallen stone and reslung the throwing stick across his body. Tagawan took to the air with a loud flourish of his strong wings, and both boys twisted around, alert to any new threat.

From around the corner of the structure, the Chief and Daryl's father strode into view, with the Shaman not far behind.

Nado stepped closer to Daryl as they stood to meet the approaching men. The men were flushed, as if they had run the entire distance from the old cave system down.

Daryl's father spoke first. "How did you do it?" he asked, looking from one boy to the other.

Daryl glanced quickly over at Nado, one eyebrow raised in question. The rest of the tribe filtered around the corner, all of them stopping just behind where the Chief stood with the Shaman at his right, and Daryl's father on his left. Daryl said nothing, not being able to truly grasp the meaning of the question.

"How did you do that?" the Shaman rephrased the father's question, but before Daryl could say anything, the Chief's deep, penetrating voice was heard.

"We saw everything from the rise." His arm waved back which they had come. "The village was lost. The Mur were going to destroy it. There was no doubt." As his low, deep voice pronounced the words, he stepped slightly forward of the two men at his side. Then he turned slowly to face the gathered tribe.

"From that place," he again gestured with the ceremonial spear, "we all watched these two youths, these outcasts—" for the first time, that word was used aloud to describe the boys' status, and the crowd rocked back uneasily from it, "—these two unfit members of our tribe, who stood together and turned the Mur, not just one, but this . . ." and he swept around, arms upraised, in a full circle, to take in the almost indescribable view of the gathered animals below them. From one end of the river to the other, the beasts moved slowly about, clumping together and then thinning out without thought or intent. There were far too many Mur to count, even if they could have been stilled for the purpose.

Both boys stood stock still, facing the village and riveted by the attention that neither had ever experienced before. Daryl felt guilty at first, until he was irresistibly drawn into two pools of deep brown warmth and reassurance. Parlon had appeared just behind the shoulder of her father, and only her eyes were visible. Daryl did not need to see the remainder of her face to feel her luminescent support, and his chest swelled.

A great, single trumpet of sound caught the attention of the entire village, and as one, they turned to the Mur gathered below near the river. Daryl saw the now-smallish Mur standing separate from the others. It faced the remainder, its trunk raised high into the air.

Without conscious thought, Daryl raised his right arm to wave.

"Goodbye, Murgatroyd," he yelled, hoping his voice would carry across the full distance of the hardened clay ground. The beat trumpeted once more, then turned and blended into the mass of moving Mur. Again the earth trembled beneath their feet as the entire herd of great beasts began their slow run up-river, giving the effect of a red river running in opposition to the waters just beyond. In complete silence, the tribe stood and watched the Mur pass.

After many heartbeats, Daryl's father was the first to speak. "You've named one of the Mur?" His voice, hushed and incredulous, also held a strong element of awe, one that Daryl had never heard from the man. His upbringing by the man had been anything but respectful or cordial. Daryl was given a place to stay out of the weather, suitable attire, and a family to belong to. There had existed nothing of an emotional relationship, certainly nothing of what the big warrior had exhibited to his wife or, in a lesser way, to Daryl's elder brothers. And since the debacle following the catastrophe, they had not spoken more than a few sentences to one another.

"The one—" Daryl began, pointing at the general departing assembly, as Murgatroyd had disappeared into the herd, "—the one you saw. Yes. His name is Murgatroyd. He's the Mur from the island, where I was trapped at the time of the catastrophe." Daryl spoke slowly, his arm dropping as he finished. The silence he had spoken into was so great that he knew every villager had heard his words. For an instant he caught his mother's eyes, but even she looked away immediately when their gazes met.

The afternoon wind started with a gust at that point, and the moment was broken. The children of the tribe ran forward to catch the last glimpses of the animals that they had only previously heard of in legends, while the villagers themselves filed back into the structure through its many openings. All walked well around the two boys, but the distance they gave in passing had changed, Daryl noted. The men nodded, and then women smiled in semi-secret smiles as they passed by, in a sort of acknowledgment that there was something special about both boys that they had known all along.

"Stop!" the Chief bellowed. The scene froze as everyone halted in an instant. The Chief reached out and took the Shaman's spear of office. He stood, his own ceremonial spear resting on the ground and held in his right hand, while he balanced the Shaman's in his left. Both decorated and feathered spears angled outward. The Chief stepped forward until he stood less than a man-length from the boys. Daryl's first instinct was to back away, but he held his ground, jaw muscles clenching with tension.

The Chief extended the Shaman's spear out to Nado. Nado glanced at Daryl, who could only mirror the dumfounded boy's look and shrug ever so slightly. Hesitantly, Nado took the weapon offered by the Chief, awkwardly clutching it to his chest, the feathers blowing full in his face. Daryl was then more prepared, and accepted the Chief's own spear in as dignified a manner as he could manage, holding it butted to the ground and out from himself, as he had seen the older man do. His eyes could not help, however, straying back into those of Parlon. Her stare never wavered, her support evident, and he longed to see the glint of the stone that hung about her neck, just above her heart.

"These men," bellowed the Chief, "now carry the authority of your Chief and your Shaman. The Council will meet tonight to decide their new place within the tribe, and until such time, these men shall be considered full warriors."

Daryl and Nado stood rooted to the ground in stunned silence. Around them, women keened small, shrill sounds into the air, while the men began to thump their spears rhythmically against the earth, one after another joining in, until the high-pitched calls and the staccato thumping merged into a single repetitive beat. Neither boy had ever heard of such a practice or witnessed anything like it.

Slowly the crowd dispersed, working its way back around the boys and into the structure. The only smiles that Daryl didn't see were on the faces of the Shaman, the Chief's son, and his own two brothers.

He wondered if they were all as shocked as he was. Finally, the boys stood alone. Parlon gave Daryl one last look, then slipped past, fondling the crystal about her neck. On the way, she leaned toward him and whispered a few words, then was gone. Daryl's face reddened.

"What did she say?" Nado asked between the feathers still blowing about his head. He batted them away, but the evening wind had picked up and they blew right back at him.

"I knew it," Daryl whispered.

"Knew what?" Nado returned, his voice growing petulant.

"That's what she said." Daryl shrugged as Nado nodded.

"What happened here?" All the stuffing had left Nado's voice, and he sounded almost as if he was a small child again.

"I don't know. I hoped you would." Daryl looked directly into Nado's eyes. "I think that they feel that I redeemed myself for somehow stopping the attack of the Mur. And you proved your worth, and that your arm does not matter, you are as brave as any warrior." His head shook from side to side as he spoke. "At least that's what I think everyone thinks."

A moment of silence passed, ended by Tagawan's usual plunge into Daryl's body, accompanied by the usual loud squawk.

"And what are you doing here?" Daryl hissed, but did not turn to regard the bird. The razor-sharp beak was only a hand's breadth away from his right eye. "I warned you never to come to the village." He shook his head. The animals in his life had somehow developed a control over events that Daryl was at a loss to understand, much less explain.

"Did we?" Nado asked, his voice still small.

"Did we what?" Daryl shot back, exasperated.

"Save the village, the structure, you know, the tribe . . ." and his voice trailed away. Daryl did not know what to say, his mind whirling with conflicting thoughts and emotions. He could only think clearly of Parlon.

"What do you suppose she meant?" he asked, changing the subject.

"What?" Nado's old, acidic tone had returned.

"That she knew, you know, what she said." Daryl inquired, embarrassed even to be discussing this subject, but unable to keep himself from doing it.

"Idiot. Only you could fail to understand that message." Nado waited for some reaction, but Daryl only looked toward the river and into the setting sun, so he went on. "She meant that she knew all along that you were of high character and quality. That you were no coward, and that one day soon you would become a warrior and that you would claim her as your own." Nado singsonged his words, sighing deeply when he was done.

"All that in those few words?" Daryl's head had come full around as the other boy had spoken, his forehead wrinkled up in an intense frown.

Nado swung the spear down, until it hung next to his small body. He shook his head. "Oh, Great Mother Earth," he said to the ground. "You know that he is dumb, so very dumb, but forgive him. He is the only friend I have." Then he laughed, and after a moment, Daryl joined him. It took many heartbeats for them to recover. The laughter was more due to release of their own fear and tension than Nalo's humorous plea.

"Come, we must talk away from here." Nado motioned with his spear downriver, as several warriors had stepped out of the structure, appearing not to notice them but obviously intent on discovering the cause of their mirth.

They walked to the small pool above the falls in silence, Daryl leading, but in reality Tagawan establishing his place out front, bobbing and weaving about as they walked. They took up their customary positions, back to the nearby great rocks, the bird on his comfortable, high perch, where he could watch everything but not seem to at all.

"What are we going to do?" Nado asked, without preamble.

"About what?" asked Daryl innocently, but then seeing Nado's expression, went on, "I don't know."

"How can we become warriors? The council meets tonight. What if they decide that we are really warriors now? What about our ruins? Our throwing sticks, even?"

"And him?" Nado pointed at the grooming bird, who immediately squawked in reply. "Useless as he is, I have grown accustomed to his bad personality and nasty habits."

"We are already warriors, and you know it. The council is never going to go against the Chief, just as they did not when we lost our status." Daryl expelled a breath of pent-up air and frustration. "It's exactly the same, you know. They thought we were worthless, and we were not. Now, they think we are heroes, and we are not. So we were outcasts, the Chief even used that word. And now we are to be honored above all. And, according to my father, it's true. Whatever the tribe decides is true and becomes the truth. How can that be?"

Daryl took his head into his hands. "Why does it all have to be so complex? Why can't things just happen and be the way they are? Why is there all this trouble?" The boy spoke to the ground between his legs, expecting no answer and getting what he expected. Tagawan flew down to preen just before him, walking back and forth, as if expecting some notice.

"Maybe he could be the tribal bird?" Nado pointed at the cooing creature, "Or maybe he would make at least one good meal." Daryl had to look up at the prancing bird and smile.

Chapter XXX

Daryl walked back to the village with Nado, the setting sun making the cliff face beyond the structure appear reddish in color, like a vast slice of some strange fruit. They did not talk to one another, although Nado provided a running commentary of what story they might tell to back up what apparently everyone had come to believe. He laughed and stabbed at imaginary Mur with the Shaman's spear, making up scenario after scenario of how they had driven the vicious beasts back. Normally, Daryl would have laughed at the other boy's antics, but he could not free his mind from darker thoughts.

Suddenly, everything in his life had changed once again. It had occurred completely beyond his ability to foresee or control, and even as they walked, carrying the authority of the tribe's two most powerful figures in their hands, he had no idea of what the consequences would be. Daryl held the spear out at arm's length, watching the sun's rich setting light reflect back from the lightly blowing feathers.

"I think we're in trouble," he said to his companion. Nado flitted back from one of his ferocious spear attacks, to again walk at his side.

"If this is trouble," Nado laughed, thumping the spear's butt solidly on the hard clay, "then I like being in trouble."

Daryl could not help smiling at the boy's enthusiasm, but his expression quickly sobered. "Now who's the idiot? You are not thinking. Do you suppose the Shaman is sitting in his room thinking wonderful thoughts about some cripple carrying around his very special spear?"

Daryl was sorry the minute the words came out. Nado stopped, a look of questioning concern and even mild fear crossing his features.

"You are right. We must be very careful," he said, more seriously than Daryl had intended him to be. Upon reaching the structure, they both leaned their spears against the wall next to Daryl's family opening.

Neither of them had ever before seen the symbols of power lain so carelessly aside for the night. Nado looked Daryl in the eyes as they stood back, but the boy just shrugged in response. It was not a time for such questions, he knew. They parted with a nod.

Daryl stepped in through the opening. His mother sat near the opposite wall, her place and countenance lit by the beautiful softness of the setting sun's last light. She was bent forward facing him, one hand working a rounded stone into the bowl-like depression of a larger one. Daryl felt the heat from the ash-covered fire from where he stood. Every so often a small flame leapt out of the gray whiteness of the flat bed, sending a spark of additional illumination into the room's darker corners.

"Sit before me," she said, her voice quiet but full of strength. Her gaze stayed on the stone-ground medication she was preparing. With a tingle of trepidation running up his spine, Daryl sat on the thatched reed rug.

"You have been through a lot." She said the words as if she had long thought them through, slowly and heavily laden with meaning. "Some of that has been awful." She looked up. "And the most awful part is not the circumstances of what has befallen you, but how you felt inside."

The boy felt his throat constrict, and fiercely fought against the moisture threatening to escape from his eyes. He could only stare at her as she continued.

"Was Murgatroyd the omen you spoke of?"

Daryl was stunned by the question. He had seen his mother only briefly in the background of the tribe when the Chief had spoken, and he was not only dumfounded that she had heard the name he had given to the Mur, but that she immediately associated it with the recollection he had told her about the island adventure. He nodded, his mouth opening to say something, and then closing again. This time, he could not force his eyes to rise to meet her gaze.

"Yes, I believe your story," she said quietly.

He then looked up, involuntarily, one brow arched high in query. "But, you . . ." and he could not finish before she cut him off.

"I know exactly what I said."

"But . . ." he tried again.

"Because no one here would have believed you. It was too far from any tribal reality. This small place where we live." Her arm waved at where the escarpment wall lay behind the structure, "has no frame of reference for such events. And it was too soon, too soon after so many had been lost in the catastrophe. The tribe needed to vent the anger and frustration they felt, and they chose you." The words rushed out of her like a strong, escaping wind. She breathed in heavily as she finished.

"Why didn't you tell me?" Daryl asked, shaking his head, his mind spinning with all that had occurred and now his mother's revelations.

"You would have resisted. It's a wonderful, yet terrible part of you. And you would have eventually been banished. Instead, you chose to find your own way apart from the tribe for awhile, and it saved both of us." Their eyes met again.

"Yes," she said, "I would have died without you. You are my son." Daryl stood and leaned over to touch the only person in the tribe who had always been true to him, even when he had believed otherwise. They said nothing as he gripped her shoulders and then hugged her. He wanted to cry, but he could only smile. They broke apart and she went back to grinding her potion while he paced back and forth in front of her.

"What will you do tonight?" she asked, a touch of innocence in her voice.

"I don't know," he said, his hand coming up to massage his jaw as he walked. Then he launched into the great concerns he had regarding such a sudden change in roles. He was not prepared to be a warrior, and had attended none of the training that his brothers had been studying for months. And he did not feel that he could give up his freedom to travel and explore with his friend Nado and the bird, Tagawan. He did not bring up either the ancient city or his desire to return to the mysterious island again.

"Perhaps, you might tell them the truth," she said when he had concluded. He looked back sharply, stopping in his tracks. "I mean just this once," she said, looking down with a small smile.

"This once?" he mouthed the words, as if saying them for the first time in his life.

"You've learned so much, and so soon. You've learned that you have to be true to yourself, I know. But the tribe is a different place. You need the tribe and it needs you, although I don't expect you to see that yet. What is true to you is not necessarily true to the tribe." She stopped speaking, seeing his strange expression.

"Oh, mother," he blurted into the sudden silence. "I'm not a hero. Nado and I simply made some foolish decisions. I didn't name Murgatroyd here, but back at the island. He's the young Mur who was my omen, yes, but back there. It was only blind luck that he now seems to lead that great herd. And it was only my experience with him on the island that saved us. We did nothing to stop the Mur." The relief at admitting the unwilling deceit came through in his voice. His mother stopped grinding and watched him closely.

"What is true to the tribe is not necessarily true to you," she repeated, but more forcefully. Daryl looked at her in puzzlement.

"You mean it's okay to lie to the tribe?" he asked, thinking back to her comment about standing before the council.

"That's not what I said at all. The tribe is not an individual, and it doesn't think like one. Its truth is different, and you must find a way to gauge it and then understand it." Her voice had become light again, and she had gone back to grinding. He was about to say that he did not understand at all, but remained silent.

"I will know?" he asked instead, but she just smiled in reply. Daryl wished then that he had Nado along to interpret for him. Nado seemed to have a talent for understanding these concepts so much better than he did.

He looked at his mother sitting before him. She was radiant, like Parlon in some way that he could not figure out. It was like there was some sort of inner light burning inside her. All his life she had seemed to be able to simply reach in and touch his very soul. Even when he thought she had deserted him, she had known what was inside of him. And he realized then just how much it must have hurt her to reject him. He wanted to say that he was sorry, but could not think of any way that he could phrase it. He shook his head slightly, looking around the room.

"Where are my father and my brothers?" he asked, realizing just now that they had not come into the room.

"They were selected to track the Mur and watch them, in case the herd changes directions," she said, looking up.

"Father will not be there tonight?" Daryl asked.

His mother regarded him for a moment before replying, "You don't need your father at that meeting. And you must consider that nothing changes the facts as they happened, as you understand them. Without you meeting the Mur on that island, and then facing the herd today, the tribe would have perished, or at least been driven back into what's left of the caves as a remnant of its former self."

Daryl stared into her eyes, understanding only that there was so very much to understand. She shook her head, and smiled softly before continuing.

"You must accept the judgment of those around you to live among them. If that judgment is against you, then you must struggle against it and change the flawed perception with your words and deeds. And if the judgment is in your favor, you must stand and attempt to live up to it." She stopped, watching him think.

"But what if the judgment is wrong?" he blurted out after many heartbeats of silence.

"It's always wrong," she replied.

"Ahhh." His voice gave out only a weak, hushed tone. The concept of what his mother had said was overwhelming. She stepped back and then returned to her work grinding the special herbs. He thought of many questions, one after another, but he said nothing. Somehow he knew that a better understanding would come with time, but he did not question her correctness. As time dragged on, she looked up once more.

"And the girl?" she asked.

"The girl?" he answered, taken aback.

"The Shaman's daughter," she said with another of her enigmatic smiles. Daryl knew Parlon's name was known by all the tribe's women, but still his mother would not violate the tribal custom of not speaking a name aloud until it was assigned at ceremony.

Daryl thought of denying his feelings, but realized immediately that he could not fool his mother. He did not understand nearly everything she said, but he understood that she did.

"Ah, I'd like to claim her," he gushed out, then waited for her reply.

"The crystal that rests beneath her throat. It was from you then?"

Daryl frowned. He wondered if she only asked questions that she already knew the answer to in order to make him uncomfortable.

He nodded, expecting her to ask him where he had found it. His hand went instinctively to the small knife pouch attached to his belt. But she asked something else entirely.

"Are you going to claim her tonight?" She said the words so innocuously, yet their impact shook Daryl to his core. He started, taking in a breath so quickly that it sounded like a grunt. Then he let it out slowly, spacing his next words quietly and evenly.

"She can't be claimed until the Solstice, still many moons away. You know that." He said the words more as a question than as a statement, once again not understanding where such a strange conversation could be headed.

She waited to answer, the air between them suddenly charged with an expectant tension. The fire spat twice into the silence. Finally, his mother spoke. "Yes, that's true. But you have watched the rules of the tribe for some time now. What rules made you an outcast? What rules allow you and your friend to carry those spears?" She nodded toward the opening, where the two items lay against the wall. She stopped her work. "The rules are made by the Chief in response to what the tribe wants or needs. They change with those needs and wants."

Her head flipped up and her dark eyes bored into him.

"Tonight will be a night without rules, unless you choose to make them. It is in the air of the people. You lose nothing by the asking. And if you do not ask, then the Chief's son may. It would be a marriage of great power and convenience to both of those families." She looked downward into the small, flickering flames of the fire. "But right now, and maybe only right now, the Chief will find it very, very difficult to refuse you."

Daryl was too stunned to speak. The Chief's son.

"Magabo," Daryl whispered softly. It was the second time that the young warrior-in-training had come up with regard to life-changing events happening to Daryl. He did not even really know the boy, and here he was again somehow inextricably tied into Daryl's own fate.

"Magabo would claim Parlon?" Daryl asked, his voice a strangled whisper. What chance could he have against the Chief's son? But his mother didn't reply, instead turning to work on one of her complex medical potions.

He nodded at her profile, then turned and left through the room's single opening. He had to find Nado.

Chapter XXXI

Daryl's journey through the dark labyrinthine interior of the tribal structure was totally unlike any other he had taken among his tribe. In each room it became a ritual to accept good-natured backslapping and re-introduction to all the residents of that particular room, as if he was from a different tribe and being presented to all the members of the tribe for the first time. Finally, he stepped into the room Nado inhabited, gingerly peering through the other openings to make sure he did not collide with either Parlon or her father. His feelings toward the girl were intense, but he was also somehow afraid of her, and certainly of Huslinth, her father.

Only the red coals from a corner cooking fire lit the smoky room. Daryl had bent ever lower as he proceeded into the structure's interior.

A layer of thick smoke drifted about very slowly, never seeming to find its way out of any of the smoke tubes. Again Daryl idly wondered if the lack of parasites was not due to the ever-present smoke than to any "freshness" of the air. The clay packing on the exterior walls had all but eliminated the terrible, cold drafts that had so chilled the interior during the long, harsh winter.

"Nado," Daryl whispered toward the particular short wall where the boy usually lay. He figured he would have to come closer and physically jostle Nado awake. Inside the structure, the boy slept like a part of the rock wall he abutted. A strong hand grabbed his biceps and pressed. It seemed to have plunged right out of the smoke layer itself.

"Will you keep quiet?" hissed his friend. Daryl pulled back, having kept from yelping only by biting one lip. He allowed himself to be pulled to an even darker corner.

"You can't call me by name like that," Nado whispered. "We haven't been given names yet." The boy was so insistent that Daryl almost laughed. He had been calling his friend Nado, not paying any mind at all to whom was around, throughout the winter and into the spring.

Nado noticed his smile, then ruefully returned one of his own. "Sorry," he murmured, "but it's not like before. Now everyone notices everything."

Daryl looked around again, smiling in spite of himself at Nado's instant new respect of the social order within the tribe. Only that very morning, he would have held everyone around him in some form of disdain.

Nothing else had to be said as Daryl turned and headed back through all the rooms he had crossed while Nado silently followed. They both moved softly but quickly, not so much in fear of disturbing the residents, but simply to keep from being congratulated all over again.

The moon was a bright, silvered slice that had just risen above the escarpment behind them. Daryl looked back at its magnified radiance, and wondered why sometimes it was bigger than at other times, but only when it was close to the horizon or just above the cliff wall, as it was at the moment. Nado had denied the obvious fact every time he had brought it up during the winter. "It's your eyes, they are crossed," was all the boy would say, and Daryl could never penetrate the humor.

They walked down toward the river, a cool, gentle wind blowing from downriver, and the light dampness of the spring's mist in the air.

"What's the plan?" Nado asked, before Daryl could get out the very same question. He shook his head instead.

"This is new. No rules, my mother said, although I'm not sure what that means either. She wants me to ask for the claiming privilege of Parlon."

Nado started spluttering. Before he could say anything, however, Daryl went on.

"I know, I know." Daryl waved the air around him with one hand. "I'm just not sure of what she meant. She says we can ask for anything we want and they can't really deny us." He said the words, but his voice lacked conviction. Then he waited. Nado padded beside him, his head down, eyes staring at the shadowed ground. They were almost to the river before he answered.

"Your mother is right, I think." He rubbed his face absently, and then phrased the question that had been on Daryl's mind since his mother had made her comment. "What else can we ask for?"

"Idiot. That is why we have to talk." Daryl relished the opportunity to use the derogatory term so near and dear to his friend. But a quiet "humph" is all he got in return.

"The meal is being served about now, I think," Nado said after a few seconds. "And I don't really feel hungry at all." He rubbed his flat stomach gently. Daryl felt the same uncomfortable stirrings in his own stomach, and had ever since the Chief had all but invited them to the council meeting. At first he had not believed that they were intended to be there at all, as the Chief had only mentioned that they would be discussed, but everyone that had greeted him since had confirmed that they were to be guests of honor.

"I don't really want to go at all. I'd rather be up in the old city." Daryl gazed longingly downriver when he said the words, lost in thought.

"I too," Nado replied, "but I would not want to miss this

either. We are just stupid and afraid. Being an outcast was easy, but this might be more fun . . ." His voice trailed off into the sounds of the river for many heartbeats before he continued, "And we might just be able to gain the benefit of both."

"Both what?" Daryl asked, immediately, only to be met with Nado's usual reply.

"Idiot. We're heroes, and we were outcasts, and now we'll be warriors. So let's ask to be special warriors. I don't want to go out with the men and search for baby bears." They both laughed at the last two words. The baby bearskin had become the subject of much humor, all behind Daryl's father's back, at the evening meals during winter.

They turned toward Tagawan's perch, stepping slower and more carefully as the path became less worn. The rushing waters were never taken lightly, although no member of the tribe had yet to make the fatal passage over the falls.

"My mind feels like it might burst with some of these thoughts," Daryl began, but Nado interrupted him before he could go on.

"Are you sure it's your head that is about to burst?" Nado laughed loudly, while Daryl was flushed. But he could not contain his thoughts.

"I mean about the stranger." His words had the intended effect, and all traces of humor faded from Nado's face.

"Oh," he said seriously. Neither boy had mentioned the horrid creature's bizarre, ugly appearance. They had not had much opportunity, but even when it had presented itself with his mother, Daryl had shied away. He wondered if even she could believe such a story. Somehow the creature had made his way upriver past the tribal area without being seen.

"There must be more of them downriver. I think I've seen the smoke from their fires, more than once and for quite some time. They are enemies. I just feel it." Daryl let out a breath as he finished. He had held the information so close that it was a relief just to be able to say the words.

"I feel it as well," Nado said, his own voice signifying relief.

"Should we . . . ?" but the words died as Daryl spoke them. Both boys looked at one another and shook their heads. "No," Daryl continued, "You're right. It's too soon. Maybe they can wait, whoever they are."

"Or whatever they are," Nado added.

The thunder of the falls was so loud here that any communication except yelling became impossible. They stood silently and looked over the edge into the black abyss. The waterfall in the daytime was a fearful sight at close range, but at night it was terrifying. Daryl shivered, the memory of his narrow escapes in the water only a few man-lengths away still fresh. After a while they turned and started back, walking slowly, neither boy particularly enthused about attending their first-ever council meeting. The day's events had numbed them, except it had not taken away their fears of their future. Nado was the first to talk when they were far enough for normal conversation to be comfortable.

"Maybe after being outcasts we just can't fit into the tribe again." His voice was wistful, without a trace of his usual cynicism or humorous arrogance.

"No," Daryl replied quietly, "I don't think it's that." He looked over at his friend. "Everyone in the tribe imitates everyone else. I think it's for survival. Everyone dresses about the same, eats the same, hunts the same, and even talks the same. We used to do that until we were cast out. We had to find our own way, that's all."

Nado stopped walking right where the two paths intersected and they would turn uphill to walk back to the structure. "I hadn't thought of that." Suddenly, his old enthusiasm was back. "That's it. You've explained everything. The catastrophe. That's when you changed and started inventing things. You weren't the same anymore. Most interesting." Then his expression turned thoughtful. "But if they imitate one another for survival, what happens to those who don't?"

"Today, we survive on our own," Daryl said. "Survival tomorrow may be different."

"Yes," said Nado. "The structure came about because the tribe was forced to change to survive. Then everyone adjusts to another method of doing everything the same again. But we need to think ahead to maybe tomorrow, and what is the best way for survival. If one can think ahead to maybe tomorrow, and what might be needed, then the actual survival tomorrow would be easier."

"How do you do that?" Daryl exclaimed in frustration, his brow furrowed and one eyebrow raised.

"Do what?" Nado answered, his own tone one of surprise.

"Make it all so complicated that I can't even understand what I was talking about." Daryl walked faster, shaking the difficult concepts Nado had brought up from his mind. The council meeting was the most important event in either of their lives, and here they were discussing things that really did not matter at all.

"Oh," Nado said, increasing his speed to catch up with the fast-moving boy ahead. Under his breath he said only a short phrase.

"Brilliant idiot."

Chapter XXXII

Both boys stood outside the opening to Daryl's family room.

The feathers from their ceremonial spears fluttered in the evening breeze, and several of the villagers had made a point to stop at the end of the evening meal and thank them for their efforts earlier in the day. Both had adopted the same method of dealing with the effusive and emotional outpouring. They bent at the waist, nodded their heads while receiving the thanks, and then only smiled and nodded some more if they were asked to elaborate. They'd decided together that they couldn't be held accountable if they did not lie, and the safest course was to say nothing at all. As Daryl's mother had taught him, the beliefs of the tribe had little to do with actual fact, and much more to do with what everyone thought about the facts.

It was dark when Nado's father came to summon them. This time their way back through the many rooms to the great open center area was made without incident, the rest of the tribe remaining quiet and withdrawn as the purposeful group passed through.

A small, bright fire lit the scene as they stepped through the last opening, its flame dancing just enough to cast sinister, moving shadows against the rough, clay-covered walls. The Chief sat in the center with a small, cleared area between himself and the cooking circle and, as was the custom at evening meals, the places to his right and left were occupied by Daryl's father and the Shaman. Senior warriors beneath his father's status sat on either side and in a row behind the more powerful men. Beyond them stood the full body of the tribe's warriors, all still and waiting. Nado's father took his place along the right side of the front line, leaving both boys standing before the gathered group, feathers faintly fluttering in the small air currents.

The Chief let the silence build its own level of tension, as no one moved or spoke for many heartbeats. Daryl felt that the noise of his own thumping chest must be audible to the whole gathering. Still the Chief did not speak, instead waving upward with one hand toward Daryl's father. The tribe's senior hunter rose and approached the boys, walking slowly before both and then retrieving the ceremonial spears. One in each hand, he turned, bent down, and placed each in its respective place before its owner. With his back to Daryl and Nado, he raised both arms and held them out. He waited a short time until the Chief signaled again. Then he spoke.

His low-timbered voice rose and fell, its vibration almost physically felt from the reverberations against the walls. He recounted the coming of the Mur and both boys' refusal to retreat. Adding such things as the courageous thoughts that had occupied the boys' minds while waiting for the Mur's approach, he told of Nado's attack with his throwing stick, and its obvious effect in stopping the great creature. Then he finished with Daryl's mysterious exercise of control and his physical handling of the beast. The last part was blended into the Mur departure, with all listeners left to assume the direct connection.

His arms did not drop until he was done. Even before they reached his sides, a rhythmic drumming began. Slowly, the sound became deeper and more pervasive. The warriors and hunters present all pounded their spear butts into the packed clay surface. Neither Daryl nor Nado had ever experienced the tribal form of honor, except from a great distance. The demonstration of support for their actions was apparent, eliminating the necessity for any decision from the council itself.

The Chief slowly worked his way to his feet, lifting his spear of office as he rose. The room fell into immediate silence. He turned to face the banked rows of warriors and hunters, looked up and down their ranks, then nodded once, as if in agreement with their unspoken decision.

"You shall be warriors from this day, and so it shall be." He thumped his feathered spear into the hard clay, then sank back to his cross-legged sitting position.

Daryl felt the fine hairs on the back of his neck beginning to relax back to their original positions. The drumming of the spears had penetrated to his very center of being. He stood, staring straight ahead, an undefined sense of well-being coursing through his body and mind.

Again it was quiet, only the fire's crackling and a whir of gentle wind breaking the silence. The Chief motioned for the boys to sit.

"Now we must consider a special selection for council membership." The Chief turned his head slightly to look at Nado directly. Daryl turned as well, his forehead wrinkling with a complexity of questions.

"For extraordinary heroism. For stopping the Mur with the well-thrown stone." The Chief stood again as he spoke, leaned forward, and grasped Nado's good shoulder with his left hand. "For this act, you are to be appointed to the council without respect to our normal rules or process." He nodded once, then sat again, allowing his ceremonial spear to fall across his folded legs.

"The Shaman has asked to be allowed to speak before this council and so shall it be."

Daryl's eyes had remained glued to Nado's profile, but the other boy's attention remained riveted on the Chief. At the mention of Huslinth's title, Daryl jerked his head back. The

Shaman stood, then turned to speak to the assembled warriors and hunters.

Huslinth made no attempt to build drama except by way of his appearance. His neck was painted a bright red, split down the center with a single stripe of gray, no wider than a finger. His face was shaven clean with the edge of a flint knife, while his hair was stained white with ash and pulled to the back of his head. Circles of deep blue surrounded both of his eyes. His torso remained bare, emphasizing the impact of the powerful decorations.

He extended his spear out from his body at an angle, its base set near his left foot. He waited for a few long heartbeats, every eye upon him. Suddenly, he pivoted around and swung the weapon with him, the shaft extending out with its point coming to rest no more than a handsbreadth from Daryl's chest.

"What say you, Da-ga-ryl, of the family Ryl?" he hissed, low and deep across the intervening space between them. A great inhalation of breath could be heard from the entire assembly. Several heartbeats passed, during which Daryl's heart seemed to stop altogether. He had no chance to answer, however, as the Shaman was not done.

"What strange power did you harness and release, to hold the Mur beast under your control?" The spear edged out to almost touch Daryl's chest when he said the final word. Daryl flinched back from the sharp point. He could not think of a single word to say. His voice was so paralyzed that he wanted to reach up and massage his throat, but he didn't move. He stared at Huslinth and, just for an instant, he thought he saw a faint smile cross the man's painted lips. Anger overcame his paralysis and a shudder went through his body. He breathed in deeply, then squared his shoulders.

"It was medicine," he began, his voice as low and steady as he could make it. "It was the medicine I learned from my mother." He forced an innocent smile to his face as he finished. Out of the corner of his eye he saw Nado turn and gape at the extraordinary comment.

The Shaman stared at him, his eyebrows rising high in confusion and question. "Medicine?" Huslinth whispered, his tone changing from attack and command into one of perplexity. "You used some strange potion of your mother's to gain control of the Mur?" The Shaman's voice rose as he spoke, his head shaking from side to side. "You want us to believe that you administered some medicine to the beast?" His tone had gone even higher, and, for the first time the spear lowered and Huslinth glanced back at the gathered council, as if to solicit its understanding and support.

"No. That's not what I did," Daryl responded, gaining more control over his roiling emotions with each word he spoke. He was frightened of the Shaman, more because of the simple fact that he was Parlon's father than because of his powerful status within the tribe. "I used my mother's knowledge, not her medications," he said, as he fumbled with the bottom of his torso jerkin. From beneath the leather covering, he extricated the remainder of the spear shaft, with its fire-hardened tip still intact. "I removed this spear remnant from the Mur's shoulder."

The only sound came from the point of Huslinth's spear sinking to the clay at his feet.

"After Nado stunned the beast with his stone, of course." Daryl glanced quickly over at his staring friend and winked very quickly.

Huslinth did not get a chance to go on. The members of the council, including the Chief, surged forward to view the strangely carved artifact, still covered with the dried, semi-clear liquid of the beast's inner skin layers. The Shaman was shouldered aside, and questions flew at the boy. He handed the fluted shaft to a nearby warrior and tried to field all the questions. There were no ready answers, however. Neither he nor any of the tribesmen had ever seen a spear tip of such unusual, yet old, design. No one could remember back to a time before flint-tipped weapons were used by a warrior or hunter from any of the valley tribes. The spear shank passed from one council member to another until finally the Shaman stood holding it up in one hand. He looked intently at the broken piece, examining and turning it over and over in his hand. Then his eyes rose to meet Daryl's. A flare of anger and deep-seated animosity transmitted itself across the short distance between them.

The questions died out and the original assemblage began to reform. Nado leaned into Daryl's shoulder.

"I didn't know you had it in you. That was a masterstroke. You should be appointed to the council just for your ability to dream up such wild stories." Daryl would have laughed, but out of the corner of his eye, he noticed Huslinth's movement to regain control of the meeting. In his hand he held high the broken spear shaft.

"This is an ominous omen," he said, his eyes peering at it intently, as if the object had proclaimed the words by its very existence alone. The sudden silence grew into a deadly stillness. The word omen was never used lightly, let alone by the Shaman himself.

"Note the workmanship," he waved the spear in a circle over his head. "Somewhere, there exists a tribe," he said, pausing for many heartbeats on the last word, his eyes swiveling to look into those of many of the tribe's more senior council members, "a tribe that hunts the deadly Mur." Once again discussion began among all the warriors and hunters until little else could be heard within the confined area.

"Hold," Huslinth shouted, and all conversation ceased. "Somewhere, possibly not far off, a tribe of strange courage and brutal insanity exists, and that is a terrible, fearful thing." A grudging assent of nods and grunts came from the assembled council.

Daryl watched Huslinth closely. He was both frightened by the man and impressed. The man drew his strength not so much from any of his manifested powers to predict or explain nature, but from his gift to gain and direct through his manner of speaking, plus his fascinating line of reasoning. Daryl and Nado both had come to the same conclusions as Huslinth was presenting, Daryl suddenly realized, but neither could have used the information with such stunning impact. And the Shaman had leapt to his conclusion in only a few heartbeats, and with only the broken shaft of the spear to guide him.

The Shaman once again raised the broken spear. "It is not the weapon itself," he began, "but the omen within," and he paused once more, making certain that he held the attention of all before going on, "and that omen is of a coming disaster." His voice trailed away with his last words and he lowered the weapon to chest level, as if to study it in more detail. "But this will take some time to manifest itself." He then jerked the weapon up, stepped right past Daryl, and plunged the broken shaft into the hard clay at the fire's edge. Then he turned and stood with his back to the offending artifact, arms crossed over his chest.

"I support the immediate initiation of Na-ga-do, the flint knapper's son, into warriorhood, and without delay. I also recommend that he be appointed, in the same fashion, to the tribal council. His exhibition of courage alone supports both of those decisions, but . . ." and once again his voice fell away into an expectant silence. Huslinth raised his right hand and paused as if in deep thought.

"I must withhold judgment on the son of Ryl. He must wait until I have had time to study the omen in more detail." He turned to nudge the imbedded spear point with his right foot.

"No, his fate should be suspended to await a decision by the council itself." In the silence that followed, he strode to his place next to the Chief and took his seat, staring balefully into the red embers of the dying fire.

Daryl had stopped breathing somewhere near the end of Huslinth's speech. Finally, he sucked in an audible gulp of air to stop his head from spinning. He could not decide, in his shocked misery, whether he was more upset with Huslinth's words or by the obvious hatred for Daryl that appeared to be building in the man. His chances with Parlon were beginning to look even grimmer than they had been when he was merely an outcast assigned to the lowest tribal errands. All he could do was look to the Chief for any assistance whatever. And the Chief seldom ever disagreed with the Shaman. It was well known that they did not necessarily like one another, but it was also well known that they did not compete with one another either.

The Chief sat as before, his back straight and large gnarled hands resting across the spear cradled atop his crossed legs. A silence dragged on for many heartbeats, the attention of everyone concentrated upon their leader. Finally, he cleared his throat, and gestured for Nado to approach the area in front of him. Nado scrambled forward and seated himself once more, so as to allow the Chief to look down upon him. The old man's fierce gaze appeared to stare right through Nado's own.

"And so shall it be, young Na-ga-do. You may cross to the side of the council. You are a warrior from this day, as I so declare. And you will sit on that council at the left hand of the Shaman himself. Your service to the tribe is rewarded and your service for the future is expected." He nodded at the boy. Nado hesitantly arose, then moved to Huslinth's side, where a space had quickly been made for him.

Daryl did not look at his friend, his stare fixed upon the Chief's face. Bagestone turned to look at Nado in his new position of honor among the tribe.

"Your father will make your warrior's spear, applying all of his skill to make your flint the sharpest in the valley. This will be awarded to you and carried by you at all times. Upon solstice you will be engraved with the tattoos of a warrior."

He nodded once again, and then turned to face Daryl. "You, Da-ga-ryl, are a most unusual member of this tribe." The Chief spoke deeply and contemplatively, while the silence around him seemed to absorb every syllable that came from his mouth. "You, whom all thought to be a coward but have never, in reality, acted as one. And yet, you accepted the mantle of cowardice without complaint. You, the same person who withdrew that spear," the old man pointed at the still buried shaft to Daryl's left, "from the injured shoulder of a living Mur and survived." He stopped and shook his massive head as a murmur was heard from the massed warriors and hunters behind him. He held up his right hand for silence before proceeding.

"No, not just survived, for we all witnessed the act. You survived and thrived in the performance of the act." Another murmur ran through the men, and once again the sound of spears striking the hard earth could be heard. The Chief waited until the noise faded away.

"Such courage, and something else that I cannot quite say, those things will see you as a member of this council one day. But the Shaman's words have been noted, and this will not be that day." He stopped briefly for his words to be fully considered, but no sound came from anyone.

"Such courage and service cannot go unrewarded. Not even for a period of time for the Shaman's or anyone else's consideration. You are a warrior. Not by proclamation, although I say it is so, but by the simple fact that you have demonstrated what a warrior is. Beyond that, and in forbearance of your appointment to this council, it is my decision to award you a wish." The murmur, which had again begun to rise behind the Chief, turned, in an instant, to complete silence.

"A wish?" Daryl blurted out, unable to stop himself.

The Chief smiled for the first time.

"Yes, a wish. Anything that it is within my power, as leader of this tribe, to allow, I shall allow this one time, to honor your bravery on behalf of all of us." He looked at Daryl expectantly.

Daryl was dumfounded. A wish. He was certain that nothing like what was happening had ever happened before. Throughout the assemblage of men, looks were exchanged, he noted, and the expressions running across the faces of the warriors and men before him were little different than his own. His mother's words came to him, as she had spoken them earlier; *"Tonight will be a night without rules, unless you choose to make them."* He nodded to himself, finally beginning to understand what she had meant.

"I wish to claim the Par-ga-lon, the Shaman's daughter," Daryl said, his voice low and fast, as if he feared that the Chief would retract his offer at any moment. A wave of noise behind the Chief, punctuated by an anguished cry from Huslinth as the man realized what Daryl had said.

"Silence," the Chief shouted, then glanced quickly over at the Shaman before speaking.

"Ah, you are a warrior now. You can lay claim to any young woman of age and circumstance in this tribe. You do not need to ask for such a thing, as it would be yours anyway. This is a special wish I have granted you, and you should consider wisely before making the request." He leaned back after he finished, again glancing over at Huslinth.

"I understand that I am a warrior now," Daryl began, his mind racing. He did not understand at all, but he fought to conceal that fact from the Chief, the council, and especially the

Shaman. "But, as I understand it, I will need more than a claim to marry Par-ga-lon. I will need her father's approval upon completion of the claiming process. And that is what I ask for now."

Bedlam broke out as everyone in the open area began to speak to everyone else. Daryl watched and listened. Rules of claiming, the Shaman and his special place in the tribe, Parlon's strange, tall appearance and remote attitude . . . he heard snippets of each subject, but sat unmoving, his gaze never leaving the Chief's face.

Huslinth leaned to whisper into the Chief's left ear, the expression on his face tight with urgency. The Chief listened carefully, the room around him awash in deep discussion. Finally, he held up one hand for silence. Into the silence the old man's back seemed to bow, as he stared down at the clay just before him. Then his craggy face rose up and his eyes stared deeply into Daryl's.

"Son of Ryl, one of the saviors of this tribe, and the recipient of a wish that I have promised on behalf of us all," he paused to breath in deeply. "That the Shaman would deny you his approval in the matter of the claiming process of his daughter is unthinkable, no matter what may be said. Your wish is granted. Upon the arrival of next summer solstice, after Par-ga-lon is of age, and after having successfully completed the claiming process, the Shaman's approval will be given. And so shall it be."

The room instantly became frenzied with the sound of thudding spear butts, although the sound quickly became deeper and more rhythmic than before. The warriors and hunters pounded their approval with their spears, and with smiles and nods. Only the Shaman remained seated.

Daryl glanced at the man as he sat unmoving. The full intensity of Huslinth's gaze penetrated through the crowd's movement to reach Daryl's eyes. And the boy knew that he had just made a terrible enemy of the second most powerful man in the tribe.

Chapter XXXIII

Daryl slept fitfully through the night, waking before dawn as a cold, strong wind blew through the unprotected opening of the family room. Skins had covered the opening during the long, hard winter, but the coming of spring had dictated that the leather be used to clothe the tribe's hunters.

He stood outside the door, moving back and forth along the wall to warm himself. He thought of Nado and Parlon from the night before. He had seen neither following the definitive council meeting. Nado had stayed on, as was his place, and Parlon had retired to her own family rooms. He tried not to think of Huslinth as he paced.

The first light of morning was not visible when he finally gave up and ran down the path leading to the river. Tagawan's small niche of rocks near the lip of the falls would provide some protection against the wind, he knew, but it was more for the activity of running that he moved, and quite possibly the bird would show up at first light. He ran easily, his body warming with the effort. On the way to the falls he realized it was not the coldness of an early spring night that had awakened him. The complexities that spun from all that had happened at the council meeting ran through his head, and sleep had not provided any respite from his fearful conclusions.

Arriving at the grotto, he pushed his back into the curved stone wall, the top of which served as Tagawan's perch. He rubbed the long, leather sleeves of his new warrior's jerkin. His mother had laid the garment out on his sleeping skins while he had been at the meeting. How she could have known that he would walk out a warrior, he could not guess. He had not been able to question her at all. When he had tried, she had simply brushed the inquiry aside to ask her own questions. And they had all been about the wish, and the Shaman's reaction, and on and on and on, until Daryl had gone to bed just to escape her never-ending questions.

The sun's light flowed over the top edge of the escarpment long before its presence could be seen. Only the change in wind speed, along with a very slight warming of the air, gave any clue about the beginning of a new day. He waited patiently for the bird to drop out of the air above him, or glide soundlessly from the white cloud of the falls' mist.

The first glimmer of light did not bring the bird. Instead, Nado and Parlon loped around the last bush protruding out into the trail they'd worn on the way to Tagawan's perch. He was so surprised that he leaped from his bent crouch and plunged his right foot into the center of the small pool. The water poured instantly into and through the soft leather of his right foot-wrap. Daryl barely was able to chop off the yelp of surprise and pain from the misstep before Nado stood before him.

"Good morning," Nado said casually, as if he spent every morning wandering about the riverbank with the Shaman's daughter. "I thought we might find you here," he went on, a small smile playing across his features. Daryl smiled back, but weakly, his mind roiling with questions he could not ask. He did not meet Parlon's gaze, instead greeting Nado only with a slight wave of his left hand. He thought about what his mother had told him of the claiming process the night before. It could not begin until he sat down face to face with the Shaman and formally announced himself.

Parlon walked forward until she stood just behind Nado's shoulder. She stared at him, after glancing at his feet. He could not avoid her direct gaze, and his eyes moved to meet hers. "Nado said you would be here early," she said, then glanced down again. "Isn't it cold wading in the river?" Her tone was so innocent that Daryl's brow winkled in question, before his eyes grew round and he looked down at his soaked foot-wrap. His face flushed red with embarrassment and he could not keep himself from moving the wet wrap back behind his other foot. He looked up to see a slight smile vanish from Parlon's face.

"What are you doing here?" he gasped.

"I'm bringing Par-ga-lon, claimed woman of Da-ga-ryl, dutifully forward to spend time with her betrothed," Nado replied, the smile never leaving his face. Daryl shook his head and sighed deeply. At that very instant, Tagawan plunged out of the air to land on the boy's right shoulder. The bird squawked loudly, then turned its head to gaze upon Parlon with its rotating left eye. Squawking once more, as if in approval, it went about its morning grooming.

Parlon flinched back from the bird's arrival and obvious appraisal. Raising one eyebrow, she once again stared deeply into Daryl's eyes.

"The claiming process is not without its rules," she said, seeming to grow taller and straighter as she spoke, "and one of those rules involves some discussion with the woman being claimed, even if it's only a brief statement. That way the woman does not hear of the event from everyone else first." Daryl recoiled somewhat from the seriousness of her delivery and was attempting to think of some apology when she abruptly turned and began to trot back up the trail.

"What was that?" he finally said to Nado, again shaking his head.

"Well," Nado said, looking in the direction that the girl had disappeared, "on the way down here she did mention the fact that you have somehow forced her father to give his approval to the process, even before it began. Her father, in turn, apparently doesn't believe that she knew nothing of the arrangement prior to your taking advantage of the Chief's wish." Nado shrugged.

"And, before you start on me, it was her idea to come down here. She's not exactly happy with me, you know."

Daryl looked over at his friend.

"You!" he exclaimed. "I thought she was mad at me! And why'd you bring her down here, anyway? She could not have known where I was."

"Ah, you see, she said that if I wasn't a cripple she'd have her father cut my tongue out as part of some special ceremony. What could I do? I haven't been real complimentary toward her since I gave her the crystal on your behalf."

Daryl stared at Nado, and wondered what he wasn't being told. Nado was not at all the type to be intimidated by any kind of threat, much less those made by the Shaman's daughter. But he could think of nothing to say that might elicit more information.

"Come on. Let's climb. The air is cold up there but it's empty of all these things." Daryl swung one arm up and around before running toward the top of the slope that ran down next to the thundering waters. Tagawan flew into the air and disappeared into the cloud of mist.

It was midmorning by the time the boys reached the extended stone overlook. They sat side by side, as the sun revealed the totality of the valley below them.

"It's so beautiful," Nado said. Both boys knew that nothing needed to be said. The tremendous panoramic view had captivated them from the very beginning and not even time could diminish the impact of the scene.

Great clouds of black and gray gathered on the far horizon

near the downriver end of the valley, adding an air of distant drama to the already idyllic setting.

Tagawan lifted rapidly toward them, rising on an updraft that rose only a few man-lengths from the face of the cliff. He had badgered and cajoled them constantly as they had made the climb up, but then disappeared as they crested the lip.

"I think it's time to move on," Nado said as he stood. "The ruins await us." He ran along the wall toward the interior of the plateau with Daryl on his heels. As they leaped from the stone and began their run through the blowing pines he reappeared ahead of them, swooping and swerving through between the branches, sometimes barely a handsbreath above the floor of thick pine needles.

They didn't stop until they had reached the open area with the pedestal on one end and the statue on the other. They walked to the pedestal. Nado stopped to take in the ruins around them.

"You found it, you know," he said, his voice soft against the whisper of the constant low wind. "I always suspected there was something somewhere beyond what we knew." He turned to look at Daryl. Daryl looked back at him, hoping the other boy would say something further to explain what he meant, but Nado stood silent, his eyes shifting back to the mounds of broken stone and lichen-covered rocks.

"Found what?" he finally said, unable to withhold himself any longer.

"You found the heart of the tribe, and it's not down there. It's right here, before us. I just know it." Nado's good hand moved to rest on the middle of his chest. "Don't you feel it?"

Daryl nodded. "Yes, there's some strange connection between this place and the tribe. I feel it too. Then, there's the carved symbol I found on the island, like nothing we've ever seen before. It too is connected. And the Mur. It can't just all be coincidence, can it?"

Nado shook his head. His hand moved from his chest to rest on Daryl's left shoulder for a brief instant. "Will you tell her about this? Bring her to this place?"

"I don't know," Daryl answered, feeling Nado's supportive hand fall away. "I'm not sure about her," he finally said, not at all certain what he meant by the statement.

"Not sure?" Nado laughed, his eyes still running over the ruins, "You could have asked for anything at all when you made your wish. Anything. And yet you asked for her. You're sure. You just don't know it yet. And what of the future? Will we ever be able to come back? Will we go to the island? Will we ever find any answers to any of this?"

Daryl shook his head, sighing deeply. He could never seem to answer the other boy's questions.

"I don't want to go on hunts. And I don't want to make war on anyone, not that anyone in the tribe ever has. I want to do this. I want to explore the far valley, and valleys, if there are more of them. I want to talk to that creature again, and find out what he is. Do you understand?"

Daryl heard the quaver in Nado's voice as he finished. This time he laid his hand upon his friend's shoulder.

"Something is ending, and something else is beginning. I don't understand almost any of it, but of one thing I am certain," Daryl stopped, watching the bird come in for one of his ungainly landings atop the flat pedestal surface, "and that is that you and I will be together for whatever that beginning brings." He lowered his hand to his side.

"Don't forget the stupid bird," Nado pointed to the animal, who squawked loudly in recognition, making both boys laugh.

ABOUT THE AUTHOR

Jim Strauss has been a marine officer, deep sea diver, shipboard physician's assistant, professor of anthropology, and currently writes for several Hollywood production companies. Having visited over 100 countries, he currently lives with his wife in the greater Chicago area.